When Shadows Fall

PATRICIA H. RUSHFORD

HELEN BRADLEY MYSTERIES

When Shadows Fall

BETHANY HOUSE PUBLISHERS
MINNEAPOLIS, MINNESOTA 55438

When Shadows Fall
Copyright © 2000
Patricia Rushford

Cover by Dan Thornberg

Published by Bethany House Publishers
A Ministry of Bethany Fellowship International
11400 Hampshire Avenue South
Minneapolis, Minnesota 55438
www.bethanyhouse.com

Printed in the United States of America by
Bethany Press International, Minneapolis, Minnesota 55438

Library of Congress Cataloging-in-Publication Data

Rushford, Patricia H.
    When shadows fall / by Patricia H. Rushford.
        p.   cm. — (Helen Bradley mysteries ; 4)
        ISBN 1-55661-733-X
        1. Bradley, Helen (Fictitious character)—Fiction. I. Title.
PS3568.U7274 W48   2000
813'.54—dc21

                                                00-008487

This fourth book in the Helen Bradley Mysteries series marks a milestone for me. During its writing, I was diagnosed with colon cancer, went through surgery, and had a toxic reaction to chemotherapy. All of this left me with very little energy and creativity. Much of the time, writing was paramount to paddling upstream without a paddle. In completing *When Shadows Fall*, I feel I have reached the shore. The process was a struggle I wouldn't care to repeat. While I felt God's continuing presence through it all, I'm not certain I'd have made it had it not been for the support of friends and family who loved and supported and encouraged me.

I'm especially thankful to Drs. Ginsberg and Lamert for pulling me through the physical and emotional crises; my husband, Ron; my family and friends for the reassurance and care, especially Lois and Del Williams, Margo Power, Sandy, Gail, Lauraine, Ruby, Birdie, Marcia, Marion, Woodene, and Elsie; my editors at Bethany House, who understood and worked with me through missed deadlines and frustrations; and for editing and advice, I'd like to thank Judy Frandsen and Howard Greer.

So at the end of this book, I not only celebrate finishing yet another mystery, I celebrate life.

Books by Patricia Rushford

Young Adult Fiction

JENNIE MCGRADY MYSTERIES
1. *Too Many Secrets*
2. *Silent Witness*
3. *Pursued*
4. *Deceived*
5. *Without a Trace*
6. *Dying to Win*
7. *Betrayed*
8. *In Too Deep*
9. *Over the Edge*
10. *From the Ashes*
11. *Desperate Measures*
12. *Abandoned*
13. *Forgotten*

Adult Fiction

Morningsong

HELEN BRADLEY MYSTERIES
1. *Now I Lay Me Down to Sleep*
2. *Red Sky in Mourning*
3. *A Haunting Refrain*
4. *When Shadows Fall*

PATRICIA RUSHFORD is an award-winning writer, speaker, and teacher who has published numerous articles and more than thirty books, including *What Kids Need Most in a Mom*, *The Jack and Jill Syndrome: Healing for Broken Children*, and *Have You Hugged Your Teenager Today?* She is a registered nurse and has a master's degree in counseling from Western Evangelical Seminary. She and her husband, Ron, live in Washington State and have two grown children, seven grandchildren, and lots of nephews and nieces.

Pat has been reading mysteries for as long as she can remember and is delighted to be writing a series of her own. She is a member of Mystery Writers of America, Sisters in Crime, Romance Writers of America, and several other writing organizations.

One

Helen Bradley wrapped her arms around herself and shivered. The Oregon coast in mid-November could be brutal. The day matched the dark gray clouds that hovered near the ground despite the wind's attempts to blow them away.

If she were into rating days on a scale of one to ten, she'd have given this one a minus three. And that was before she found the body.

The day had started out a ten with J.B. kissing her awake and telling her how much he adored her. She loved these languorous moments. Savored them. With J.B. retired after recently suffering a mild heart attack, who knew how much more time they would have together? His encounter with death had left her reeling. Helen snuggled against him, reveling in the feel of his solid warm body against her back.

"Have I told you how lovely you are in the morning, luv?" he'd whispered against her neck.

"Yes, but I don't mind hearing it again." Turning to face him, she whispered, "You look pretty wonderful yourself." She closed her eyes and wove her fingers into his thick silver hair, then kissed him thoroughly.

The phone interrupted what promised to be one of their more exquisite mornings.

"Let the answering machine pick it up," J.B. murmured against her lips.

"Mmm." She'd have liked nothing better, but the mood was broken. Besides, she couldn't ignore a ringing telephone. "We should get it. Might be one of the children."

Helen had two grown children from her first marriage and four grandchildren, with another on the way. Seven in the morning was too early to call for a chat. What if something had gone wrong with Susan's pregnancy? Her daughter-in-law was only five months along.

J.B. sighed, rolled away from her, and grabbed the phone. "Hello," he barked into it.

Helen snuggled against him.

"Right." His voice softened. He turned onto his back, then grasped her hand and brought it to his lips. Raising a roguish eyebrow, J.B. grinned at her, his Irish blue eyes alight with a promise that they'd pick up where they'd left off as soon as the call ended.

As he listened to the caller, J.B.'s smile disappeared. The light drained from his eyes. "Are you sure?"

Helen frowned and mouthed, "Is it one of the children? Susan?"

J.B. shook his head and averted his eyes. "I see. When do you want me to come in?" He withdrew his hand, then sat up, dangling his legs over the bed. "I'll be there by noon." After hanging up, J.B. turned and looked at her for a moment, his gaze filled with longing. He opened his mouth as though he wanted to tell her something, then leaned over and kissed her. Without a backward glance, he got up and strode into the bathroom.

Helen stared at the closed door for several moments, then tossed her covers aside. "J.B.?" She tried the door, but he'd locked it. *Locked it.* "What's going on?"

She listened intently, hearing only the sound of running water. The shower curtain swished across the rod.

Leaning against the door, she yelled, "J.B., what was that all about?"

Still J.B. said nothing. He either hadn't heard or hadn't wanted to.

"Fine. Don't tell me. You'd better not be thinking about going back to work." Helen shoved aside her annoyance and slipped into her white velour robe, then shuffled downstairs and into the kitchen to make their morning tea.

"Men," she muttered as she filled the teakettle. Then, not wanting to wait for the water to boil, she filled a mug, put in a tea bag, and set it in the microwave. In the three minutes it took for the water to heat and turn into tea, Helen came to the conclusion that J.B.'s phone call had not been a request to return to work. For one thing the FBI wouldn't rehire a man who'd suffered a heart attack—unless it was for consultation. And if that were the case, J.B. would have been elated.

No, she decided, this was something else entirely.

Could the phone call have been from his doctor? J.B. had gone in for a checkup a few days before. Maybe they'd found something. It would have to be serious to garner that kind of disturbing response from J.B. Very serious.

Helen didn't like the direction her thoughts were taking. "Don't be jumping to conclusions," she muttered. The doctor probably wouldn't be calling this early. True, they often made phone calls and hospital visits before they started seeing patients at the clinic, but . . . no. It could be anything. Though Helen couldn't imagine what, J.B. would tell her soon enough. Then again, if it was health related, he might not.

For weeks following his heart attack, he'd been sullen, keeping his emotions under lock and key. It had taken some doing to get him to open up to her. Never having married before, J.B. wasn't used to sharing his concerns with a wife. He'd always been, and apparently still was, the strong silent type.

Helen understood that kind of man all too well. Her first husband had been even more closemouthed. She didn't like it in him and disliked it even more in J.B. Maybe if Ian had been more open with her, he wouldn't have been killed. He might have told her where he was going, and she could have insisted he refuse the assignment.

"That isn't true and you know it," she mumbled, sipping her Earl Grey tea. Besides, the government frowned on agents who disclosed their secrets—even to family. And she could never have talked Ian into quitting his job and going into another line of work. Ian had lived for his work as a government agent—had loved the thrill of facing death at every turn. If the bombing in Beirut hadn't taken his life, something else eventually would have. Helen tucked her guilt and pain away as she had time and again for the eleven years since his death. *Even if you'd known, he wouldn't have listened. He never did.*

What's done is done. You couldn't have changed Ian any more than you can change J.B.

Any more than he can change you.

Helen smiled at the thought. She had little room for criticism. She'd gone from being an agent in her younger days to being a homemaker and mother. Then, feeling at loose ends, she'd returned to school and in due course became a police officer. Shortly after Ian's death, she'd retired from the police bureau in Portland and done some traveling. That led to a career in travel writing—something she still enjoyed. Even with her career change, Helen had never really given up her work in law enforcement. She still did odd jobs for the various government agencies and managed to solve a crime every now and then. It was in her blood.

Taking her tea into the living room, she stood at the window and watched the waves smash against the jagged rocks that separated the house from the ocean. Their home sat well above the pounding surf. The remodeled Cape Cod was one of several houses nestled in the fifteen acres of woods just north of Bay Village.

Normally the view soothed her. Today it only made her more restless. Her insides churned with the powerful waves as she listened to J.B. walking around on the floor above.

Maybe he just needs time to think, she reminded herself. Bad news could do that to a person. Undoubtedly he'd mull things over and tell her all about the phone call when he came down for breakfast. Speaking of which, she had better get it made.

Several minutes later J.B. entered the kitchen, wearing casual khakis and a beige cardigan over a neatly pressed shirt that brought out the blue in his eyes. He set his overnight bag on the floor beside the door, his sad gaze roving from it to her face. "I'll be heading into Portland this morning, luv." His brogue was heavier than usual—a sure sign of distress. "May need to stay over a night or two." He cleared his throat. "Could be longer." He unfolded the newspaper Helen had placed on the table earlier and scanned the front page.

She set the teapot, two bowls of oatmeal, juice, and grapefruit on the kitchen table, then poured J.B.'s tea and refilled her own. "Why?"

His expression grim, he said, "Nothing for you to be concernin' yourself about." He settled into his chair, sprinkled brown sugar on his oats, and poured on a dab of milk, then began reading in earnest.

"I see." She sat down across from him. It was all she could do to keep from picking up her bowl and dumping the oatmeal on his head. They finished their meal in silence, with J.B. reading the paper and Helen fuming. Until his retirement she might have accepted his refusal to tell her about his trip. Secrecy had been part of his job. She understood that. Normally he'd have told her it was job related—that he'd been called by this or that agency. Now, it seemed, he couldn't tell her anything.

When they'd eaten, Helen cleared the table. "Could you at least tell me who called? Was it the doctor? Did something show up on the tests?"

He cleared his throat. His anguished look settled on her. He seemed to struggle with what to say, then set his paper aside. "Can't a man take a trip into the city without his wife harassing him?"

"Harassing! Jason Bradley, that is so unfair. I'm your wife. I've a right to know what's going on with you."

"And I've a right to some privacy. Wasn't that part of our agreement? That we would give each other space?"

"Fine. You can have all the privacy and *space* you want." She spun around and stomped through the living room, out the French doors, across the breezeway, and into the new addition.

But by the time she'd run up the stairs to her office, slammed the door, and started a fire in the gas fireplace, most of her fury had been spent. In place of the anger came an overwhelming sense of loss. Helen brushed at the sudden tears as she stood at the window and watched J.B. toss his bag in the backseat of his Cadillac. He climbed inside, then started the engine and backed out with not so much as a glance her way.

Helen hadn't known what to expect from their first real argument as husband and wife but certainly not this. Wasn't he supposed to come after her and apologize? Weren't they supposed to kiss and make up?

Helen watched the road long after his taillights had disappeared. Would he be back?

"Of course he will." She scolded herself for feeling so insecure. He loved her as much as she loved him. Whatever had come between them would pass. He'd apologize for shutting her out, and everything would be all right. Wouldn't it?

Helen took a deep, calming breath and turned from the window. Glancing at her computer, she reassured herself again that all couples argued from time to time and that J.B. would indeed come home. She needed to pull herself together.

Look on the bright side, she told herself. *With J.B. gone you can catch up on your writing. Begin those articles on the San Juan Islands.*

Helen turned on her computer. While she waited for it to boot up, she made another cup of tea in the small kitchen.

She loved the new addition to their home. The first floor served as a garage and workshop. The second was made up of two large offices, an adjoining bath, and kitchen. The addition had been J.B.'s idea. Helen had needed her own space to write. Now that J.B. had taken it upon himself to write a book about his experiences as a government agent—one for which he was being paid very well—he needed his space too.

Space. Not long ago she'd pleaded for it. *Well, Helen Bradley, like it or not, you have plenty of it now.*

Taking the tea to her desk, she sank into her plush leather chair. Time to stop worrying about J.B. and get to work. Something she hadn't done for far too long. Not that she needed to these days, as she'd recently come into a great deal of money. She owned a resort in the San Juan Islands with her cousins, Claire and Richard O'Donnell, Uncle Paddy's grown children. There were other resorts as well—in France and the Caribbean. Her uncle had been a very wealthy man. Still, she'd much rather have him than his money.

Even with her newly acquired wealth, Helen was determined to continue working—at least with the writing. She needed excitement and a sense of purpose. Truth be known, she was far more like Ian and J.B. than she cared to admit.

Helen pulled up her files and clicked open the *San Juan* folder. She'd recently come back from a visit to the islands and planned to write two articles. The first would be about the different ferry routes through the area along with a travelogue on each of the major islands the ferries passed or stopped at. The second was a piece on Paradise Island, a world-class health resort and spa, of which she was now part owner. She'd been skeptical about writing about the resort, as it would also be free advertising, but her editor wanted both pieces for the same issue.

She'd managed to work up an outline and write two pages when the phone rang.

"Helen, this is Eleanor Crane."

"Eleanor, what a surprise." Eleanor was Bay Village's first lady and Ethan Crane's wife. Ethan had been sworn in as mayor only two months before. Since she was always chairing some fundraising event, Helen suspected the call was probably a request for money for one of St. Matthew's many community outreach programs. "I haven't talked with you in ages. How are you?"

"I . . . um . . . fine. I'm so glad I caught you. I hope you're not busy."

She didn't sound fine. Hearing the tension in Eleanor's voice, Helen revised her earlier impression. This wasn't a social call. "What is it, Eleanor? What's wrong?"

"Oh, Helen," she gasped. "I don't know what to do. Ethan is missing."

Two

"M issing?" Helen responded after getting beyond her initial shock. "Why are you calling me? You should be talking to the sheriff."

"No, I couldn't do that. Not yet. You see, I don't know for certain. He didn't come home last night." She hesitated. "It's not something I want to discuss on the phone. Could you come here?"

Helen was tempted to tell her again to call the authorities but didn't. If Eleanor didn't plan to alert the police, Helen might need to. To do that, she'd need far more information than she had gotten so far.

"Please, Helen. I need to talk with you. I wouldn't ask if it weren't important."

That was true enough. Eleanor was not the type to ask for help. "Of course. I'll be there within the hour."

It took Helen less than twenty minutes to shower and dress. Wearing jeans and a classic white shirt under a blue cotton sweater, she grabbed her jacket from the coatrack in the entry. She picked up her bag and headed out the door and was just opening the trunk when someone in a muddy black utility van pulled in alongside her car.

An attractive young man, perhaps in his mid-thirties, emerged from the vehicle. In his heavy flannel shirt, denim jacket, and jeans, he looked ready for work.

"Can I help you?" Helen asked.

"Hope so." He grinned and checked the form on his clip-board. "You Helen Bradley?"

"I am."

He gave her an even wider smile. "Got a work order here to repair a leaky roof."

"It's about time. I called Chuck several weeks ago." She and J.B. had hired Chuck Daniels to remodel their home and build the new addition. He'd come highly recommended, and though he did excellent work, Chuck was often late, making promises he rarely kept. She'd only recently discovered why. Bay Village's most sought-after builder was an alcoholic.

"Yes, ma'am. We got a lot of work piled up."

"That may be, but Chuck assured me it would be done two weeks ago."

"Sorry about that." He ran a hand through his thick dark hair and down the back of his neck.

Helen backed off. "I'm sorry. I shouldn't have snapped at you. It's not your fault."

He shrugged. "Hey, it's not a problem. I get this a lot. Things should get better for them. They hired a couple new guys to help them catch up—I'm one of them." He reached out a hand. "Alex Jordan."

"Hi, Alex. Thanks for coming. Better late than never, I guess." Helen quickly took him into the addition and up the stairs to show him the damaged ceiling. After discussing the work needing to be done, she instructed him to lock up when he finished and gave him her cell phone number if he had any problems.

Jordan went right to work, whistling an engaging John Den-ver tune. One of her favorites. He seemed like a nice enough fellow, but before Helen entrusted him to the care of her home, she decided to check him out. With so many ruthless characters hanging about these days, she didn't want to take any chances. A call to Chuck's home office where his wife, Lynn, acted as secretary, affirmed that Alex was indeed legitimate.

"I'm sorry, Helen. Chuck shouldn't have promised it so soon. We've been having a terrible time keeping up." There was a hard edge to Lynn's voice. Helen had gotten to know Lynn fairly well during the remodeling project. Seemed the poor woman was always apologizing for her husband's schedule—or lack of one. They'd talked several times at length about her husband's drinking problem.

"You sound upset. Is everything all right?"

"Not really." Lynn cleared her throat.

"Is there anything I can do?"

"No, I don't think so. Chuck is drinking more than ever. Since the city council turned down his proposal to build a housing development on that stretch of beachfront property at the north end of town, he's been hitting the bottle pretty heavily. Last night he was supposed to meet me for dinner after work, but he never showed up. One of the men said they saw him at Bagley's Tavern. I don't know where he went from there, but he never came home. Probably stayed with one of his drinking buddies so he wouldn't have to listen to me yell at him."

"I'm sorry to hear that, Lynn. Have you talked to a counselor?"

"No—I keep hoping . . ." She paused. "I shouldn't be telling you this. I'm sorry."

"Don't be. You need someone to talk to. I've mentioned this before, but you're enabling him. Chuck is an alcoholic, and trying to ignore that is like trying to ignore an elephant in your living room. You might want to start going to the Al-Anon or Alcoholics Anonymous meetings at St. Matthew's on Monday nights. I understand they have an excellent program."

"We . . . we're not members and . . ."

"It's open to everyone. Besides, if you feel uncomfortable there, you can find a number of other places. Um . . . I don't mean to sound pushy, but these programs can help. They'll give you some answers as to how to handle the situation. Waiting just compounds the problems."

"I know. And you're right. You're not the only one who's mentioned it. Just this morning Alex was telling me the same thing." She sighed. "I need to do something. Chuck and I have worked too hard to develop the company to have his drinking mess things up. Anyway, I shouldn't be burdening you with my troubles. Alex will take care of the roof for you. He's a good worker." She paused. "Cute too."

Helen glanced out her window as the subject of their conversation came around the corner of the building with a ladder. "I noticed. He seems very nice."

"And he's single. Too bad I'm taken."

"Now, Lynn." Helen couldn't help but smile. "I'll admit he's a hunk, but he's a little young for you, don't you think?"

"Well, a person can dream, can't they?"

Helen turned serious. When problems arose in a marriage, it was all too easy to look to another person as a way out. "I wouldn't dream too much, Lynn—like all men, I suspect Alex has his flaws. Everyone comes with their own set of problems."

"I suppose you're right about that. But don't worry. I'm not ready to dump Chuck. He has a lot of good qualities—when he's sober."

Helen politely ended their conversation, saying she had errands to run. She then left the house in what she hoped were Alex Jordan's capable hands.

Minutes later she was in her restored 1955 T-bird convertible heading south on Highway 101 toward Ethan and Eleanor Crane's home. On the drive she mulled over her conversations with Eleanor and Lynn. How odd that neither man had come home last night. Did one incident have anything to do with the other? *Probably not*, Helen mused. Lynn had most likely been on target about Chuck's sleeping it off at a friend's home.

Ethan, however, was a different story. Over the phone, she had reassured Eleanor, telling her not to worry. Yet Helen couldn't seem to take her own advice. Ethan had been selected as the mayor of Bay Village to complete the term vacated by Mayor Ames. Ames had been poisoned at the big charitable art auction he and his wife hosted this past summer. With his killer behind bars and the ordeal over, the small coastal town of Bay Village needed someone to fill Ames's shoes and had chosen Ethan by an overwhelming majority.

He's most likely been detained, Helen told herself. *Still, wouldn't he have called?*

To keep her imagination from creating tragic scenarios, Helen trained her thoughts on the raw beauty of the breakers as they battered the rugged coastline. The waves pounded the rocks, sending plumes of white spray as high as forty and fifty feet into the air.

Bay Village was a small, narrow town with the ocean on one side and the Cascade Mountains on the other. Businesses lined the east side of the highway, while a seawall and walkway lined the west. Behind the businesses, homes crept up the steep hill. Nearly every home had a view. Helen loved this particular stretch of beach, and shortly after her first husband's death, she would come here on weekends for respite. She began staying for longer and longer periods and finally bought the house. She'd lived here for eleven years and never tired of it. Even if it did rain too much at times, it was the perfect setting for writing and healing wounds.

Soon after she'd moved in, she began attending St. Matthew's, one of two churches in Bay Village. That's when she met Ethan and Eleanor. Helen murmured a prayer for Ethan's safekeeping as she turned into a private drive, punched the security code into the number pad, and waited for the gate to slide open. When it did, she nosed her car in and crept along the meandering wooded lane. The houses on either side suggested moderate wealth. The posh development of twenty-five or so homes had been built on a bluff similar to the area in which she and J.B. lived. That's where the similarity ended. When the lane split into a Y, Helen veered left on Ocean Ridge Way and drove to the end.

The Cranes' elegant two-story colonial sat on two acres atop a ridge and offered a spectacular view of the ocean. The same builder who'd renovated Helen's home had built it and many of the other homes in the development five years before.

Helen growled out loud just thinking again about Chuck Daniels. His carelessness had caused her and J.B. weeks of grief. Alex Jordan's appearance this morning appeased her some, but Chuck was a scoundrel. It had been hard enough to put up with him during the remodeling, but to have to deal with him while he built their entire house? Helen shuddered at the thought. Eleanor must have considerably more patience than she did.

Helen brushed the pesky thoughts aside. She wasn't being entirely fair to the man. Just because she didn't care for his chauvinistic attitude and lackadaisical manner, or the fact that he drank too much, didn't mean he wasn't a good contractor. The beautiful homes around her attested to the man's talents. Besides, when he wanted to, Chuck could be quite charming. Though she held reservations about his character, Helen wished him the best. Alcoholism could be debilitating, and she sincerely hoped he'd get help before he ended up losing everything—including his wife.

Dismissing further thoughts of Chuck, she pulled into the circular driveway. A cyclist shot past her. Helen didn't see the girl's face, only the blur of a helmet, black spandex, and neon pink windbreaker.

"Melissa!" a woman shouted from an open upstairs window. "Get back here. Now!"

The girl ignored the order and kept riding. Helen glanced up at the woman in the window with what she hoped was an empathetic response. It was Nancy Belmont, the Cranes' daughter. Nancy's angry gaze met hers for an instant. Then, in obvious embarrassment, she raked a hand through disheveled hair, retreated inside, and closed the window.

Not certain what she was getting into, Helen took her time going up the walk, pausing to admire the landscaping. Everything was lush and green and very wet.

"There you are." Eleanor opened the door before Helen had a chance to ring the bell. "Thank you for coming. Come in, please. Um . . . I suppose you heard. I swear that girl is more headstrong than her mother used to be at that age."

"She's certainly grown up since the last time I saw her."

"Yes. Melissa is fourteen and taking her parents' divorce very badly."

"Divorce? I'm so sorry."

"Don't be. It's for the best. I never did like Bob. And I like him even less now." She gave Helen a thin smile. "I know that's not a very Christian attitude, but the man . . . well, I won't bore you with the sordid details. Nancy and Melissa are staying here for a few weeks—for their protection. Ethan and I thought it best."

Eleanor ushered her into the living room. In her expensive-looking silk lounging ensemble, Eleanor resembled Ingrid Bergman. She was shorter than Helen, but her wiry frame made her look as tall. Or maybe it was the regal way she carried herself. She wore her platinum hair in a moderate pageboy, which was now pulled back and held in place by an elegant clip. Her pastel pink silks perfectly matched the soft beige carpet, the creamy leather furniture, and the pastel pillows. Helen sank into the chair near the fireplace and settled her bag on the floor.

"Would you like some tea? I seem to remember you prefer it to coffee."

"I'd love some, thanks."

Eleanor had already prepared it and poured the tea into gold-trimmed teacups and saucers decorated with yellow and red roses. Replacing the tea cozy on the matching teapot, she said, "I still haven't heard from Ethan." She appeared more angry than concerned. "I can't believe he hasn't called."

"You said he was due back last night?"

"Yes. His plane was due in yesterday afternoon." Eleanor handed Helen her tea, then glanced toward the stairs in the entry and frowned. "I haven't said anything to Nancy or Melissa. No sense in worrying them."

"Have you checked with the airlines to see if his plane might have been delayed?"

She lowered herself into the sofa. "His flight came into Portland yesterday afternoon at three."

"Did he have business in Portland?"

"Not that I know of. Our son, Brian, lives there. I tried calling, but he wasn't home." She pinched her lips together. "Ethan usually calls if he's going to be late."

Helen took a tentative sip of the hot brew. It smelled faintly of vanilla, and she savored the smooth taste of it. "I really don't know how I can help. Like I said on the phone, you really should call the authorities."

"No." Eleanor fingered the large diamond ring on her left hand. "I don't want the police involved."

"But if he's missing . . ."

"There are things you don't know."

"Maybe you'd better explain."

Eleanor sighed and drew herself up. "He always calls me when he's been *detained.*"

The hesitancy and sarcasm in her voice when she said the word triggered Helen's curiosity and concern even more.

"And he doesn't usually stay out all night."

Helen gave her an expectant look. "Eleanor, what's going on? You seem to be tossing out a lot of hints, and so far they aren't coming together very well. Why don't you just come out and tell me what you're getting at?"

She clasped her hands on her lap and let out a rush of air. Helen had never seen her so flustered. Eleanor was the rock. The one to call in a crisis.

"I think Ethan is seeing another woman."

"Oh no." Helen rubbed her forehead to ease out the beginnings of a headache. "Are you sure?"

"No. That is . . . I have no proof, but he spends so much time away. Almost every night he calls and says he has to work late. Several times I've called him and he's not there. Once a woman answered."

"Could it have been his secretary?"

"I suppose. He has several women working for him. She didn't give me her name. Just said he'd left the office."

"Ethan doesn't seem like the kind of man who would have an affair—except maybe with his work. It can't be easy stepping into the mayor's position on such short notice. It's a big job."

"Don't you think I know that?" Eleanor's voice was uncharacteristically harsh. "I wish you would stop siding with him. Being a deacon in the church doesn't make him a saint."

"Of course not, but . . ."

"I shouldn't have said anything." She pinched the bridge of her nose and after several thoughtful moments said, "I was hoping you might be able to find him. I need to know if he's having an affair and who it is. With your being a detective and all."

"I'm not a licensed private detective."

"But you do take cases sometimes. And you are a consultant for the sheriff's office."

"I do some investigating." Even though she didn't actively work as a private eye, Helen had been known to get involved in an investigation now and then. But she had no interest in hiring herself out to dig up dirt on an unfaithful spouse. "I can't. You and Ethan are my friends."

"You're right. I'm sorry. I shouldn't have asked. It's just . . . I'm so worried."

Helen settled her cup in the saucer. "You need to call the authorities and report it."

"No." Eleanor set her cup on the coffee table without drinking from it.

"Whyever not?"

"I don't want a scandal. The press would get ahold of the story and it would be all over the news. If he is with his . . . his girlfriend, I . . . couldn't take the embarrassment. He couldn't either."

"For heaven's sake, Eleanor, what if something has happened to him?"

"I don't think *that's* the problem. He's with *her*. I just want you to find him and follow him. I want to know for sure if he's cheating on me. And I want to know with whom."

"Based on what you've told me, I don't see any reason to suspect him of being unfaithful." Helen started to pick up her bag. "I'd be more worried that he'd had an accident on the way home. Coming through the mountains can be treacherous at night. His car may have gone off the road. There are a number of explanations." Helen sighed. "Call the sheriff's office. They'll be able to locate him far more quickly than I."

"I can't. Don't you see?"

Helen stood and swung her bag over her shoulder. "I should go."

Tears gathered in Eleanor's eyes, turning them a grayish blue. "Wait. Please. I'm sorry. I had no right to be upset with you. Maybe you're right, and he really has been working. I tried his office, but no one there has seen him. He doesn't have any appointments scheduled for today, and they didn't expect him in until tomorrow. He told me he'd be home last night."

"You need to talk to Joe Adams," Helen urged. "Tell him you haven't heard from Ethan and that you're getting worried. You don't need to mention the possibility of an affair. If it turns out you're right and he has been seeing someone, Joe will be discreet." Helen trusted the young sheriff and had worked with him on several investigations. Joe had an office in Bay Village and usually had one or two deputies working with him.

"I suppose you're right." Tears filled her eyes. "There might not be a woman at all. It's just that when he didn't come home, I began to assume the worst. I was afraid he'd been in an accident or something. Then I started thinking about all the times he's been away lately and how different he's seemed. He's been so distant and . . . I couldn't bear it if anything has happened to him."

Helen went to sit beside her friend and settled an arm across her shoulders. "I understand how frantic you must be. But all this speculation isn't helping one bit." Maybe she'd been too hasty in refusing to help. Maybe she should investigate. If something had happened to Ethan . . . no. The authorities were more than capable of handling it. "You're doing the right thing by alerting Joe. And please, keep me posted."

Eleanor dabbed at her eyes with a tissue. "Yes, I'll do that. I'm sorry I troubled you. Um . . . you won't say anything . . . about . . ?"

"Of course not."

After saying good-bye, Helen drove her vintage car around in the circular driveway and headed home. She thought about calling Joe herself to tell him about Ethan, then decided against it. Maybe she'd check with him later to make sure Eleanor followed through.

Driving back through Bay Village, thoughts of Ethan, Chuck, and J.B. tumbled through her mind like a landslide of rocks down a mountain.

Helen didn't like thinking of Ethan as being unfaithful to Eleanor—couldn't fathom it. But she'd been wrong about people before. She didn't want to see Chuck sinking into the mire of addiction. And she saw no point whatsoever in dredging up worries over J.B.'s health or his whereabouts. Yet she couldn't seem to put the negative thoughts about the three men out of her head.

Be not anxious. The familiar Bible verse drifted into her mind. *The day has enough troubles of its own.*

"You're right about that, Lord. This one is turning out to be a doozy."

Noticing the sun breaks in heavy cloud cover, Helen drove on to the house. What she needed was a good long walk on the beach to clear her head. As the Bible verse said, her worrying over things wouldn't help in the least. *By this afternoon,* she told herself, *everything will be ironed out and you'll wonder what all the fuss was about.*

In the meantime she decided to take advantage of what appeared to be a brief but welcome window of opportunity to walk on her favorite stretch of beach near Siletz Bay. After her walk she'd check back in with Eleanor and Lynn.

Three

Helen stopped at the house, checked her answering machine, and changed into a pair of warm sweats. Alex Jordan was still working on the roof. She went out to see how he was progressing. He had stripped off several square feet of roofing and was laying down new tarpaper. A bundle of shingles sat nearby.

"Looks like you're making progress."

"Hope so." White teeth glistened from his tanned face. "That's what I'm here for. Should have this done in twenty minutes—then I'll repair the damaged ceiling."

"I just stopped by for a few minutes. I'll be leaving again unless you need something."

"Not a problem, Mrs. Bradley." He took a drink from the canteen that hung on a belt around his waist. "I should be through in an hour or so."

"Great." Helen went back inside. J.B. would be happy, since the leak had been in his office.

J.B. Helen swallowed back the lump in her throat. Concern for him started anew. Her concern quickly turned to annoyance and determination not to let his mysterious departure ruin her day. She had to keep her mind on other things. Like going to the beach.

Digging through her closet, she found her beach bag and tossed in the essentials: binoculars, a towel, paper and pen, and change of clothes in case she got wet. She then dumped a bowlful of agates she'd collected over the past year into a canvas bag and escaped into the sunshine. She'd been meaning to return the agates for several weeks, and now was as good a time as any. Not that they needed returning. It was just something she did on occasion. One could only collect and enjoy so many agates. After a while the collection overran the house, and it was time to clean them out, toss them back, and start over again.

She threw her beach bag into the trunk and drove north of town on Highway 101, going past Salishan and the Siletz River. At the light she made a left onto the beach-access road and drove by the new condominiums and hotel. Seeing the new buildings still rankled her. Helen hated watching the area develop so rapidly. Condos, hotels, and shopping centers seemed to pop up every day like unwanted weeds in a flower garden. The coast was becoming far too crowded—especially during the summer and on weekends.

Helen thought about stopping at the Clam Digger Restaurant for a latte and lunch but opted instead to wait until after her walk. The Clam Digger was a popular eatery known for its view, as well as for the fish chowder and seafood fare.

Helen parked in the public lot at the end of the road. Before leaving her car, she grabbed her cell phone. She stuffed the phone in her beach bag and cut through the driftwood-studded sand to the water's edge.

This scene where the bay and river mingled with the ocean had captured her heart. She'd often sit on a piece of driftwood and watch the seals sunning themselves on the sand spit across the narrow inlet or bobbing in the restless waters, playing and fishing in the strong currents.

Helen tossed a handful of agates into the surf, then another. She chuckled to herself, thinking anyone who saw her would wonder about her sanity. Glancing around, she noted only one other person on the beach. An obviously pregnant woman, legs outstretched, was leaning back on her arms, with eyes closed and face to the sun.

Helen looked up at the sky and grimaced. *Enjoy it while you can.* The wind was picking up again, bringing in another bank of clouds from the northwest and probably more rain. Not unusual, just disappointing. Summer had come and gone much too quickly this year. She'd often thought of joining the throngs of snowbirds who headed south for the winter—maybe to Laguna Beach or the Keys. Maybe she'd talk to J.B. about the possibility. Now that he was retired . . . She stopped her thoughts before they could drift and tossed out another handful of agates. A large wave pressed in, forcing her up the bank. It was then she spotted a little boy.

Helen felt a moment's irritation at the woman, who was still basking in the sun, oblivious to the danger her child might be in. At least she assumed the child was hers, as there were no other adults nearby. The boy, perhaps three or four, sat at the water's edge, filling the back of a red dump truck with wet sand. Neither mother nor child appeared to have any concern for the incoming tide.

A wave knocked the child to his knees and swept over him. He came up gasping for air, with another bigger wave bearing down on him. Helen tossed her beach bag aside and raced into the water in an attempt to pull him to safety.

She grabbed him around the middle and held him tight against her as she struggled against the receding water. The second wave crashed against her thighs, dragging her back. For several long and frightening moments she feared the severe undertow would drag them both out to sea.

In a temporary reprieve between swells, she staggered forward out of the ocean's reach. "It's all right," she gasped. "You're safe now."

Her words were lost in his frantic attempts to escape. "No. . . ." He flailed against her, pummeling her with his fists and shoes. Once they reached dry sand, Helen set him down.

"Mommy," he sobbed, stretching up his arms to the young woman lumbering toward them.

"Joshua! I told you not to go in the water."

"I didn't," he wailed. "The water came and got me and pushed me down."

"It wouldn't have if . . ." His mother sighed. "Never mind. You're safe, that's all that matters." She scooped up her son and straightened, a look of relief on her face. "Thank you so much." The woman, who seemed not much more than a child herself, stroked Joshua's sopping hair and wrapped her arms around him. "I . . . he got away from me. Josh was playing. . . . I saw him fall. I was afraid we'd lost him."

"Glad I could help." Helen couldn't resist a brief lecture. "The surf is dangerous here. We have a lot of sneaker waves coming in that toss logs around as if they were toothpicks. And the current is treacherous in places."

"I've read about that. You're right. I should have been paying more attention."

"Yes, you should have. If I hadn't . . . well, never mind. I just hope you'll watch him more closely in the future."

"I will."

Joshua struggled to be put down, but his mother kept a tight hold. "Be still. You're hurting Mommy's tummy."

"But my truck. That mean lady made me lose my truck."

"Joshua! That's no way to talk. You tell the nice lady you're sorry. If she hadn't pulled you out, you could have drowned."

He pouted in response, his blue lips quivering.

"I don't think he has a clue as to what drowning is," Helen said. "You'd better get him out of those wet clothes."

"No," he whined. "I want my truck."

"We'll get you a new one." His mother thanked Helen again and headed toward a rumpled blanket lying in the sand.

Helen glanced at the surging sea that had almost claimed the child's life. Seeing the red toy tumbling in on a wave, she hurried back and scooped it up. As she did she spotted something trapped beneath a grotesque and misshapen tree stump. Her insides twisted in revulsion. She stifled a scream.

Thinking she'd imagined it, Helen closed her eyes. When she opened them again, she fully expected to see a snarled root extending into the sand like human fingers. Unfortunately, she'd been right the first time. They were fingers, all right . . . on a very human hand.

Four

Helen wasn't normally given to hysterics, but then she'd never discovered a body on the beach before. She felt as though she'd been rammed in the stomach with a two-by-four. Helen turned away and, with her left hand, gripped one of the roots above her head to keep her balance. She straightened and at the same time tried to pull her scattered senses together.

Closing her eyes again, she hauled in a deep breath of salt air. Helen wasn't a stranger to death and as an ex-homicide detective had seen more than her share of bodies. But here, on the beach. . . . This was her sanctuary, her peace. She swallowed back the bile rising in her throat and tried to concentrate. She had to call the sheriff.

Helen twisted around and looked at the hand again. Left hand. Palm down. Fingers curled. No rings or watch or identifying marks. The waves continued to dig into the sand beneath a large tree trunk of driftwood, revealing more of the victim's arm and a sneaker-clad foot. The arm had wet strands of dark hair. *Ethan has dark hair. So does Chuck Daniels.* And neither man had come home the night before. *There's no reason to think the hand belongs to either of them,* Helen reminded herself.

Most of the victim's body had been buried beneath the wood, but she could see the remnant of a saturated gray wool sweater. She suspected the man had been walking or jogging. A sneaker wave must have heaved the enormous tree stump onto the beach, catching him unawares. As she'd told the young woman only a few minutes before, accidents like this happened far more often than they should.

The fingers were long and tapered. Not like Chuck's, she decided. He was stockier, wasn't he?

Helen closed her mind to the possibilities and refused to speculate on who the victim might be. Probably a tourist. Not someone she knew. She'd know for sure as soon as the authorities uncovered the body. Helen reached up to run a hand through her already disheveled hair and clunked her forehead with something hard. Staring at the toy truck in her hand, she frowned—momentarily blank as to what it was doing there.

"Oh good. You found it." The pregnant woman came toward her with her little boy in tow.

"Yes . . ." Helen looked at the truck again, then at the victim, and hurried around the driftwood. "Stay there. I'll be right up."

She scrambled over the sand dune and handed the truck over to its owner. The boy reached out from the colorful beach towel his mother had wrapped around him and grabbed it. A smile curled his trembling blue lips.

"Tell her thank you, Joshua," his mother coaxed.

In response, he clutched the truck tighter and ducked his head against his mom's shoulder.

"It's all right," Helen said. "Um . . . something has come up. I have to make a phone call." Helen didn't mention the body. The woman had more than enough to deal with already.

"Oh, sure. Guess I'd better get him to the car. I can't believe how quickly the weather changes here. One minute it's sunny and the next it's pouring. We just moved up from California and I'm not used to all this rain—or the cold."

"Welcome to Oregon."

"Thanks again. I owe you big time."

"Don't mention it." The young woman looked overburdened, and Helen felt a twinge of guilt for not offering to help her. Unfortunately, she had a burden of her own.

She wished the woman well and jogged back to where she'd dropped her beach bag. Pulling out her cellular phone, Helen dialed 9-1-1 and reported her discovery.

Once she'd given directions and advised the operator to send the appropriate equipment and manpower to pull the tree stump off the body, Helen went back to the scene to wait.

Her lovely patch of blue sky had been overtaken by clouds. Her heart settled into a normal rhythm as she paced back and forth on the sand dune above the body and the tree stump that held it prisoner. She felt helpless and at odds. The sheriff and his crew would be here soon. Ten minutes max. Not soon enough. There was no urgency, though—except within her own restless spirit. The man was dead. Yet even in his death he seemed to cry out for attention.

She didn't want to look at the body again. Didn't want to think about it. But her gaze kept drifting back. Was it Ethan? Or Chuck? Why did she keep thinking that? Other than the fact neither had come home the night before, she had no reason to believe either of them might be the victim. Refusing to think about either man's possible demise, she switched her thoughts to J.B., which didn't make her feel much better.

Helen closed her eyes, wishing her handsome Irish husband were there beside her, warming her inside and out with his smile and his arms. Only that wasn't to be. At least not today. After the argument they'd had this morning, she wondered if he'd ever come back. Ian hadn't.

This is different, Helen tried to reassure herself. *J.B. isn't an agent anymore.*

Anger flared again at the way J.B. had dismissed her questions. "What's the matter with you?" she muttered. It wasn't like her to be so negative.

Two sheriff's cars pulled into the public parking area, drawing Helen away from her morbid regressions. She watched the two officers emerge and jog around an obstacle course of driftwood and through the quarter of a mile of soft sand that lay between the patrol cars and where she waited.

"Hey, Mrs. Bradley. What's going on?" Joe paused to catch his breath. His dark hair was already damp and curling from the thick, steady mist. He brushed back a lock of hair that had fallen onto his forehead, and the moisture dripped onto his olive green rain slicker.

Helen told him what she'd found. "You're going to need a four-by-four with a winch to get that tree stump off him."

"Right. We've got one on the way." Joe introduced the officer who'd accompanied him as Tom Blackwell. Helen knew some of the officers in the area, but Tom was new to her.

"I transferred in from Seattle." Tom Blackwell grinned and shook her hand. He was a beefy-looking fellow in his mid-forties with thinning sandy brown hair and hazel eyes. "Pleasure to meet you. Joe was just telling me about you."

Seeming anxious now to get down to business, Joe asked, "Where is the body?"

"Over here." Helen led the officers to the massive chunk of driftwood. "I was fishing a kid's toy out of the water when I found it."

Tom looked away and shook his head. "Poor guy."

Joe grimaced. "Must have been caught by a sneaker wave."

"I was thinking the same thing." She kept her thoughts of Chuck and Ethan to herself.

"We'll need to tape off the area."

Tom agreed. "I'll bring the camera down. Better get some photos before the water gets too deep."

Joe's dark gaze drifted back to Helen. "Thanks for the call. Sorry you had to be the one to find him."

Helen shrugged. "Better me than some tourist." She wondered briefly if the little boy had seen it. Probably not. He'd been playing several yards away from where his truck had washed up.

"You're right about that. We'll take it from here," Joe said with a compassionate smile. "You look like you could use some warm clothes and a hot drink. You can go on home if you want. I'll swing by later to let you know the details."

"Sounds good, but I'd just as soon hang around if you don't mind. Still, I think I will get changed and maybe grab a bowl of soup at the Clam Digger."

"Don't mind at all." Joe shifted his attention to Tom. "See what's keeping Clarkston. Tell him we need that winch right away."

"I'm on it."

Joe waited until the water receded, then moved in for a closer look, intent on searching for clues.

Chilled to the bone, Helen hurried back to her car, passing Tom on the way. He tipped his head slightly in acknowledgment.

When she reached the edge of the parking lot, Helen noticed a forest green Bonneville pull in beside the patrol cars. An older man, thin with silver-gray hair, got out. Opening the trunk, he brought out a worn leather bag and slipped into a gray-green rain slicker. He'd aged some and gotten a lot more wrinkles and more gray hair. Helen hurried toward him. "George?"

He turned and closed the trunk in one graceful move. A wide smile graced his lips and moved into his silvery blue eyes. "Helen. My goodness, is it really you?" He dropped the bag and spread out his arms in a welcoming embrace.

Helen hugged him long and hard. "It's so good to see you. What are you doing here?" George Fisher had been a medical examiner in Portland while she'd worked for the police bureau there.

He picked up his bag. "Moved to Bay Village about two weeks ago. I'm in the process of retiring, so I thought I'd work on call down here. So far they've been keeping me pretty busy. What about you? I knew you'd quit police work, but . . ."

"I moved to Bay Village after Ian died."

"I heard about that." He looked her over, his eyes filling with concern. "You're soaked."

"Yes, I'm the one who found the body. Had to wait for the sheriff."

"Too bad about that. Did you know him—the victim, I mean?"

"So far there isn't enough of him showing to make any kind of identification." She told him about the tree stump. "I was just going to the restaurant to change and get something hot to eat."

"You do that. I'd better get to work. Can we talk later? We have a lot of catching up to do."

"I'd like nothing better."

The Clam Digger was warm and noisy with its usual lunch crowd. The tempting smells set her tummy to rumbling. After ordering a bowl of fish stew and a chamomile tea, Helen headed for the bathroom.

Once she'd changed, she returned to her table by the window at the west end. From there she could see the officers working in the distance. They'd drawn several curious onlookers, who were kept at bay by an officer outside the taped area. A corner of the tape had broken loose and now waved in the wind like a grounded kite's tail.

The waitress brought her order, and Helen concentrated on easing the dull ache in her stomach. The stew was excellent, and while it satisfied her hunger, it did nothing to ease her concerns. She sipped at her tea, willing herself to stay put and relax. That lasted about two minutes. She couldn't stand sitting there doing nothing with all the action out on the beach.

Helen paid her bill, transferred her tea to a takeout cup, and headed toward the door. On her way to the car she pulled out her cell phone and made a call to Eleanor Crane.

"Eleanor, it's me, Helen. I just wondered if you'd heard from Ethan."

"Not yet. I did as you suggested and called Joe. He wasn't in, so I left a message to have him call me."

"That's good. He's tied up right now. But I'm sure he'll call as soon as he's free."

"You've seen him, then. You didn't . . ."

"No, I haven't said anything." Helen rang off without telling her what Joe was tied up with.

She then called Lynn Daniels. Lynn hadn't heard from Chuck either.

"I think you're more worried than I am, Helen. He'll come home when he's sober."

"I'm sure you're right." Ending the call, Helen tucked her phone and bag into the trunk and zipped up her jacket.

Though a thick cloud cover persisted and the air was still damp and cold, the rain had stopped. Helen walked back to where the officers were still working to extricate the corpse from its root-bound prison. Several people stood on the periphery, eager to learn firsthand about the body on the beach. A couple of reporters had already shown up. A cameraman panned the area several times while a man Helen recognized from one of the news stations spoke into a microphone. She wondered how they'd managed to respond so quickly. Before long the area would be saturated with reporters clamoring for details.

Helen diverted her gaze and hoisted herself onto a nearby piece of driftwood—a log about three feet in diameter and some twenty feet long. Dampness from the rain-soaked log seeped into the seat of her jeans. She stood and brushed off the sand, then leaned against the log instead.

Since she'd been gone, two officers, a man and a woman neither of whom she knew, had joined Joe and Tom. Two paramedics stood to one side waiting to transport the body to the morgue once it was freed. Tom and Joe now had on scuba gear and stood knee-deep in the soupy surf. They'd apparently been trying to shovel the sand out from under the tree stump—an impossible task with the incoming tide extinguishing their efforts.

George stood near the paramedics. One of the new officers, probably Clarkston, stood behind an all-terrain vehicle, securing the hook from his winch to a chain they'd put around the narrower part of the enormous stump.

Tom heaved his shovel onto dry sand. "Try it again," he yelled to Clarkston.

The deputy jumped inside the four-by-four and switched on the ignition. Revving up the engine, he engaged the winch. The others moved aside and watched the cable tighten. The stump inched forward.

"That's enough." Tom and Joe pulled the body free and carried it out of the surf, laying it in the dry sand, well away from the water.

The reporters snapped photos while the camera whirred. The newsman spoke excitedly into his microphone and pressed in for a closer look.

George hunkered down to examine the victim.

Dread filled Helen as she speculated again on the victim's identity. She wanted to know, yet at the same time she didn't. Tearing her gaze away, she watched a boat riding the swells on the distant horizon.

Twenty minutes later, Helen still waited on the dreary, cold, and windy beach. Joe and George had apparently completed their on-site investigation. The paramedics loaded the body into the back of the four-by-four and draped a blanket over it. Clarkston drove them back to the parking lot, where they transferred the corpse to a stretcher and put him into the waiting ambulance.

Helen hadn't been able to see much from her vantage point. Several times she'd thought about moving closer. Joe and George would have welcomed her presence. But Helen had already seen more than she wanted to.

The crowd then broke up. The reporters and cameraman managed to get a statement from Joe. Helen heard snatches of the conversation: "Yes, we've been able to ID the victim. We'll release the information as soon as we've notified the family."

Helen's stomach churned. They'd identified him. That meant he was probably a local.

The reporters seemed satisfied with the report and left. Helen straightened and walked out to meet Joe and George.

"Well . . . ?"

Joe's dark eyes met hers for an instant before moving toward the surf.

"It's Ethan."

"Oh no!" She closed her eyes. "I was afraid of that."

Joe looked surprised. "You were? Why would you think it might be Ethan?"

"I talked to Eleanor this morning. Ethan didn't come home last night. She was going to talk to you about it."

He shook his head. "But she didn't."

"She left you a message." Helen buried her hands deeper into the pockets of her jacket. "Any idea how long he's been dead?"

"Hard to say. I suspect it was sometime last night." George put an arm across her shoulders. "I take it he was a friend."

"Yes. Yes, he was."

"I'm so sorry, Helen. If there's anything I can do . . ."

"You two know each other?" Joe asked.

"We sure do." George tightened his hold for a moment, then

released her. "We collaborated on a lot of cases. Are you still working in an official capacity, Helen?"

"Not exactly."

"Not for money, anyway," Joe corrected. "We call her in as a consultant—she helps out when we're overloaded or short-handed."

"What's that?" Helen asked, frowning at the plastic bag swinging from Joe's hand.

He held it up to give her a closer look. "A knife of some kind."

"I can see that, but what . . . ?"

"Helen," George said, "I don't think the tree stump killed Ethan. Looks like he was murdered."

Five

Helen's stomach rolled and pitched like a ship at sea, her mind a jumble of wild and random thoughts and questions.

George excused himself, saying he needed to get back to work. "I'll call you sometime today, Joe. Helen, I'll catch you later. Maybe we can have dinner."

She nodded absently. "That sounds good."

"Hard to believe, isn't it?" Joe lowered the bag containing the weapon to his side.

"Unthinkable. Who would want to kill Ethan? And why? He was one of the kindest men I know." While part of her refused to accept his death, another part—the homicide detective—had already begun to look at motives and suspects. Helen pushed her thoughts aside, reminding herself not to get involved. The last time she'd taken on an investigation, she'd nearly gotten herself killed.

Still, Ethan had been murdered. Helen looked at the weapon again. Though the wet sand in the bag limited her view, it looked oddly familiar. The handle had an unusual rectangular shape. The blade was narrow, maybe half an inch wide and about six inches long. "It doesn't look particularly lethal."

"Maybe not, but the fact still remains, someone was trying to kill him."

"Joe, if you don't mind, I'd like to take a closer look at the weapon when you're through with it."

He raised an eyebrow. "Sure. You planning to come in on this one?"

Not wanting to commit herself, Helen ignored his question. "I have the oddest sense I've seen it somewhere. Just can't place it."

"Well, think hard. It's about the only physical evidence we have so far. Surf washed almost everything away. This is going to be a tough one. We'll keep looking—check out the area more thoroughly, but it doesn't look good." Joe shook the water off his hat, then replaced it. "Unfortunately, the killer has had a lot of time to disappear. That tree stump coming in probably kept anyone from finding the body sooner." He frowned. "Look, I need to tell Eleanor. Um . . . I hate to ask, but could you come along? You're her friend and . . . she might need some moral support."

"Of course, but I think you're the one who needs the moral support."

"You got that right," Joe muttered.

Helen understood his reluctance. Informing the family had always been the hardest part of being a police officer. "Poor Eleanor." She thought briefly of telling Joe about Eleanor's suspicion of an affair but decided against it—at least for now. There wasn't much point in bringing it up, since Eleanor had no proof—none that she'd shared anyway.

Helen trudged through the soft sand with Joe, making what she hoped were appropriate responses to his statements of disbelief.

"This is too much," Joe said as Helen tuned him back in. "Two mayors murdered within two months. Makes you wonder."

"You don't think they're related, do you? Mayor Ames's killer is in jail awaiting trial—isn't he?"

"Yes, but two mayors . . . ?" He shook his head. "What are the odds?"

"Maybe there was more to Ames's death than we thought."

"Meaning our suspect might not have been working alone."

"It's possible." By the time they reached the parking lot the drizzle had become a steady shower. She pulled her keys out of her pocket. "I'll see you there."

He nodded and ducked into the patrol car.

Helen folded her long, slender frame into her own car, setting her now-empty cup in the drink holder. Pulling a towel from the backseat, she dabbed at the moisture on her face and rubbed most of the wetness from her hair. She vigorously shook her head, then finger-combed her short salt-and-pepper hair and started the car. Cold air from the heater blasted her as she backed out of the lot.

She flipped off the air and shivered. Helen loved her vintage car, but it took forever to warm up. She was nearly to Bay Village before the engine warmed enough to turn on the heater.

Helen eyed the empty cup, wishing she had something hot and comforting to drink. As she spotted Past Times, her favorite hangout, her foot went to the brake. She wanted a latte in the worst way and imagined herself curled up in one of Rosie Monahan's wonderful overstuffed chairs, sipping a hot creamy drink and talking to her good friend. Bad days and problems always seemed to diminish when she and Rosie chatted. They made a good pair, sharing both good times and bad and managing to cheer each other up when the dark gray days threatened to send them into depression.

Helen looked longingly at the beautifully restored Victorian and drove on by, promising herself that the moment she left Eleanor's, she would go straight to Rosie's. Besides, Rosie would want to know about Ethan. The two of them could commiserate together.

Thinking about Rosie got Helen to considering what Eleanor had said about Ethan's late nights. She hated the direction her thoughts had taken, but she didn't stop them. Instead she began looking for connections. Rosie had been one of Ethan's strongest advocates when he was being considered as a replacement for Mayor Ames. Could she have been the other woman? *Rosie and Ethan?*

Helen had never particularly noticed it before, but now the clues seemed to pour down like the rain pummeling her windshield. How often had she gone to the bookstore and found Rosie and Ethan chatting, or Ethan buying a book and lingering over a cup of coffee? Helen had seen them talking at various get-togethers at church and charity functions. No one would argue the fact that they were friends. But lovers?

"Don't be ridiculous," Helen said aloud, chiding herself for her groundless speculation. She wouldn't have even made the connection if Eleanor hadn't mentioned the possibility of another woman. Being an avid reader didn't make Ethan guilty of cheating on his wife. Still, Eleanor's suspicions had to count for something, didn't they?

Not necessarily, she answered her own question. *How many times have you and Ethan talked?* He was friendly with everyone.

The idea of Ethan having a romantic tryst had been born out of Eleanor's fears. She'd as much as admitted that. Helen certainly understood how wild the imagination could be. Hadn't she been building scenarios out of thin air about the mysterious phone call and J.B.'s reaction to it? Given enough time she might have come up with the *other-woman* theory herself.

J.B. would never be unfaithful to you.

Never say never.

Thankfully, her imaginings came to an end when she turned into the Cranes' driveway.

Helen pulled in beside Joe, then, slipping the keys into her jacket pocket, hurried to catch up with him. When they reached the wide porch, he rang the bell.

"Joe, hi." Annie Costello, Bay Village's finest and only caterer, opened the door. "And Helen. What a nice surprise."

Helen didn't miss the way Annie's admiring gaze lingered on the handsome sheriff. The petite strawberry blonde brushed short, wild curls from her forehead.

"The surprise is seeing you here," Helen said.

Annie's smile diminished. "Oh, I guess it would be. Ever since the fiasco at the art auction, business hasn't been so good. I mean . . . everyone knows I didn't poison poor Mayor Ames, but when it's your food, people are hesitant to hire you. Anyway, I needed a job, and Eleanor needed an extra hand over the holidays, so here I am."

"It's only temporary," Joe said. "Before long your business will be booming again."

"I'm sure it will," Helen added. "Just give it time. Which reminds me, I'm on the committee for the women's luncheon this month. I'd like to talk with you later about catering it."

Annie's dazzling smile was back. "Thanks. I'd love to. Come into the kitchen before you leave and we'll discuss the menu. Is Eleanor expecting you?"

"No." Joe sighed heavily. "She's not."

"What's wrong? It's Melissa, isn't it?" Annie's green eyes clouded. "Eleanor and Nancy have been worried. She's been gone for—"

"It isn't Melissa." Joe settled a hand on her shoulder.

"Then what?" She covered her mouth. "Oh no, not Ethan."

"I really need to talk to Eleanor." Joe stepped past her into the entry.

"Of course." Annie bit into her lower lip and glanced toward the wide, curved staircase. "She's upstairs with Nancy. I'll get her."

Helen closed the door. Memories washed over her, taking her back nearly twelve years to the day she'd opened her own door to two men in black suits, identifying themselves as CIA agents. Now Eleanor would hear the same words: *"Your husband is dead."*

Helen shoved the thoughts back into the musty corner of her mind. Joe had asked her to come, and Eleanor would need someone strong to lean on.

Moments later, Eleanor joined them in the living room. Since Helen's morning visit, she'd changed into jeans and a long-sleeved coral jersey knit. "I've asked Annie to bring us some tea and cookies." She led the way into a sitting room.

Once they were seated, Eleanor looked from one to the other, letting her confused gaze linger on Joe. "I assume you're here about Ethan." Turning to Helen, she asked, "You told him?"

"About Ethan being missing, yes," Helen answered, letting her know she hadn't mentioned their discussion about the alleged affair.

"I tried to call you earlier, Joe."

"I know."

"I suppose I should have called you sooner," Eleanor said,

"but I kept hoping he'd show up. Helen told you he should have been here last night?"

Joe nodded.

"I know an adult isn't considered missing for twenty-four hours, but I think you should make an exception. It isn't like him not to call."

"Eleanor," Joe interrupted. "Ethan isn't missing."

"Well, of course he is. . . ." She stopped. "I don't understand. Have you found him?"

Joe took a deep breath and let it out in a rush. "There's no easy way to say this. Ethan is dead."

Eleanor stared at him with a blank expression as his words sank in. "That's not possible. He can't be."

Helen moved to Eleanor's chair. Hunkering down, she placed what she hoped was a comforting hand on her friend's arm. "It's true, Eleanor. I'm sorry."

"There must be some mistake."

"No mistake," Joe answered. "I wish there were."

Eleanor closed her eyes and folded her arms as if trying to hold herself together. "How . . . how did it happen?"

Joe cleared his throat. "His body was found on the beach—under a tree stump."

"On the beach? Under . . . you think he was caught by a sneaker wave?"

"That's what we thought at first. But when we pulled him out, we saw that he'd been stabbed. The medical examiner will do an autopsy to determine the exact cause of death."

Her eyes widened in horror. "Stabbed? I don't understand. Are you saying someone killed him and buried him under a . . . a tree stump?"

"We don't know what happened yet." Joe turned his hat in his hands. "I'll need to ask you some questions."

Eleanor's eyes held a mixture of shock and disbelief. She clasped her hands and straightened. "Of course. But I don't know what I can tell you."

"When did you last see Ethan?"

Eleanor glanced at Helen. "Thursday afternoon. He was flying to Washington, D.C., for a special meeting with our state senator."

"Do you know whether he arrived in Washington?"

She nodded. "He called me Thursday night from the hotel."

"You're certain he was in D.C.?"

"Yes. I looked at the number on the Caller ID."

"Was that the last time you talked to him?"

She nodded again. "He said he'd be home Sunday. Told me not to wait dinner and that he'd grab something on the way and see me around nine. He never came." Eleanor's shoulders sagged. Pulling a tissue from a decorative box on the end table, she dabbed at the corners of her eyes, catching her tears before they spilled. "This can't be happening."

"Did Ethan have any enemies?" Joe asked. "Someone who might want to see him dead?"

Lines knitted her forehead. "Not that I know of. I suppose he's made a few enemies being mayor—you can't please everyone. No one that would kill him. I . . . I'm sorry. Can we do this later? I can't think." She folded her arms again, pressing them against her stomach, then leaned forward and back in a rocking motion.

"Yeah," Joe said. "I can come back later."

"Thank you."

"I can stay with you for a while if you'd like," Helen said. "I know how devastating this must be."

"Would you?"

Annie arrived with the tea and cookies. "You're leaving?" she asked as Joe stood.

"I have to get back," Joe said.

Annie set the tray down on the coffee table in front of Eleanor and Helen. "I'll walk you to the door."

He told Helen and Eleanor he'd see them later and turned his attention to Annie.

Eleanor dabbed at her eyes again, then busied herself with the ritual of pouring tea. With shaking hands, she offered Helen a cup before taking one for herself. "There's something soothing about a cup of tea, don't you think?"

"Yes." Helen wrapped her hands around the cup, gathering its warmth.

Eleanor took a sip of the hot brew, then, setting her cup and saucer on the table, picked up a small throw pillow and fidgeted with the fringe on one corner. "You were right."

"About what?"

"I should have alerted the sheriff last night when Ethan didn't come home. Instead I let my fear of the gossip mills stand in the way of my better judgment. We're supposed to grow wiser with age." She rose and paced to the window, staring out at the churning water. "I don't know what to do. Should I tell Joe that Ethan might have been seeing someone?"

"Do you really think he was?"

She covered her eyes. "I don't know anything for certain. Maybe he *was* working all those evenings. When he didn't come home last night, I let my suspicions get the best of me. Poor Ethan. Do you think I was wrong about his having a mistress?" Eleanor turned back to Helen. "What should I do? Part of me wants to know for sure. The other part wants to look the other way and pretend nothing was going on."

Helen nodded. "I understand. While I hate to think of Ethan as being unfaithful to you, if there was another woman, we need to know."

Eleanor bit her lower lip. Tears gathered in her eyes again and she blinked them back. She was trying so hard to hold herself together.

Helen cleared her throat. "Earlier today when you asked me to investigate the possibility that Ethan was having an affair, I said no. But in light of what's happened, I think it might be a good idea if I looked into the matter. Whatever or whomever Ethan was spending so much time with may have something to do with his death."

"Do you think she might be the one who killed him?"

"Let's just say if she does exist, she'd be a person of interest."

"I don't want Ethan's name dragged through the mud."

"Nor do I. If it turns out that Ethan didn't have a mistress, then fine. Only you and I need to know about your suspicions.

If we find evidence that he was seeing someone, we'll have to tell Joe."

Eleanor nodded wearily. "I suppose you're right." She sat back down and picked up her teacup. "I need to tell Nancy about her father. This is going to be hard for her. She's dealing with so much already."

"Would you like me to stay while you tell her?"

"That's kind of you, but no. I'd better deal with this myself. I'll tell her, then call Brian." She rubbed her forehead. "Oh, Helen, they'll be devastated. They loved Ethan so much. And Melissa. She adored her grandfather."

"I know. When Ian died, I think the hardest part was telling the children." At least in the beginning. Later came the aching loneliness that no one could fill. Healing had been a long time coming.

"Then you know what it's like." Eleanor drew herself up and stood and eyed the sweeping staircase.

Helen picked up her jacket and reached into her pocket for her keys. "Call me if you need anything."

"I will." They walked together into the entryway.

Helen gave her a hug. "I mean it. If you need help with funeral arrangements or—"

"Mother?" Nancy yelled from the top of the stairs. "Is Melissa back yet?"

"Not yet, but I'm sure she'll be here soon. You know how kids are." Eleanor's voice belied the pained expression on her face. She gripped the banister and leaned heavily against it.

"I'm going out to try to find her." Nancy came down the steps and stopped when she saw Helen. "Oh, you're still here. I thought I heard someone leave."

"That was Joe," Eleanor said. "Nancy, there's something I need to tell you."

Shifting her gaze to Eleanor, Nancy frowned. "Mother, what is it? Why are you crying? You never cry."

"I'll try to stop by later." Helen closed the door and stepped into the rain. Once in the car, she rested her forehead on the steering wheel, letting reality settle around her. Ethan was dead.

Eleanor's husband, the town's mayor, her friend, had been murdered.

Straightening her shoulders, she drew in a deep breath and
exhaled slowly, then started the car. As she pulled out of the
driveway she remembered her promise to talk to Annie about
the catering. Deciding to call later, Helen drove on. She really
needed that latte. But more than that, she needed to talk to
Rosie.

Six

Unbidden thoughts linking Ethan and Rosie surfaced again on the drive through town. "This is crazy," Helen mumbled as she parked her car in the gravel parking lot to the side of Past Times. "Eleanor *thinks* Ethan might be having an affair, and you suspect your best friend of being the other woman."

Helen felt both justified in her thinking and ashamed at the same time. She needed answers, not speculation. But right now, she needed to let Rosie know about Ethan, and then they'd drown their mutual sorrows in hot coffee and hazelnut-and-chocolate-chip scones. Hopefully Rosie would be in a less frantic mode than she'd been during Helen's last visit. She'd been unusually flighty and short-tempered. When Helen tried to pin her down and get her to talk about what was bothering her, Rosie just attributed it to stress and money problems. Helen had suspected something else at the time, since Rosie had financial problems every year in the off-season and it had never sent her into a dither before.

Helen opened her car door and took her time going inside, letting the feel of the place work its magic. Unlike most of the modern buildings in Bay Village that housed art galleries and gift shops, Rosie's establishment, Past Times, was a restored three-story Victorian. The third floor served as Rosie's home. The rooms on the first and second floors were filled with books—mostly used ones—and miscellaneous gift items that suited the room. Rosie had a theme for each room: one for romance, another for mystery, and yet another for the classics.

She loved entering the store, especially on cold, blustery days like this one. Helen paused on the lovely wraparound porch before going inside. A familiar Celtic tune by one of her favorite artists drifted out of the speakers at either end of the porch. *"Music and books complement each other,"* Rosie had said more than once. Celtic was her preferred style. Helen's too. The ancient sounds drew her back to her Irish roots.

Patches of sunlight pushing through the gray sky made the store look even more springlike than it already did. Even on the bleakest of winter days, Rosie's place never failed to brighten Helen's spirits. There were planter boxes and hanging baskets everywhere, filled with real flowers in season and silk or plastic plants when nothing in Bay Village grew except rain clouds. It looked like something straight out of *Better Homes & Gardens*.

On the porch to her right sat a lovely white wicker chair-and-sofa set with mint green and rosebud cushions and matching throw pillows. Pink and white geraniums filled the window box. Buttermilk, a mottled gray cat, lay coiled in the chair. "Her Majesty's Chair," according to Rosie. The cat cast Helen a bored, don't-even-think-about-sitting-here look, then closed her large blue-gray eyes and ignored her. Buttermilk, Rosie claimed, actually read books, and especially liked mysteries. *The Cat Who . . .* series by Lillian Jackson Braun were Buttermilk's favorites.

A cold ocean breeze tinkled the chimes that hung from the ceiling as the door swung open—a sweet, happy sound, so at odds with the turmoil in the pit of Helen's stomach. The fragrant scent of vanilla and spice mingled with coffee and baked goodies.

"Excuse me." A plus-sized woman in a long gray raincoat brushed past Helen and opened her umbrella. She tossed Helen a thin smile and mumbled something about wishing the weather would make up its mind. Helen watched her descend the steps and turn toward the only other car in the parking lot.

Helen grasped the edge of the still-open door, forcing her mind back to the reason she'd come. Somehow she'd have to inform Rosie of Ethan's death and at the same time maintain her objectivity to read Rosie's reaction. She'd always been good at judging correctly people's nonverbal communication. Helen took a deep breath and closed the door, then leaned against it for a moment, gathering her strength and resolve.

But the store's atmosphere made it hard to concentrate on Ethan's being murdered, when all her senses told her to relax and enjoy the surroundings. Paradoxically, the sun peeking through the curtained windows made her mission seem all the more obscure and the death of their friend unreal.

The music was softer now. Melancholy. Or maybe it was just the singer's tone as she sang about a woman in love with a man about to die on the gallows. Helen tuned out the morbid words and glanced around, looking for her friend and, at the same time, hoping she wouldn't find her.

She scanned the former living room with its overstuffed chairs and end tables. The cozy niches provided customers with places to sit and browse. Rosie had recently put in an espresso bar and several small round patio tables with café chairs. On the other side of the café was the children's corner, where an orange tabby kitten sunned herself on top of one of the many bookshelves. The kitten, a stray that Rosie had taken in, stretched, turned, and settled back down without so much as brushing against the fanciful display of *Alice in Wonderland* books and ceramic figurines.

Helen finally spotted her friend behind the counter, nearly hidden from view by stacks of books on the counter. Rosie's dark head was, as usual, bent over a book. She sat in a platform rocker with her stockinged feet propped up on a matching hassock. Rosie's bohemian tendencies were evident in the flowing, colorful clothing she wore. She reminded Helen of a rainbow in her floor-length gauze dress splashed with vivid greens, reds, blues, and yellows. Rosie made no excuses for having been a flower child in the sixties.

Rosie glanced up and greeted her with a dimpled grin. "Helen, I was just thinking about calling you." She set her glasses and the book she'd been reading aside, slipped into a pair of leather clogs, and came out from behind the counter. Giving Helen a hug, she said, "It's been ages. I was beginning to think that gorgeous husband of yours was holding you captive in an ivory tower somewhere."

Helen laughed despite the seriousness of her visit. "You've been reading too many romances."

"You can never read too many of those—or any book for that matter. How is J.B.?" Rosie beamed up at her. Her deep brown eyes shone with elfish delight.

"Okay, I guess."

"Uh-oh. Sounds like the honeymoon is over."

Helen shrugged. "It happens. We had an argument this morning. He left for Portland in a huff and wouldn't tell me where he was going or why."

"Wow. I don't blame you for being upset." Rosie leaned against the counter, her gaze lingering on Helen's face. "You're really torn up about this, aren't you?"

"It isn't just J.B., Rosie. Something has happened."

"What is it?"

Tears gathered in Helen's eyes as she started to speak. Annoyed with herself, she dug a tissue out of her jacket pocket and wiped them away. Straightening her shoulders, Helen glanced around the store. "Are we alone?"

"Yeah—it's been dead today. What's wrong?"

"I found a body on the beach this morning. It was trapped under a tree trunk."

"Oh, Helen, are you serious? Who was it? Another sneaker wave? That'll be eight this year. It wasn't another kid, was it?"

Helen bit into her lower lip. "It was Ethan."

Rosie stared openmouthed. "Ethan? But that's not possible. Why, just last night he—"

"You saw Ethan last night?" Helen grabbed the statement and threw it back.

"Oh . . . um . . . no, I mean, he came into the store the other day." She swayed and leaned against the counter.

Helen's heart hammered. Rosie was lying. She had been with Ethan last night. And judging from her response, she and Ethan may well have been more than friends.

"He was murdered." Helen watched Rosie's face, her eyes. "Stabbed in the back with . . ." As Helen visualized the familiar-looking knife, with its book-shaped handle, she suddenly remembered where she'd seen it. The murder weapon had come from Rosie's mystery room. ". . . your dagger." The words slipped out before Helen could stop them.

"My what?" Rosie's hand flew to her throat.

Helen's mouth went dry as the implications set in. How had Rosie's letter opener ended up in Ethan's back? Had Rosie killed him? Not likely. The genuine look of shock on her friend's face attested to her innocence. Besides, Rosie wouldn't be stupid enough to use such an easily identifiable weapon. Helen couldn't see her using a weapon at all—of any kind. Just the same, she needed to proceed with caution. "Ethan was killed with the dagger you got from that world mystery convention you went to a few years ago. The one advertising some book."

"*Letter to a Dead Man.*" Rosie frowned and shook her head. "My letter opener killed Ethan?"

"Unless someone else in town has one just like it, yes."

Rosie moved from the counter to her chair and sank into it. "I don't understand. How could my . . . ?" She hesitated. The color drained from her face. "Oh no. You . . . you don't think I . . . ?" Her eyes searched Helen's. "You do. Oh my. . . . You think I killed him."

"I didn't say that."

"You didn't have to," Rosie gasped. "Ethan was here. I didn't. I swear. I couldn't kill Ethan. I loved . . . he was . . . my friend."

"Rosie, stop. I'm trying not to jump to conclusions here. But the murderer used a letter opener like the one you have in your memorabilia upstairs in the mystery room." Helen started for the steps. "Look, we can check this out right now. If yours is there—"

"You don't need to look. It's gone. I thought I'd misplaced it." She held on to her desk with a white-knuckled grip. "I can't believe this. I'd been keeping it on my desk and using it to open the mail. I broke the wooden one—you know the one my brother made with the bird carved into the handle. I went to grab it one day and it was gone."

Rosie loved him. "When did you notice it was missing?"

"Last week . . . Tuesday, I think. Like I said, at first I thought maybe I'd misplaced it, then I got to wondering if it might have been one of the tourists. There was a whole busload in that day." She frowned. "But that doesn't make sense, does it? It's not worth anything to anyone but me. It was a letter opener. I didn't think . . . I never dreamed someone would use it as a weapon." Her eyes widened. "Someone's trying to frame me. That must be it. They stole the letter opener from me and used it to kill Ethan so I'd get the blame."

"Rosie, stop. We don't know that. Let's sit down a minute and think this through."

"What am I going to do?"

"First, we have to tell Joe."

Rosie looked horrified. "No, please. He'll put me in jail. I didn't kill him, but my fingerprints will be on it." Her tearful gaze flitted around the room, reminding Helen of a frightened bird desperate to escape.

Helen doubted there would still be identifiable prints but didn't say so. "Rosie, please. Calm down. If it's any consolation, I don't think you killed Ethan."

Rosie clasped her hands. "Thank goodness for that."

"But you're not being honest with me. You were with Ethan last night, weren't you?"

"No, I . . ." She hesitated. "All right. Yes. He came by around five-thirty. I was just closing up. Um . . . he was looking for a book."

"What kind of book?"

She shrugged. "Something to do with the environmental impact on wetlands. He said he was preparing a statement for a meeting he had with some corporation wanting to build a shopping center north of here."

Helen knew about the proposal. She and J.B. were prepared to fight it. If approved, it would go in across the highway from their neighborhood and extend into a designated wetland area. The mall would negatively impact the environment and basically ruin their easterly view of the hills, as well as their peace of mind. Yes, it would generate jobs and possibly bring in more tourists, but at what cost?

The already-established retail businesses would suffer, and it was so unnecessary. The area had plenty of shops and restaurants. Helen tucked away the information and her annoyance with the project. It was something she'd have to look at later. Ethan had probably made a few enemies there, but would getting rid of him strengthen the investors' cause? Helen doubted it. And the idea of using Rosie's letter opener made no sense whatsoever.

"Did Ethan say where he was going when he left here?"

Rosie hesitated, frowning. "No . . . just home. He hadn't eaten."

Helen bit the inside of her cheek. "Eleanor told me Ethan wasn't going to be home for dinner last night."

"She did?" Rosie's gaze slid to her desk, then back to Helen. "Maybe I just assumed that. He may have been meeting someone."

"Who?"

"I don't know."

"You make a lousy liar, Rosie." Helen heaved an exasperated sigh. "I'd like to help you, but you've got to tell me the truth."

"I am. He came in for a book—and left. Why can't you believe that? He was fine when he left here." Rosie buried her face in her hands. Several moments passed before she brought her hands down and hauled in a deep breath. "I didn't kill him."

Helen placed a gentle hand on her friend's shoulder. "We need to call Joe. The sooner he knows about the letter opener the better."

"I can't." Fear glistened in her eyes.

"You have to, Rosie. If you don't, I will." Helen softened her plea with reassurance. "It will be all right. Just tell Joe what you told me. And be honest about your relationship with Ethan. He needs all the facts if he's going to find out who killed him."

"I suppose you're right. I'll call him." Rosie moved toward the phone she kept on her desk. She picked up the receiver and punched in the numbers. Then in one fluid motion she opened the top drawer and pulled out a gun.

Seven

R osie!" Helen gasped. "What are you thinking? Put that thing away before one of us gets hurt."

"No. I can't talk to Joe. Not yet!" Rosie's voice hung on the edge of hysteria.

Helen held her breath and took a step toward her. "Come on, Rosie. This is crazy. Put the gun down."

"Don't come any closer." She waved the gun for emphasis. "I mean it. I don't want to hurt you. That dagger was mine. You know what that means. They'll think I did it."

"Did you?"

"Of course not. I told you I didn't."

"Then for goodness' sake, talk to Joe."

"He'll never believe me. I need time to think. I can't let anyone find out about . . ."

"About what?"

Tears gathered in her eyes again, and Helen moved closer. "Rosie, please. Let the authorities handle this."

"Stay back! I'll use this. I mean it. You're my friend, but there are things you don't understand."

"Then explain it to me. And while you're at it, you can tell me why you have a gun. I thought you hated guns." Rosie's actions were so out of character, Helen wondered if her friend might be in the middle of a mental breakdown.

"I can't. Not now." She waved the gun toward the door. "Move."

"You're taking me with you?" Helen hoped that would be

the case. It would give her time to talk some sense into her. And if that didn't work, maybe she could get the upper hand.

"No. Do I look like an idiot? You'd have me on the floor with one of your karate moves before we got to the car." Rosie glanced at Helen's bag, which was still lying on the floor where she'd set it when she came in. "You don't have your gun in there, do you?"

Fat lot of good it would do. Even if she had her gun, she couldn't get to it.

"Rosie—"

"No! Don't say any more. Get into the storage room behind you."

Helen glanced back. The door to the room in question was slightly ajar.

"Open it and get inside."

"Rosie, please don't do this."

"I mean it, Helen. Don't make me use this. Just get in there."

Helen pulled open the door. Storeroom nothing. It was a closet, lined with shelves. It still had a dowel reaching from one side to the other. Rosie's jacket hung there along with a clear plastic rain slicker. "You're not going to lock me in there, are you?"

"I have no choice. There's something I need to do. You wouldn't understand." She waved the gun again and Helen complied.

She doubted Rosie would actually shoot her but didn't want to take any chances. As far as Helen knew, Rosie had little or no training in using the weapon. That and her present state made her extremely dangerous. She quickly assessed the situation. The door to the storage room was an original. It had a tendency to swing open, so Rosie had installed a latch on the outside to keep it shut.

She considered throwing the door open before Rosie had a chance to lock it but decided against it. She didn't want the gun to accidentally go off and hit either one of them.

"You'll be sorry, Rosie," Helen yelled as the door snapped shut and Rosie slipped the hook in place. "You'd be much better off going to Joe."

"Maybe, but I don't have much choice."

Grasping the antique knob, Helen made a final plea. "Yes, you do. Come on, Rosie. Let me out. Let's talk about this."

Something heavy scraped across the floor, then hit the closet door.

Helen could hear Rosie securing the front door, then ascending the stairs to her apartment. Moments later, she heard the garage door open and the car start.

Stepping back a couple feet, Helen rammed her shoulder against the old wooden door.

Big mistake. Pain coursed through her shoulder and radiated down through her entire body. Helen grabbed her right arm, sank to her knees, and rocked back and forth. She'd temporarily forgotten about the injury she'd incurred earlier last summer in an ambush. The bullet had been surgically removed, and she'd spent several weeks in therapy. She massaged the painful area, hoping she hadn't caused any permanent damage.

Helen kicked at the door in disgust. Several hefty kicks later, she still hadn't dislodged the screws holding the latch in place. Probably because she was kicking too low. She needed to move her efforts up nearer the latch. She felt along the wall next to the door for a light switch. Nothing. She then reached above her for a light chain and found only air. Widening her search, her hand connected with a shelf toward the back of the closet, and under it was the rod she'd noticed on her earlier inspection. Helen closed her hands around the thick wooden dowel, thinking maybe she could hang from it and use more of her body weight in hitting the door above the knob. The dowel sagged and creaked under her weight. She closed her eyes to the pain in her shoulder and delivered one swift and furious kick. The door seemed to give a bit, but it wasn't enough. Finally, she released the rod and groaned as her shoulder spasmed in rebellion. Helen sank to the floor in defeat.

How could you have been so stupid? Stupid, stupid, stupid. You shouldn't have confronted her. As soon as you realized the murder weapon was hers, you should have gone straight to the authorities.

You couldn't have known she'd react that way, a kinder, more empathetic side of her argued. *Or that she'd have a gun.* Had she misjudged Rosie all this time?

Of course not. Rosie has always been a kind and decent person. She'll do anything for people. She couldn't have killed Ethan.

So why did she pull a gun on you?

Helen released a long sigh and drew her knees against her chest. Berating herself would do no good whatsoever. Wrapping her arms around her legs, she rested her head on her knees. Her anger, both with Rosie and herself, faded along with the adrenaline rush. Her painful joints settled into a dull ache. She'd have to give her body a rest, then try again.

"Now what?" she asked aloud. No one was at home to miss her. Rosie had probably locked up the store. It could be days before anyone found her. She swallowed back an anguished cry. An overwhelming darkness permeated the closet, sucking the oxygen out and filling her with a deep inexplainable fear. She hated the dark, hated small spaces. Always had.

Some time ago she'd decided it had something to do with her childhood, yet she had no recollection of anything so traumatic as being locked away in a small space. About the only thing she could think to blame was the ongoing eruption of violence in her homeland.

Trying not to think about the tightness in her chest, Helen concentrated on the light slivers filtering in under the door and willed them to expand. *Everything will be all right*, she assured herself. Rosie wouldn't leave her here for long, would she? Surely not.

The Rosie she knew would never have locked her up in the first place.

Helen frowned as she thought again about her so-called friend. What would have caused her to behave so rashly? *Could I have been wrong about you, Rosie? Did you kill Ethan?*

No. Helen couldn't believe that. Maybe Rosie hadn't killed him, but running away certainly wasn't going to convince the authorities of her innocence. She'd panicked, but why? It wasn't just her fear of being a suspect or being arrested. Rosie knew much more than she was telling. And she had seen Ethan after he'd returned from his trip. Was she protecting someone? Did she know who killed Ethan? If so, wouldn't she be eager to share that information? Rosie's actions simply didn't make sense.

"Lord," she whispered, "please get me out of this. And keep Rosie safe." She closed her eyes, meaning only to catch her breath before trying to break out again. She tried to relax and think positive thoughts. Eventually Joe would figure out where the murder weapon had come from and would question Rosie himself. Not many people would have a letter opener with a book-shaped handle. He'd see her easy-to-spot candy-apple red T-bird in the parking lot and notice that the store was closed. If Joe didn't come to her rescue, surely someone else would eventually notice it and realize something was wrong. With that assurance, Helen closed her eyes and dozed.

Soon a shuffling noise woke her. She scrambled to her feet. Mice? Her heart hammered against her chest. The sound hadn't come from inside the closet. Someone was walking around on the front porch. A customer?

"Is someone there?" Helen called. "Help! I'm locked in. Can you get in?"

"Hang on!" a masculine voice yelled back. "I'm coming."

"Joe." Helen rested her forehead on the door. "Thank you, Lord," she murmured.

Several minutes later Joe moved whatever Rosie had shoved in front of the door and unlatched the hook. Helen stumbled out and flung her arms around the surprised sheriff. "I'm so glad to see you!"

"Yeah, I'll bet." Joe stepped back and lowered his hands to his sides, looking annoyed. "What happened?"

"I came to tell Rosie about Ethan." Helen gave him a quick rundown of what had transpired.

He stared at Helen in disbelief. "You knew that knife was Rosie's and you didn't tell me?"

Helen shook her head. "I didn't know—not until Rosie and I started talking. I tried to get her to call you. I thought she was going to, but she pulled a gun on me instead."

Joe ran a hand through his hair. "I knew that gun would be trouble. Tried to talk her out of it."

"You knew she had it?"

"While you were up north, she called to ask about getting a permit. Her brother-in-law bought it for her. Thought with so many crazies showing up these days, she needed protection."

"But Rosie's not a gun person."

"Tell me about it. She got all of one lesson on using it."

"I thought as much. The fact that she pulled it on me—Joe, she must be terrified."

"Hmm. She did sound pretty upset when she called to tell me you were here."

"Rosie called you?"

"Yeah. To tell me where to find you. She kept saying she didn't have anything to do with Ethan's death."

"I'm sure she didn't. Her shock was genuine. Judging from her reaction, though, I think she's hiding something. Or protecting someone." Helen stepped away from the closet and closed the door. In doing so, she noted that she'd pushed the screw holding the latch out about a quarter of an inch. She shouldn't have given up so easily.

"I'm not convinced that Rosie didn't do it."

"Joe—"

"Look, Helen. I like Rosie. But I have to look at the evidence. We have a witness who says he saw the mayor's car parked in front of the store here last night around five-thirty."

"You can't seriously be considering her as a suspect."

"Give me one good reason why I shouldn't. Just because she's Rosie?"

"Yes." Helen rubbed the back of her neck. "She told me he'd been here. He'd come in for a book."

"And you believe her?"

"I do." *At least in part.* "What possible reason would she have to kill Ethan?"

"Maybe she just got tired of waiting."

"What do you mean?"

"Look, it's no secret the two of them were friends. My hunch is there was a lot more going on."

"I asked Rosie if she and Ethan were having an affair, and she denied it."

"One of the deputies that went to school with them says Rosie and Ethan dated in high school. He was surprised when Rosie left town. A few months later Ethan up and married Eleanor. Personally, I think the flame was still burning. Something was going on between the two of them, that's for sure."

She sighed. "To be honest, I wondered about that myself. There's something else you should know. Eleanor suspected Ethan was having an affair. I told her I wouldn't say anything just yet. I wanted to check it out. She may have known it was Rosie."

"Are you suggesting Eleanor killed him?"

"I don't know." Helen closed her eyes and folded her arms. "I can't imagine either Eleanor or Rosie killing anyone."

"Yeah, well, we both know how that goes. With enough provocation, just about anyone could do just about anything."

"I realize that we can't assume anything, but just the same . . ." She stifled a yawn.

Joe's lips twisted in a reticent grin. "Go on home. I hoped you would work with us on this one, but I'm not sure you can be objective enough."

Helen managed a smile. "You may be right. Don't give up on me just yet, though. I need time to think on it. Rosie took me by surprise." She shrugged into her jacket and grabbed her bag from the spot on the floor where she'd set it when she came in. "You'll keep me posted?"

"Will do." Joe stood on the porch with his hands on his hips and watched her drive away.

Helen didn't need to think too long about being part of the investigation. By the time she pulled into her driveway, she knew she'd have to see it through. She had to find out who had killed Ethan, even if that person was her best friend.

Eight

O nce home, Helen tossed her keys onto the coffee table, dropped her bag on the floor, and dragged herself upstairs. Depositing articles of clothing on the way, she padded into the bathroom and turned on the shower. With the temperature to her liking, she stepped under the spray. The hot water pelted her shoulder, easing some of the nagging ache, but not enough. After shampooing, she filled the tub, dropped in a fizzy ball of mineral salts, then settled in to soak away the soreness and, hopefully, her concerns about Rosie.

It didn't happen. Helen kept envisioning Rosie's reaction to Ethan's death. Though Rosie had denied it, there had obviously been something between them. Were they lovers, as Joe suspected?

Joe had been right when he questioned her ability to remain objective. Helen couldn't cast Rosie as a killer and so far hadn't come up with a motive. Joe had suggested that maybe she just got tired of waiting. Helen didn't buy that. Yet, in a love triangle, jealousy provided a strong motive for Rosie and perhaps even more for Eleanor.

Not wanting to think about Rosie, Eleanor, or Ethan, Helen closed her eyes and took several long, lingering breaths.

She began singing a favorite hymn. Eventually the voices in her head took their battle elsewhere, but in their place trooped in concerns about J.B. Then Ethan and even Chuck. She tried to come up with something to be thankful for, but her mind refused to empty itself of the day's troubles. The roof, she decided. Alex Jordan was gone, and that most likely meant their roof no longer leaked.

❖   ❖   ❖

Twenty minutes later Helen blow-dried her hair, then slipped into her favorite sweats. J.B. had given her the pale pink reverse terry top and pants as a birthday gift. Wearing it made her feel closer to him. She ran a hand over the plush fabric and hugged herself. She'd come to several decisions during her soak. First, she trusted J.B. and knew he would not intentionally hurt her. Second, she refused to expend too much energy worrying about him. He'd probably come back pleading forgiveness. She just wished he'd do it soon. Third, she would not try to find Rosie—at least not today. It was already four P.M. and rainy. Dark clouds covered the sky, nearly occluding what little light the day had left. Besides, the hot water had left her so relaxed, she could barely walk.

Picking up a novel from the nightstand, Helen went downstairs and into the kitchen in search of a snack. She drank a glass of vegetable juice and ate a piece of string cheese. A motherly voice in the back of her mind told her she should eat a proper meal, but she ignored it. She wasn't in the mood for anything substantial, and the snack would take the edge off her hunger. She made peppermint tea, then turned on the gas fireplace in the living room and settled into her Brentwood rocker, putting her feet up on the matching ottoman. Using the remote, she turned on the stereo. It clunked from disk to disk and finally settled on Vivaldi's *The Four Seasons*.

Helen thought about calling Joe to get the status on Rosie but decided against it. She'd promised herself a quiet afternoon and evening, and that was exactly what she intended to have. Hopefully, reading would take her mind off everything, including J.B.

The book was a beautifully crafted story: a historical suspense set in the highlands of the Great Smoky Mountains. Helen found it captivating and was soon lost in the drama and the characters.

After about an hour of reading and sipping tea, Helen rose

from the chair when she noticed the blinking red light on her answering machine. She hadn't seen it earlier when she'd come in. But then she'd been too tired to notice much of anything.

"You have one message," the automated voice announced. "Monday, eleven-ten." That was about the time she'd found Ethan's body.

"Hello, luv, it's me. Sorry to have missed you." J.B.'s deep melancholy voice sent her heart skittering. "I was hoping to catch you before . . ." After a long pause, he said, "I wanted to tell you how sorry I am about the way I acted this morning. The call took me by surprise. I'll try to reach you later. I-I'll be away for another day or two."

"Before what?" Helen asked aloud when the machine clicked off. Another day or two doing what? She tipped her head back. "Where are you, J.B.? What are you up to?"

Grabbing the receiver, she punched out the number on the Caller ID. The prefix identified it as a Portland number. A few rings later a woman answered.

"Hello," Helen said. "Is . . . is J.B. there?"

"Hang on a sec. I'll check." Helen heard a shuffling sound, then a muffled, "Hey, anybody here named J.B.?"

Helen could hear the clatter of dishes, laughing, and talking. He'd called from a restaurant pay phone. At least a full minute went by before the woman came back on the line. "Sorry, nobody's answering. What's he look like? Maybe I waited on him."

"Tall, silver hair, blue eyes."

"Big guy and gorgeous—I know who you mean. For an old dude, he was pretty awesome. He and his lady friend had lunch around one."

Lady friend? J.B. had lunch with a woman? "This woman. Can you describe her?"

"Blond. Pretty—if you're into tall and skinny. I remember thinking she looked a little too young for him, but whatever. They seemed pretty taken with each other, if you know what I mean. Left around one-thirty—maybe a little before."

"I see." Helen swallowed back the sudden lump in her

throat. "Um . . . thank you. Oh, what was the name of your restaurant?"

"Antonio's Deli. We're down on the waterfront."

"Thanks." Helen hung up, feeling as if she'd been split open and hung upside down to drain. J.B. with another woman.

"No," she told herself firmly. "Don't even think it. J.B. wouldn't be having an affair. He loves you." There had to be a perfectly reasonable explanation for his being on the waterfront in a deli—with a woman. Perfectly reasonable.

She picked up the phone again and dialed the number to J.B.'s condo in Portland. It was also on the waterfront, not far from the deli. They'd talked about giving up the condo after he retired but had never gotten around to listing it with a Realtor. Maybe J.B. hadn't wanted to. Maybe he still used it for . . .

Don't even think it, Helen Bradley. J.B. wouldn't do that to you.

After nine rings Helen settled the receiver back in its holder. She played the message again, this time listening specifically to sounds other than his voice. Near the end of the message she heard a woman's voice, distant yet plaintive: "We'd better hurry, J.B. We don't want to miss . . ." There the message ended.

Helen's hopes fell. What was going on? What didn't the woman want him to miss?

She listened to the tape again, now concentrating on J.B.'s words, his tone. "I was hoping to catch you before . . ." Helen stopped it.

"Before what? Leaving me?" Though she fought against it, her mind dug up old tapes of Ian talking about J.B.'s many relationships—the women he kept in every port. But J.B. had sworn that, although he'd dated on occasion, there had never been a serious relationship.

"There were no women," J.B. assured her when he'd asked her to marry him. "At least no one who really mattered. I let people believe I was a womanizer so I'd never be expected to get serious about anyone. You were the only woman I ever wanted, Helen." His Irish blue eyes had fastened on hers, filled with love and desire. "I fell in love with you the day Ian introduced us. But Ian spoke first and I couldn't stand in the way. He was my best friend."

J.B. had been Helen's best friend as well. The trio had gone on one spy mission after another. Inseparable. Invincible. She and Ian had even named their son after him. Jason McGrady.

"There has never been anyone but you," he'd said. And like a fool, she'd believed him.

Jason Bradley. How often she'd teased him about his initials being the same as the roguish movie character James Bond. And oh, how well J.B. fit the part—he even had a similar accent. Handsome and sexy. In his younger days, J.B. could easily have doubled for her favorite Bond actor, Sean Connery. Was it possible he had lied to her about his philandering?

She didn't want to believe it. Helen directed her thoughts back to her original suspicions—that J.B.'s leaving had something to do with his health. She again played the tape. J.B. had apologized and said he'd phone later. He sounded as though he was truly sorry for not finding her home. *"The call took me by surprise,"* he'd said. *"I'll try to reach you later. I'll be away for another day or two."*

He was planning to come back. She scolded herself for jumping to conclusions. It could easily have been a business lunch. Or perhaps the woman was an old acquaintance, someone he'd bumped into.

Before what? Surgery? She recalled the tests he'd undergone during his last checkup. Of course. She'd call J.B.'s doctor. Surely he'd let her know what was going on. When she couldn't find Dr. Lewis's card in the Rolodex, she called information and after what seemed an eternity finally got through to his office.

"I'm sorry," the receptionist said in a stern tone when Helen told her what she wanted. "We can't release any information without the patient's consent."

"But I'm his wife."

"Right. I wish I could help, but I can't. Those records are confidential."

"Look, I just want to know if J.B. is scheduled for any tests or surgery."

"Um . . . maybe you should just consider asking him."

"Oh, now why didn't I think of that?" Helen snarled. "I told you he's not here."

"Well, I'm sorry. I can leave a message for Dr. Lewis to call you. Would that be all right?"

"I suppose—yes, please." Helen thanked her and threw the phone at the couch. It bounced out and hit the floor. Surprised at her reaction, Helen retrieved it and settled it back where it belonged.

Running both hands through her hair, she sucked in shallow breaths until her rage subsided. She was angry, not at the receptionist who was only doing her job, but at J.B. for keeping secrets. And at herself for letting her emotions get so far out of line. She rarely lost her temper. After Ian's death she'd been as steady as a rock. Or maybe she'd just been numb. When J.B. had come back into her life three years later, he'd elicited emotions she thought she'd never feel again. He'd brought her passions back to the surface. He had the ability to melt her with one look—or one phone call.

Maybe what she felt wasn't anger at all, but fear. She didn't want to lose him—not because of a health problem or because of another woman. "I am not going to let you get away with this, J.B."

She called the hospital where Dr. Lewis usually admitted his patients, but J.B. hadn't checked in. Maybe he'd been referred to another doctor. That meant he could be in any of the area hospitals. It was as good a place as any to start her search. She picked up the phone again and rang her daughter, Kate.

"Oh, hi, Mom. It's about time you called."

"Kate, it's so good to hear your voice."

"Is everything okay?"

"Not exactly. J.B. got a phone call this morning. I think it may have been from his doctor." She focused on the health issue. It was the only option she allowed herself to deal with at the moment.

"You *think*? You mean he didn't tell you?"

"I'm afraid there might be a serious problem and he doesn't want to worry me. He went into Portland this morning. He's not at the condo and . . . well, I'm wondering if you'd call the hospitals and see if he's a patient at any. If he is, call me."

"I can't believe he'd do something like that."

"He probably thinks he's being noble. The men in our family seem to be good at that sort of thing." They were also loyal and faithful, she reminded herself.

"Could he have gotten an assignment? He's really looking good these days."

"I thought about that possibility, but no way is the government going to rehire a man who has recently had a heart attack. You know how they are. I can't imagine any of the agencies he's worked for involving him in another espionage situation."

"I see your point."

"I'm worried it might be something really serious, Kate. Maybe I'm being paranoid. I don't know. After seeing Richard . . . he'd been diagnosed with cancer for months before telling anyone. Went through all that chemotherapy and radiation alone." Her cousin hadn't wanted his family to know, and his silence had almost destroyed his marriage.

"I guess it's a guy thing. Try not to worry. Have you called Jason?"

"Not yet. I didn't want to bother him. He's so busy with his job and Susan. How is she, by the way?"

"Doing great," Kate said. "She and Jason are happier than ever."

"That's good. And the children?"

While Kate brought her up-to-date on her grandchildren, Helen paced. When she'd finished her report, Kate added, "Everyone misses you. You really need to come in and stay for a few days. Hmm. Maybe you should come now. You could track down J.B. yourself. In fact, I'm surprised you aren't here."

Helen went on to tell her about her day—the conversation with Eleanor, her walk on the beach, and her confrontation with Rosie.

"Oh, Mom, how awful. We'd love to see you, but it sounds as though you need to rest, for tonight at least. Think about coming tomorrow."

"I will. And if not then, soon." After Kate promised to call if she learned anything about J.B., they hung up.

Then on a whim, Helen called Tom Chambers, an old

friend of hers and colleague of J.B.'s at the FBI office in Port-land.

"Helen, what a surprise. Bet you're looking for J.B., right?"

"Yes. How did you know?"

"He was in here this morning."

"Then you know where he is?"

"Nope. I'm sorry, Helen. I don't have a clue. He didn't tell me anything."

"And you wouldn't tell me if he had, am I right?"

"Hey, that's not true—well. It might be if he was involved in some sort of covert operation, but that's not the case. He's retired, and as far as I know he won't be coming back. He's not going to want a desk job and—"

"Did he want back in?"

"No. He just came by to say hello and see how things were going. That's all, Helen, I swear. I'll admit he seemed preoccu-pied, like he was worried about something, but he didn't let on what it might be. I'm telling you all I know—which is a big fat zero."

"All right, Tom. Thanks anyway. If you hear from him again, will you call?"

"Sure."

Helen had no sooner disconnected with Tom than the phone rang. She snatched it up.

"Hi, Helen. This is Rosie."

Nine

T hank goodness you're okay," Rosie said.

"No thanks to you," Helen snapped. "What you did was . . . stupid."

"I'm sorry. It . . . it was such a shock, and I didn't know what else to do."

"You could have talked to me. You didn't have to start waving around that gun!"

"I . . . I know. I still can't believe I did that. I never should have let Dave talk me into keeping it." Dave was her brother-in-law, a contractor in Lincoln City. Which is probably where she was staying.

"Where are you?"

"I can't tell you that," Rosie responded incredulously. "Not yet."

"You're just making things worse for yourself, you know. It's only a matter of time before the authorities find you."

"I know, but I need that time."

"For what? Talk to me, Rosie. I thought we were friends. If you're in trouble, maybe I can help."

"It's not me. Oh, Helen. I'm so sorry. I can't tell you. I can't let you get involved in this. I . . . I have to go."

At the sound of the dial tone, Helen returned the phone to its cradle. The Caller ID read *unavailable*. "You won't be for long. Not if I have anything to say about it."

Helen immediately called Joe to let him know about Rosie's phone call. "She may be staying with her sister."

"She wasn't earlier," Joe said, "but then neither was anyone else. Rosie has family in Portland, but they claim she hasn't been in touch with them. Of course they could be protecting her. I was planning to head up to her sister's place in Lincoln City to have a look around myself, but there just hasn't been time. I could use a couple more deputies, but that's not going to happen. These budget cuts are killing us. I'm about ready to resign myself."

"You don't mean that, Joe. If it will help, I could do some snooping around. I may be able to find Rosie where your people can't."

"Go for it. Just be careful. She pulled a gun on you once. . . ."

"She caught me by surprise. I don't intend to let her do it again." Helen paced back and forth across the living room.

"So . . . our usual arrangement."

"That works for me." Helen had the credentials and could have easily become a deputy, but she preferred acting as a consultant, where she had more versatility.

"What's your plan?" Joe asked.

"I thought I'd check out Rosie's place tonight. See if I can turn up anything that might give us a clue as to what's going on. Then I'll drive up to Adele and Dave's."

"We don't have a warrant to search Rosie's."

"I don't need a warrant."

"Helen"—she noted the warning in his voice—"you're not thinking of breaking and entering?"

"Of course not. I have a key. And someone needs to check on the cats."

He chuckled. "Be careful," he cautioned again. "We don't know what we're dealing with here."

Helen watched as the sun descended and the clouds on the horizon broke up enough to let the pink and gold colors shine through. While she loved sunsets, she hated the shorter days of fall. She took another bite of her tuna-and-sprout sandwich. Helen had no appetite, but knowing she was going to need more energy than the snack of V8 and cheese offered, she'd fixed a sandwich and carrot sticks and washed them down with a cup of strong coffee.

After setting her dishes in the dishwasher and brushing the crumbs from her black turtleneck shirt, Helen walked into the entryway. She then donned a black jacket and tucked her salt-and-pepper hair into a black knit hat.

She felt a little like a spy again. Her mother had always taught her the importance of including a basic black dress in her wardrobe. She did have a dress, but she also kept black pants, a turtleneck, jacket, and cap. One never knew when they'd come in handy.

Helen's mouth turned up in a half smile. "Somehow I don't think this is what you had in mind, Mother." She'd recently re-placed the black turtleneck she was wearing when she was shot. A shudder went through her and she rubbed her still sore shoulder. She thought about taking her service revolver but decided against it.

This is different, she told herself. She wouldn't be running along the waterfront in Portland. She wouldn't be meeting any-one at midnight. She was just going to Rosie's to feed the cats and see if she could find some clue as to what had upset Rosie to the point of desperation.

Helen spun around and headed back to her room. Minutes later she was in the hallway with her holster and gun in place and feeling slightly more secure. Going outside, Helen checked her pockets for her penlight and clicked it on. The beam was small but efficient. She fingered the key Rosie had given her several years ago. Helen occasionally watered the plants and fed the cats while Rosie was away. Now she had another mission.

Joe's caution had spurred her into entering Rosie's under cover of darkness. *"We don't know what we're dealing with here."* Ethan had been murdered. His killer could be anywhere, and Rosie was somehow involved. Someone could be watching the house, and she preferred not to advertise her presence by turn-ing on lights.

Instead of taking her car, Helen walked into town. She avoided the road by cutting through some woods and climbing along a ledge of rocks until she emerged onto the side street that bordered Rosie's place. It was a long way around, but Helen didn't want to take the chance of being seen. Besides, the cold, moist air invigorated her. Gave her a chance to think. She felt certain her friend was innocent, and after the phone call, Helen felt even more certain Rosie was protecting someone. A search through Rosie's apartment and desk just might provide the answer.

By the time she got to Rosie's, she was sweating and the wool cap was itching her head. She avoided the lighted parking area, went around to the back door, and reached in her pocket for the key.

Something let out an unearthly cry. A streak of gray flashed around the corner and headed straight for her. Helen flattened against the door. Her heart hammered like an automatic rifle. "Buttermilk," she gasped. "You scared me to death."

The cat whined in a mournful tone. "Poor baby." Helen reached down to pet the cat. "Are you hungry? Rosie must really be in a dither to forget about you. Come on. Let's go inside." She dug into her pocket again. Her hand closed around the tiny flashlight but not the key. She tried the other side. Nothing. She'd had the key in her hand when Buttermilk showed up. Maybe it had fallen in the commotion. Helen dropped to her hands and knees on the welcome mat and felt around it and the wooden slats beyond. Nothing but granules of sand and grit.

The two-by-six planks of the wraparound porch were separated by half an inch. Wide enough for a key to slip through. With her hands pressed against her thighs, she straightened.

Maybe she should give up her mission and go home. Helen brushed her cowardly thoughts aside. She was not about to be deterred by something so insignificant as losing a key. Anyway, the cats needed attention. Who knew when Rosie would be coming back?

The back of Rosie's place faced a stand of trees that separated the house from the ocean. The only light came from the yard lights at the far corner of the parking lot near the street and the porch light by the front door. No one was likely to see her. Helen made a quick assessment. It wouldn't be difficult to get in; all she needed to do was break one of the six panes of glass in the door.

Staying in the shadows, Helen skulked down the stairs and picked up one of the average-sized rocks that lined the gravel path. She crept back to the door, pulled her hand inside her sleeve and gripped the rock, and hit the lower left windowpane nearest the doorknob. It shattered. Helen glanced around. Satisfied that the noise hadn't been loud enough to attract attention, she quickly brushed the glass out of the frame and reached inside to unlock the door.

Once inside, Helen took a few seconds to catch her breath, then hurried up the enclosed stairs to Rosie's apartment. In her hurry to leave, Rosie had left the blinds and curtains open. Light from the street and side yard spilled into the living room, kitchen, and bedroom, making it unnecessary to use her penlight. She closed the door and stood for a moment, admiring the warm, subtle glow of the place.

As with the rest of the Victorian, Rosie had taken great care to maintain the integrity of her rooms. She had an eclectic taste that blended old with new. Rosie's unique talent for creating beauty out of the most simple and outdated things was especially evident here. On a round cherrywood table, she'd placed an old hat, wire-rimmed eyeglasses and antique case, and a pair of white gloves among a spray of dried rosebuds. On top of the wardrobe, she'd set an obviously used violin, with a music stand and yellowed sheet music. In one corner Rosie had arranged a trio of old lightning rods with long, pointed metal tips sticking out of white globes, all braced on a metal tripod. The arrangements clamored for an artist to paint them. She could imagine Kate standing in front of her easel working to capture the nostalgia emanating from the place.

The entire apartment was like that: tidy, with discarded treasures set around in artistic eye-catching arrangements. Rosie created magic out of things others had thrown away or sold cheaply at garage sales. She said it was because she'd grown up poor. Her mother had taught her the importance of finding beauty in whatever she had at hand. It was the perfect place to take tea and reminisce about her home in Ireland and her own dear mother. At least it used to be.

Buttermilk meowed and brushed against her legs. The kitten sat about three feet away, head tipped to one side. Helen reluctantly pulled her mind away from the sweet memories and back to the task at hand. *You're not here to admire Rosie's handiwork.*

"Right," she whispered. "Okay, guys, let's get you fed. I've got work to do."

After removing her coat and the itchy hat and setting them on the back of a chair, Helen found cat food in the utility room. Once she'd poured the dried morsels into their dishes and given them fresh water, she went to the address book lying beside Rosie's phone. Her sister Adele was listed under the *F*'s—Feldman. Since she'd forgotten to get it from Joe, Helen jotted the address and phone number on a note pad and stuffed it into her pocket.

Feeling somewhat guilty, Helen dug through several drawers. She didn't know exactly what she was looking for but, hopefully, would know when she found it. Only one drawer looked interesting. But even it turned out to be a disappointment. Like her own junk drawer at home, it contained the usual—miscellaneous keys, pens, coupons, batteries.

She systematically moved through the house, ending her search in the bedroom. Here, on a dresser that had once graced a 1930 farmhouse, Helen found several framed photographs. One was of Rosie with Adele's family: a husband, three teen-aged kids, and a miniature collie. Another was of a nice-looking young man in a graduation picture. His handsome features and friendly smile undoubtedly had girls standing in line for his attention. He looked familiar, but Helen couldn't place him. A nephew? Helen seemed to remember Rosie mentioning an older sister living in the Midwest. Another photo of Adele, Rosie, and a third woman—with Rosie's coloring—confirmed her suspicions.

It was the third photo that especially caught Helen's eye. A young couple standing in front of an arch that had been decorated with white roses. Senior prom at Bay Village High. 1963. The girl was Rosie, no doubt about that. The young man was equally easy to recognize. Ethan Crane.

Joe had said they'd dated in high school. But why would Rosie keep the photo in such a prominent place after all these years? How sad. Rosie had never married. Did she still love Ethan? What had happened to separate them? Probably the same thing that separated most high-school sweethearts. College, other interests, growing up, coming to one's senses. Had Rosie and Ethan tried to reclaim those high-school years?

Helen set the frame back in its place on the dresser and was about to head downstairs when she heard a thump coming from the floor below. The cats? A quick glance into the kitchen showed them both still eating. The scrape of a shoe on wooden stairs. A creak. The same sound she'd made on the third step coming in. Helen swallowed hard and drew her .38. What kind of a mess had she gotten herself into this time?

Ten

The door to Rosie's apartment banged open. Helen peeked from behind the nearly closed bedroom door. A bulky figure stepped inside. Gun drawn, the man flattened himself against the door.

Helen released the breath she'd been holding and holstered the gun. It was Tom, the officer she'd met on the beach. He moved inside, hugging the wall as he made his way through the living room and into the kitchen. Any minute he'd open the bedroom door. What would he do if he found her? *Not if, when.* Would he shoot first and ask questions later? While Joe had encouraged her to snoop around, she doubted Tom knew about their arrangement.

Not wanting to take that chance, Helen shouted, "Who's there?"

Tom whipped around to face her. "Okay, lady, come out with your hands above your head!"

"Oh my," Helen said in the most innocent tone she could push past her tightened throat. She raised her hands and let the door drift open, then slowly moved into the light. "I take it this isn't a social visit."

"Mrs. Bradley? What are you doing here?" The deputy looked her up and down, frowning as his gaze latched on to her holster. "I take it you have a permit for that?"

"I do." Helen lowered her hands and brushed a hand through her mussed-up hair, thankful she'd taken off her cap. "I might ask you the same thing. I came to feed the cats and have a look around." She motioned toward the animals, now sitting next to their bowls licking themselves. "I had a key and—"

"A key? Then you didn't break in?" He glanced toward the stairs. "The glass was broken in the back door. That's why I decided to check things out. Since the only access from the stairs is to the apartment, I figured there might be a prowler. Was the window broken when you came in?" Tom asked.

This was going to be difficult to explain. "No. I dropped my key on the porch, and it must have fallen between the boards. But don't worry. I'll make certain the window is repaired."

He didn't seem convinced. "Why didn't you turn on the lights?"

"No need, really. The streetlights were all I needed." Helen stepped over to the table and the chair where she'd set her jacket and hat.

"Where's your car?"

Helen smiled. "I walked. It's not far from my house, and I needed the fresh air." She couldn't fault the man for his thoroughness. She'd have done the same thing.

He frowned. "Why do I have the feeling you're not being completely honest with me? Looks to me like you might be up to something. I know Joe has a lot of respect for you, but breaking and entering . . ."

"I did come to feed the cats." Helen spread out her hands and nodded toward the utility room. "And I had a key."

"You don't need a weapon to feed cats."

Her grin spread. "No. And, you're right. That wasn't all I came for. I was hoping to find some clue as to why Rosie felt she had to pull a gun on me and run away. You might want to call Joe. I told him I was coming to have a look around."

"Joe knows you're here?"

"In a manner of speaking, yes. He asked me to assist in the investigation."

"But I thought you had retired. That makes you a civilian."

"I'm a consultant."

Tom then called, but Joe didn't respond. Replacing the cell phone on his belt, he added, "Joe didn't say anything earlier about your being here. In fact, he told me to check the place out and that he was on his way over."

Helen went to the window. "He didn't expect that I'd have to break in—I didn't either. He's pulling in now."

Seconds after Joe entered through the front door, a crash came from one of the floors below.

Tom drew his gun and headed back down the stairs. "Sounds like trouble. Stay here."

"Wait. There's a faster way down." Her words tumbled into an empty stairwell as Tom ducked outside.

Helen hurried to a door on the opposite side of the living room. It opened into a hallway, then to the main staircase and the bookstore. Helen hugged the wall as she descended the carpeted stairs to the second floor. She stepped into the first room, where Rosie housed all of the romances. Decorated in flowers and lace, the room usually held a warm romantic charm. But at the moment, it held no charm whatsoever. Light from the windows cast eerie shadows over the bookshelves and gift items.

The front-door chimes tinkled as the door opened again. She heard the door slam followed by a loud groan, then footsteps running across the porch. Helen rushed to the window in time to see a dark figure race across the side yard. A piece of paper flew out from under his arm as he ran. He disappeared into the woods not far from where she had come just minutes before. Her heart lurched. Worried about how he'd managed to escape Joe and Tom, Helen hurried into the hall and down the remaining steps.

At the bottom of the stairs she found Joe groaning as he gripped the banister and hauled himself upright. "He's getting away." Joe gasped and staggered toward the door before falling to his knees.

"What happened?" Helen flipped on a light switch. The intruder had been looking for something. No doubt about it. Rosie's desk was bare, its contents scattered across the floor. Even her penholder—a pottery vase—lay on its side, pens and pencils strewn amongst the broken pieces of ceramic.

"Got me from behind." Joe rubbed the back of his head.

"You're in no condition to go after him." She glanced at the moaning sheriff, whose bulk filled the doorway as he held his stomach.

"Neither is Tom. Get me some backup. He went into the woods. Have them approach the water from the condominiums just south of here."

Helen pushed past Joe and headed across the lot and into the woods where she'd last seen the intruder.

Because she'd walked the path a number of times with Rosie, Helen didn't have too much trouble at first. But as the streetlight diminished, the going became painfully slow or at least it seemed that way. The woods were only about sixty feet deep, and once she got through them, she'd be on the ocean's edge. The floodlights from the nearby condos would afford some visibility. Helen emerged from the trees and scanned the area. Not surprisingly, the man had disappeared.

There were only two ways the guy could have gone. Well, three, if you counted going straight ahead, which would send him over the cliff into ocean and rocks. Not an option unless he planned to kill himself. He could have doubled back into the woods, but the most obvious way was south toward the condos. Hopefully, deputies would head him off there.

Helen scrambled over the slick, jagged rocks. Hopes of catching the guy faded by the second. She hesitated before jumping across a three-foot gap between the rock surfaces.

Twenty feet below, the churning water pummeled the rocks. A wave crashed in and sent up a wall of seawater, then another. Icy salt water stung her face and hands. Helen waited for the next wave to recede, but before she could jump, someone grabbed her from behind. A scream tore from her throat, only to be caught by the wind and carried out to sea. Helen jabbed her attacker in the stomach, then heard him grunt and gasp for air.

Just as she would have spun around to deliver a kick, her foot slipped, sending her headlong into the boiling cauldron below.

Eleven

The wind and sea roared over the sound of Helen's scream. She grasped at the slippery rocks, trying to get a grip and push herself back. Though an outcropping of rocks about four feet down had stopped her fall, she saw no way of retreating fast enough to escape the surging waves below. In seconds, she'd be picked off the cliff like a toothpick and flung into the water.

Helen cried out again for help, pleading with God to save her. The water swelled, and Helen held her breath as she waited for the end. Saying good-bye to J.B. in her mind, she then closed her eyes and prayed.

Miracles happened every day. In her lifetime she'd witnessed quite a few. Most would have termed them normal, everyday things, like the birth of a child, or the emergence of a butterfly from a cocoon. She'd seen people, including herself, live when the circumstances had dictated death.

At the moment, Helen marveled at the miracle she was still alive. And in the fact that someone had grabbed her ankles and was pulling her up to safety. Soon she was high above the thundering wave that hammered against the place she'd just been lying.

Helen rolled over onto her back, offering a prayer of thanks. She managed to get to her feet, anxious to thank whoever had pulled her to safety. He was gone. Two possibilities swept through her mind: God had sent an angel, or the man who'd attacked her had experienced a change of heart.

Wet and cold, she headed for the condos and the officers now coming toward her. "Did you see him?"

Neither had. Tom gave her an odd look. "How'd you get so wet?"

Helen told them what had happened, then added, "He stopped to help me. Can't have gotten too far."

"We'll scour the area," Tom said. "We have a couple more units coming to help—no need for you to stay."

"Good. How's Joe?"

"Okay. He's still at the shop. Wants to talk to you."

Helen left the manhunt to the deputies and walked back to Rosie's place. Another officer, a young woman, had joined Joe to help gather evidence. Joe's pride had been injured more than his head, Helen decided, as he gave her a surly greeting. He introduced the officer as Stephanie Jones.

"Stephanie used to work in Portland," Joe said. "She knows your son."

"Glad to meet you, Mrs. Bradley."

"So you know Jason?"

"Right," Stephanie said. "Detective McGrady was my mentor before . . . well, my husband got transferred to Lincoln City and . . ." She shrugged. "I quit and got a job here." She then grinned. "Speaking of which, I'd better get back to it."

Joe's dark eyes swung from Helen to the papers strewn across the floor. "I take it you didn't do this."

"Not my style. And I hadn't worked my way down here yet." Helen huddled under her wet jacket, while Joe picked his way through the scattered papers and office supplies.

"Did you see who it was?" Joe asked.

"Yes and no. I wouldn't be able to pick him out in a crowd."

"It was a man?"

She nodded. "He had a build similar to Tom's. Dark hair. I couldn't see his face."

"Well, let's hope we find him."

Helen hoped so, too, in a way. At the same time she felt an overwhelming flood of compassion. The man had saved her life. After telling Joe about her close encounter with death, Helen excused herself. "I'm freezing. If you don't mind, I'm going to go upstairs and find something warm in Rosie's closet." Without waiting for an answer, Helen jogged up the stairs and proceeded to strip out of her wet clothes and towel down. She put on a pair of pants and a sweater, threw her wet things in the dryer, then hurried back downstairs. Joe was still going through the mess, and Stephanie seemed intent on checking for prints.

Helen stopped on the lower step. "Tom told me you had a suspect in Ethan's murder."

"We're closing in. The guy who ransacked this place might have been him. Description fits."

"So who is he?" Helen asked.

"We were checking out Ethan's office this afternoon and found an interesting message on his voice mail." Joe hunkered down to get a closer look at a batch of canceled checks. "A guy named Alex Jordan left a message for Ethan to meet him at the Clam Digger at seven last night."

Alex Jordan? Helen sank onto the stairs.

Joe went on. "He wasn't too hard to track down. The guy works for Chuck. One of the gals at the Clam Digger remembered waiting on him and Ethan last night. They left together. Jordan just moved into the area a month ago."

"I . . . I know. I talked to him this morning. He was working on my house. Was there most of the day fixing the roof." Helen frowned. "So what connection could he have to Ethan—and why would he break into Rosie's?"

"Haven't figured that out yet."

"Have you talked to Chuck?" Helen asked.

"No, that's another problem. Lynn says he hasn't been around since Sunday night."

Helen moved closer to the desk. "I don't think that's a coincidence, do you? Seems to me one might have to do with the other." Thinking aloud, she added, "Do you think Chuck could have hired Alex to do more than pound nails?"

"What do you mean?"

"It's no secret how Chuck felt about the city council's decision to deny him permission to build on his beachfront property. Ethan came out strongly opposed to the variance. Chuck insisted there's no danger of erosion, but Ethan didn't want to take any chances."

"So Chuck hires a hit man?" Joe tossed her a skeptical look. "I don't think so. Daniels might have his faults, but killing somebody—or having them killed—to get some houses built isn't one of them."

"Hmm. *Now* who isn't being objective?"

Joe didn't find her comment the least bit amusing. "I'm using common sense."

"I was using common sense with Rosie too."

"Helen." Joe sighed. "Rosie pulled a gun on you."

"That may be, but she was scared. With Chuck . . . you have to admit, the timing is right. The council turned down Chuck's proposal a little over a month ago. By the way, have you checked Alex out?"

He shook his head. "Lynn says the guy just showed up one day needing a job. Chuck needed some extra help that day and signed him on. Spur-of-the-moment thing. She says he's been a good worker—has some real talent for finishing work. Couple of other guys backed up her story. But nice guy or not, he had dinner with Ethan."

"Which makes him a suspect." Helen remembered Alex's easy smile and grace. His dark hair and build. He certainly could have been the man she'd seen fleeing into the woods. And he could have pulled her from the rocks. But a killer?

"Right now we just want him for questioning," Joe said. "But something is definitely wrong. The guy didn't check in with Lynn this afternoon like he was supposed to. And he hasn't been home. Looks like he might have moved out in a hurry. Closets stripped clean—didn't tell his landlord he was going."

"Where did he live?"

"Lincoln City. Had a small rental a block off the beach." With the eraser end of a pencil, Joe flipped over a couple of pages in the checkbook that lay open on the floor.

"Okay, say Alex Jordan did kill Ethan. How do you explain why Rosie reacted as she did? And why would Alex—if it was Alex—break into her place? She must know something. Maybe she's afraid Ethan's killer will come after her."

"Or maybe *she* hired Jordan to kill Ethan."

"Joe . . ." But before Helen could express her indignation, Joe interrupted.

"Hey, take a look at this." He pointed to an entry in the checkbook's ledger. "Looks like Rosie recently came into a nice little nest egg. I could be wrong, but I don't think she makes this much in a month selling books and knickknacks."

Helen came around to peer over Joe's shoulder. "Especially not this time of the year."

"There's a deposit listed here for a hundred thousand made a couple weeks ago. That's in addition to the daily entries."

"Maybe Rosie wrote down the wrong amount," Helen said. "There's a line through it."

"I don't think so. The deposit may have been lined out, but it's still added in to the balance. All the other deposits are in odd amounts."

"You're right. The $147.53, $165.26, $78.39, and $120.89 were in line with her daily sales."

"Has Rosie mentioned anything to you about coming into an inheritance?" Joe asked.

"No. And she would have . . . I think." In truth, Helen didn't know what to think about Rosie anymore. She stifled a yawn. "Looks like it's going to be a long night. You two want a cup of tea or coffee? I don't think Rosie will mind if I make some."

"No thanks," Stephanie answered. "Never drink the stuff. Um, Joe, I'm finished with the prints—I'll take them in and run them if it's okay with you."

"That's fine. When you're finished you can go home. Can you come in tomorrow?"

"Um . . . not until ten—if that's okay." Stephanie gathered her equipment and started for the door.

Joe grunted his approval.

After saying their good-byes, Helen asked Joe again about coffee.

"Sounds good. How about a latte? Double. Use soymilk instead of regular."

Helen grimaced. "Soy?"

"Hey, don't knock it. Annie's been working with me on my

diet. I'm gaining weight. My blood pressure's up, and cholesterol's not doing so great either. She's turning me into a vegetarian."

Helen chuckled. "You two must be getting serious."

"Oh yeah." He looked up at her and grinned. "I'll tell you about it sometime. Now hurry up with that latte."

"Sorry. I'm making coffee—straight up. I have no idea how to work the cappuccino machine and have no intention of learning the trade. How about if I put some milk in yours?"

"Whatever."

Joe seemed intent on the papers he was examining, so Helen made her way to the espresso bar. She scooped the Starbucks coffee grains into the filter and pushed it into its slot on the coffee maker, then filled the reservoir with water and plugged it in. Within a few seconds it began steaming and dripping into the glass carafe. While she waited, Helen pulled out a box of soymilk.

Helen felt at odds, waiting and watching Joe. She thought about her job with the Portland Bureau and for a moment wondered if she'd made a mistake in retiring. Of course she'd kept her fingers in all these years, but it wasn't the same.

She'd been a driven woman back then. At times too much so. She'd heard that passion diminishes with age. But that hadn't been the case for her—neither in her relationship with J.B., nor in her work. The yearning and restlessness returned full force as she paced the floor behind the counter. Maybe she should take a full-time job again. The sheriff's department could certainly use another deputy. In the end, she came full circle. She loved her freedom. Loved her writing career and loved being married to J.B.—most of the time.

The coffee machine sputtered, signaling an end to its perk. Helen poured coffee into the two mugs and took one to Joe. As she handed it off, the door opened. Chimes tinkled wildly as the rain and wind hit them.

"They got him," Stephanie panted. "Tom's putting him in the car. It's Alex Jordan."

"Good." Joe grabbed his hat and headed outside.

Helen followed, stopping short when she saw Jordan's face.

The dome light in the squad car revealed his features all too clearly. His dark, thick hair curled slightly and dripped water onto his forehead. For an instant his pleading blue eyes met hers. Where had she seen that face before? Of course she'd seen him at her house that very morning. But that wasn't the only place. She remembered a younger face. . . .

Then she put the two together. Alex Jordan and the young man whose photo sat on the bureau in Rosie's bedroom were one and the same.

Twelve

I didn't do anything." Alex Jordan looked from Joe to Helen. "Please, you have to believe me."

"You'll have a chance to make your statement." Joe turned to Tom. "Where did you find him?"

Tom closed the car door, shutting his prisoner inside. "We caught him out on the rocks—guy nearly killed himself trying to get away."

Jordan buried his face in his hands, a look of anguish on his face.

"Found this in his pocket." Tom handed Joe a slip of paper and opened the driver's side. "It has Mayor Crane's name, address, and phone numbers for his house and office."

Joe held it to the light. Turning to Helen, he asked, "Is this the guy you saw run out of here?"

"I'm not sure. I didn't see his face." Though Helen couldn't say for certain, she had a hunch Jordan was the man she'd seen leaving Rosie's. He had changed his clothes since she'd seen him earlier in the day. He still wore jeans, but instead of the flannel shirt, he had on a navy sweater and turtleneck with a lightweight black jacket. The photo upstairs showed an obvious connection to Rosie. If he knew Rosie and hadn't broken in, why wasn't he offering any sort of explanation?

"Book him," Joe told Tom. "I'll be in as soon as I finish up here."

"Jones." He nodded in the deputy's direction. "I thought you were on your way home."

"I'm going."

Turning to Helen, Joe said, "You may as well go home too. I'm nearly finished here."

"In a minute. There's something you need to see first."

Joe rubbed the back of his neck. "Can't it wait?"

"I don't think so. When I was looking around upstairs earlier, I found something that might shed some light on this."

"And you're only just now telling me about it?"

"I didn't make the connection until just now. Apparently Rosie knows Alex Jordan. She has a photo of him in her bedroom." Once inside, Helen showed him the graduation photo she'd found earlier. "I realized as soon as I saw him it was the same guy. He may not have broken into Rosie's at all, Joe. I think he may be some sort of relative—a nephew or something." She cringed as Joe's gaze traveled over to the picture of Rosie and Ethan on their prom night.

"Much as I hate to say it, Helen, this connection—Rosie to Jordan and Jordan having Ethan's name and number . . ." He shook his head. "She's in this up to her neck."

"I'll admit the photo links them together, but that doesn't mean Rosie or Alex had anything to do with Ethan's death."

"Maybe not, but it gives us a place to start." Heading for the stairs, Joe asked, "Find anything else I should know about?"

"Nothing." Helen frowned. "Except that Alex Jordan saved my life. I have a hard time seeing him or Rosie as killers."

Joe didn't comment.

When they reached the first floor, Helen headed for the coffee bar to unplug the coffee maker. "I take it you still haven't found Rosie."

"Still working on it." Joe opened the door, sending the chimes into motion.

"I'll talk to Adele in the morning." Helen paused to scoop up and pet the orange tabby, who'd jumped off the back of the sofa and onto the counter. She settled the cat back on the chair, then straightened and rubbed a sore spot in her back. "Joe? Did you ever find Ethan's car?"

"No trace of it. My hunch is that his killer ditched it after he killed him."

"Hmm. Or Ethan may have driven it somewhere after his meeting with Alex."

"Want a ride home?" Joe offered.

"No thanks. I need to get my things out of the dryer. You go ahead. I can close up."

"Are you sure? It's getting late."

"Thanks, but no. The walk will do me good."

"Suit yourself." Joe closed the door behind him. Seconds later headlights flashed through the windows as he backed around.

Helen finished cleaning up the espresso bar and turned out the lights as she made her way back upstairs. Her clothes were toasty warm from the dryer. Once she got them on, she thought seriously about curling up in one of Rosie's outrageously comfortable chairs with a good book. With any luck at all, Rosie would come back. Then again, maybe she wouldn't. Quite possibly she'd sent Alex Jordan to get something for her.

Helen dismissed the idea of staying. She needed to be home in case J.B. called. More than that, she needed some sleep.

Before leaving, she put a piece of cardboard over the hole she'd made in the glass, then let herself out. Helen buttoned her jacket and pulled the hat over her ears. She then walked from the porch around front to make certain she'd locked the door. Heading around to the back of the house again, she remembered seeing the intruder drop a piece of paper as he escaped.

She searched the area, finding nothing but an old gum wrapper. Perhaps the deputies had picked it up. The only paper they'd mentioned was one they'd found in Jordan's pocket.

There was another possibility. The wind had been and still was blowing toward the house, which meant the paper could be tucked in the shrubbery. Helen fumbled in her pocket for her penlight and hunkered down to examine the thick green border of leafy plants. Her penlight revealed a light piece of paper slapped up against the trunk of a large rhododendron. On closer inspection, her heart took a dive. It was a canceled check from Past Times, made out to Alex Jordan in the amount of one hundred thousand dollars.

Helen let out a long, soft whistle. "Oh, Rosie. What in the world is going on?" Slipping the check into her pocket, she ran all the way home.

⁘　⁘　⁘

Morning brought sunshine and a smile to her lips. She reached across the queen-sized bed to snuggle with J.B. Cold sheets greeted her empty arms. Memories of the day before tumbled back onto her sleep-dulled brain like angry waves on the rocks. The mystery caller. Their argument. The possibility of a health problem. *The other woman.*

Helen shot out of bed, forcing her suspicions back into the dark, musty corner from which they'd come. She wouldn't— couldn't let herself think of J.B. cheating on her. He was gone and she needed to trust him. He'd be back. He always came back. She desperately wanted to believe that. Only this trip hadn't been like the others. There had been no "I love you." No lingering kiss good-bye.

In the shower, Helen forced concerns about J.B. into the background and drew out the circumstances surrounding Ethan's death. Strangely, the murder investigation seemed easier to deal with. She dressed in her usual beach attire—jeans, a purple turtleneck, and baggy white cotton sweater—and went downstairs to make breakfast.

Helen wasn't especially hungry and so settled on a bagel with cream cheese, tea, and orange juice. Sipping at her tea, she spread open the *Oregonian* on the table in front of her. They'd given Ethan's death a slot on the front page under a story about another murder—one involving a property dispute. She read it first. The dispute had turned ugly after one neighbor had dumped a load of concrete into the other neighbor's garden, which he claimed infringed upon his property by two feet.

Helen shook her head. At least that killing, senseless as it was, would be an easy one to solve. There had been a number of witnesses and the neighbor, a seventy-year-old man, had been taken into custody.

Helen drained her cup and perused the article about Ethan. It was short and to the point: *Mayor of Bay Village found dead on the beach near Lincoln City. Local resident finds body.* Apparently the sheriff's office hadn't given the press her name. *Thank goodness for that.* Helen set the paper aside, cleared the table, and rinsed the dishes.

❖   ❖   ❖

The doorbell rang as she was putting on her jacket.

"Mrs. Bradley. Good morning."

"Stephanie. What a nice surprise. Would you like to come in?" Helen opened the door wider and stepped back.

"No thanks. This will only take a minute. Joe wanted me to come by and pick up that check you found last night at Rosie's."

"I'll get it." Helen had left a message for Joe the night before as she was getting ready for bed. She picked up the envelope she'd slipped it into off the small table in the entryway and handed it to the deputy.

"Thanks. Oh, Joe also said to let you know that we found Jordan's prints all over Rosie's place. You were taking a big chance going there last night. I mean—if you'd gotten there a few minutes earlier, or we hadn't shown up when we did, he might have killed you."

Helen didn't think that was likely but didn't say so.

"Joe's charging him with murder."

"Really?"

"Yeah."

Helen ran a hand through her hair. "He has enough evidence to make a case?"

Stephanie shrugged. "Tom found a set of keys in Jordan's van that go to the mayor's Jaguar. Mrs. Crane identified them this morning."

Helen opened her mouth, but nothing came out. She finally managed to say, "I can't believe it."

"I couldn't either, Mrs. Bradley." Stephanie looked as disappointed as Helen felt. "I don't think we have much choice. He just confessed."

Thirteen

Helen stepped back. She didn't know what to say. When Stephanie made no move to go, Helen asked, "Are you sure you don't want something to drink? Tea? Juice?"

Stephanie hesitated, then agreed. Following Helen through the living room and into the kitchen, she said, "Tea does sound pretty good about now. Had a hard time sleeping last night."

Helen nodded at a chair and told Stephanie to make herself at home. While Helen set the teakettle on, she asked Stephanie about her position with the sheriff's department in Multnomah County.

The young officer began to relax as she talked about her job. "Portland is just too big a town. When my husband was offered a position in Lincoln City, I applied."

"So you like being in law enforcement?"

"Yeah, it's challenging and every day is different."

"That it is." Helen briefly told her about her past jobs.

"How long were you a cop?" Stephanie rested her arms on the table.

"About sixteen years."

"That seems like a long time," Stephanie said. "No wonder you can't get it out of your system. Do you miss it?"

"Not really, but then I haven't entirely given up the part I liked best—tracking down the bad guys." She gave Stephanie a wry smile. "I'm not sure I'll ever be able to stop getting involved. As long as I remain in good health, I'll probably keep dipping my fingers into an investigation now and again—

especially those cases with people I care about."

"And you cared about Ethan."

"Very much so."

Stephanie stared at her hands for a moment before raising her eyes to meet Helen's. "So what's your take on the mayor's murder? I noticed you didn't seem too happy about Jordan's arrest last night."

"That's true enough. We seem to be missing an important element here—motive. When he confessed, did he happen to say why he killed Ethan?"

She shook her head. "Joe says he'll find one. Right now he has enough physical evidence to hang the guy."

"That's what worries me. He just might." Chuck Daniels' face flashed through her mind. Helen leaned against the counter and studied the scattering of fall leaves on the wet grass beyond her kitchen window. She would have to get outside one of these days and rake them. "Frankly, I'm not sure what to think about Alex Jordan. A confession is hard to argue against. I suppose you have to go along with him—at least for now."

"But you don't."

Helen shook her head. "Part of me says I read the guy wrong and he's guilty as sin. After all, he ransacked Rosie's office, and we know he had contact with Ethan the night of his death. Another part tells me my instincts couldn't be that wrong."

"Yes, but no one we've talked to saw the mayor after his dinner with Jordan."

"Anything could've happened during the time between that dinner and Ethan's getting murdered."

"Right," Stephanie said, "but why did Jordan have the mayor's car keys?"

Helen massaged the stiff muscles in her neck and shoulder, then poured out two cups of tea from the kettle. Setting the cups on the table, she said, "Time will tell and, hopefully, so will the evidence."

"Um . . . Mrs. Bradley, if it's any consolation, I don't think Jordan did it either."

"Really?" Now that surprised her. Stephanie had seemed pleased about the department's success in apprehending the suspect so quickly, and Helen told her so.

Stephanie flushed with apparent embarrassment. "I thought we had our guy, but after watching Joe interrogate him and hearing his responses . . . well, I don't know. At first he denied everything. Then when Joe told him about Ethan's murder, he looked surprised. He covered his face with his hands and asked how it had happened. Joe said, 'You know how it happened. You did it.'" Stephanie blew on her tea and took a tentative sip. "When Joe showed him the weapon and Ethan's keys, the guy went white. Maybe it was then I knew he hadn't done it. A few minutes later—boom. He confesses and asks for a lawyer. I'm sitting there thinking, 'no way.'"

"Was there anything specific in what he said or did to make you think that?"

"Not really." She pressed her fist to her midsection. "I just felt it."

"Mmm. Unfortunately, feelings don't hold up in court." Helen stared at the handmade doily in the center of her table. "I've been forced to back off a number of cases because the evidence didn't bear out my suspicions." Helen sighed. "There was one case in particular. Happened about a year before I retired. I never did resolve it. Haunts me to this day."

"That must be tough."

"Mmm. It happens all too often. The case never went to trial. In fact, we couldn't even get enough to arrest him."

"What happened?"

"This couple had been rock climbing. He was experienced, his wife a novice. She'd supposedly fallen while trying to negotiate a sheer rock wall. Not the sort of place you'd take a beginner. I felt certain he'd killed her, but we couldn't prove it. He seemed pretty broken up about it at the time. Said he tried to talk her out of making that climb, but she insisted. I never did believe him. A few months later he married his wife's sister." Helen frowned at the reflection in her tea and set the cup down. "But that's ancient history. We were talking about Ethan's supposed killer. Did you tell Joe about your concerns?"

"No. I'm a coward. Don't tell anyone I said so, though. I'd

rather gloat over being right than say something and then be proved wrong."

"Your secret is safe with me, Stephanie. Though I'd personally like to see you stand behind your convictions."

"I might do that—when I'm more sure of myself. The last thing I need is for these guys to think I'm a sympathetic flake. They're already talking about how Jordan snowed you and Lynn Daniels."

"Lynn?" It took a moment for Helen to make the connection. "Of course, Joe would have questioned her about Alex."

"Actually she came in to file a missing person's report on her husband. I guess he never did come home, and none of his friends have seen him since he was at Bagley's Tavern night before last. When Joe told Lynn they'd arrested Alex, she broke down and cried. Looks like something was going on between her and Alex. The guys are saying he's the kind of man who can get a woman to agree to just about anything."

They sat in silence for a few moments. Helen wanted to reassure the deputy, tell her to trust her instincts, but how could she? At the moment she wasn't even sure she trusted her own.

"There is something I noticed when we first got the mayor's body out," Stephanie said, leaning forward and setting her empty cup on the table. "I'm no forensics expert, but it looked to me like the weapon went straight in. The way I see it is Alex Jordan is about six-two—close to the mayor's height. If he was going to stab him, he'd have brought the blade up, or down. Either way it would have been angled more."

"Maybe. If Ethan was bending over or . . . had fallen . . ." The image of Jordan or anyone stabbing Ethan in the back set Helen's stomach churning. "I don't suppose we'll have any real answers there until the medical examiner's report comes in."

"Joe's expecting a preliminary report this afternoon."

Helen nodded. "Then I'll have to make a point of stopping by the office."

"Hey, I gotta run. I'm glad we had this talk." Stephanie thanked her again and waved as she ducked into her car. "I'll keep you posted."

Helen stood in the doorway until the patrol car disappeared

from view. She then shut the door, padded to the living room, and sank onto the couch. So Alex had confessed. She thought about the impression he'd made the day before when he'd been at the house. He was a nice-looking, clean-cut man and had the face—the smile—of someone kind and loving. But it was more than his looks. There were plenty of guys in prison who looked like ordinary nice guys and yet had committed heinous crimes. Could her instincts be so completely wrong? Did she simply want him to be innocent because of Rosie?

Helen leaned back against the cushions and closed her eyes, thinking of the Alex Jordan she'd seen in the patrol car the night before. The pleading eyes. The look of fear. *"I didn't do anything,"* he'd said. *"Please, you have to believe me."*

She'd believed him then. And God help her, she still did. She was a good judge of character—always had been. So why had he confessed? Had Joe forced a confession? She doubted that. Helen decided it wasn't really Alex's guilt or innocence that had her so concerned. It was his connection with Rosie—the check Rosie had written to Alex in the same amount as the deposit made to her account.

Planting her hands on her knees, she stood. "There's only one thing to do," she said aloud. "Find Rosie."

Fourteen

Helen gathered the items she needed for her trip to Lincoln City—her extra clothes, towel, binoculars, sunglasses, a novel, water bottle, and protein bar—and stuffed them into her denim beach bag. Regardless of how the day unfolded, she intended to take full advantage of the sunshine.

Hopefully, she'd find Rosie and get the mess straightened out, and then locate a quiet beach and take a leisurely walk. She hadn't had a good walk or run in many days; her fitness regimen was practically nonexistent. Since being shot, she'd been remiss about exercising. Not a good thing.

Sitting in her car at the end of her driveway, Helen hesitated before taking a left toward Lincoln City. Instead, she hung a right. Soon she was driving into a private residential area on her way to the Crane home. The slight alteration in plans came as a result of two things. First, she felt guilty for not calling Eleanor the evening before, and second, she'd completely forgotten about talking with Annie regarding the women's luncheon. The stop wouldn't take long, and she felt compelled to check on the family.

She pulled into Eleanor's driveway at ten sharp. One of the doors on the three-car garage was left open, and inside was Eleanor's Mercedes. Two other cars were parked in front of the other doors. A bike leaned against the center support. It looked as though Nancy's daughter had returned to the fold.

Nancy came around from the side of the house, her shoulder-length ash brown hair tossing in the wind like a horse's mane. Her two-inch heels clicked and scraped on the sidewalk as she approached Helen. Nancy glanced at the cigarette in her hand as if she wasn't sure what to do with it. Looking at Helen, she took a puff and blew the smoke into the wind. "Mrs. Bradley."

From the almost hostile look on Nancy's face, Helen could tell she wasn't exactly thrilled about having a visitor—at least not Helen.

"Why are you here?" Nancy apparently had not inherited her mother's ability to spread out the welcome mat regardless of the situation.

Helen found the woman's attitude an odd blend of honesty and sarcasm, but she decided not to take it personally. Nancy stood about six feet away. She wore no makeup, but Helen doubted it would have done much good. The dark semicircles under her eyes and the dazed look indicated not only grief but a string of sleepless nights. She had the gray pallor of a woman who'd been on an all-night binge. Her outfit—black slacks and blazer with a dull, rust-colored print blouse—sucked the color out of her skin.

"I came by to see if there's anything you need." Helen now stood on the porch waiting for Nancy to join her.

"That's kind of you," she said in a husky voice. "But we have everything under control. Mother and Brian have seen to all the details."

Helen raised an eyebrow at the sarcastic note. "Brian. Your brother?"

"He came in last night and took over." She took one last draw from the cigarette, screwing up her face as if it were the most vile-tasting substance on earth. "He almost acts like he's glad Dad is gone." Throwing the butt to the ground, she joined Helen on the porch. "You can come in if you want. Mother will be glad you came." She tossed her head and finger-combed her hair away from her face. "Grief becomes her."

"What an odd thing to say."

With her hand on the doorknob, she turned back to face Helen. "I didn't mean it as a criticism—not really. She's as miserable as the rest of us on the inside. I just don't see how she can stay so calm and put-together like she does. People come around and you'd think she was throwing a tea party instead of getting ready for a funeral."

"Your mother has the gift of hospitality. She's used to caring for others. I suppose it's difficult for her to have things turned around. She's always been a strong woman."

"I suppose." Opening the door, Nancy added, "Joe called this morning. They think they have the guy who killed my father."

"Yes, I heard they'd made an arrest."

"Helen." Eleanor came toward them, elegant as usual in black suit and white silk shell. A diamond brooch on the jacket created a stunning effect. Helen understood more fully what Nancy meant. Helen felt a twinge of jealousy—then pity. How terrible it must be to feel you had to hold yourself together like that.

Memories forced their way into Helen's thoughts. She'd been much the same way after Ian's death—determined to put up a good front, comforting the children and grandchildren, playing hostess. Holding death at bay because it was simply too painful to bear. She'd gone back to work, kept busy. The days had been bearable. But the nights—being alone in that dark, empty house—almost undid her. A year later, with the help of a counselor, she finally allowed herself to grieve. She'd cried, really cried, for the first time since the funeral. Gut-wrenching sobs that tore her inside out. Grief, she'd come to realize, could be stuffed down for a time, but eventually, it rose to the surface, more fierce and persistent than it had a right to be. As these memories assaulted her, Helen wished there were something she could do to keep Eleanor from making the same mistakes. To reassure her that time would heal the wounds. That God would bring light into her darkness.

However, now wasn't the time to talk or even think about that. Maybe she'd broach the subject later—after the funeral and after the kids were gone.

"I'm going upstairs to check on Melissa," Nancy said.

Eleanor spread her arms and gave Helen the kind of comforting hug she should have been receiving.

"How are you holding up?" Helen asked, then wished she hadn't. It was such a tired cliché.

Eleanor assured her that all was under control. "Annie will cater a light lunch at the church following the interment. We don't have a date yet. The medical examiner says he can't release Ethan's body until he's had a chance to do a thorough exam. Maybe Friday. You are coming, aren't you, Helen? To the funeral, I mean."

"Yes, of course."

"Forgive me for not offering you coffee, but we're on our way to pick out the casket and cards and guest register. . . . There are so many details to attend to. We're using Woodland Estates, that new funeral home just northeast of town."

Helen nodded. "I know where it is."

"Ethan and I had talked about buying a plot and making arrangements before . . ." Eleanor blinked back tears and then turned to pick up her handbag from the half-round table in the entry. She stood in front of the oval mirror above the table adjusting her already perfect hair.

"Are you guys ready to go?" Brian, looking as handsome as ever, bounded down the stairs. His hair was the same ashy shade of brown as his sister's but with blond streaks. The black leather jacket and jeans couldn't have been more out of place as he stood next to Eleanor, but he didn't seem to notice or care. His gray-green eyes caught Helen's and for a moment held a puzzled expression.

"Brian, you remember Helen Bradley?" His mother adjusted his collar.

"Oh, right, the ex-cop." He pulled away from his mother and shook Helen's hand. "Mom tells me you're the one who found my father's body."

"Yes, I did."

"Why didn't you tell me that yesterday when you were here? I didn't know until Joe mentioned it this morning." Eleanor opened her bag and withdrew a tissue.

"I didn't see any reason to go into the details at the time," Helen said.

"It must have been terrible for you. But then having been a

police officer, I imagine you get used to such things."

"One never gets used to it. But you do learn to cope."

"Yes." Eleanor looked in the mirror again, rubbing her lips together. "Well, the main thing is that they have the killer."

"He's a suspect. We don't know for certain that he's guilty."

"Of course he is. That man had Ethan's keys."

"We're ready whenever you are." Nancy came down the stairs with her daughter dragging along behind. Melissa plunked down on the last step. Her dark eyes and hair reminded Helen of Ethan. She was a gangly girl—all arms and legs. The long floral-patterned skirt and short knit top accentuated her slender frame.

"You might be ready, but I'm not." Melissa folded her arms. "I don't see why you can't let me stay here. I don't want to go to a place that's full of dead bodies. It totally grosses me out."

"We aren't going to be seeing any bodies." Nancy rolled her eyes.

Melissa lowered her gaze to the floor. "Besides, if Grandpa is really in heaven like you say, why do we need to go through all this anyway?"

"I'm not crazy about going either, Mel," Brian said. "But Mom wants us all to go. It's called moral support."

Melissa leaned her head against the banister. "Please, Grams. You know I love you and Grandpa—it's just that I don't see why I have to help pick out the casket."

Eleanor sighed. "I don't want to force anyone. Perhaps it would be best if Melissa stayed. Annie's here. I don't think she'd mind looking out for her."

Melissa jumped up and flung her arms around her grandmother's neck. "Thank you." Without waiting for a response from her mother and uncle, she fled upstairs.

Eleanor stared at the now-empty stairway for a moment and then turned to Helen. "I'm sorry, but we need to be going."

"Don't apologize. You go ahead. I want to talk to Annie before I leave, so, if you don't mind, I'll just go find her."

"Of course. She's in the kitchen."

Helen stood in the entryway for a while till they got into the Mercedes and backed out of the garage. She then headed for the kitchen, but halfway there, did an about-face. As if her feet had a mind of their own, Helen detoured into the den, which she knew to be Ethan's home office. With Annie busy in the kitchen and Melissa upstairs, it seemed the perfect opportunity to look through Ethan's desk and perhaps find some clues as to who may have wanted Ethan dead. Joe or one of his deputies would undoubtedly have done a thorough search, but it never hurt to have a fresh perspective.

The desk was spotless. Even the in-out trays were empty. Helen checked the desk calendar. It hadn't been turned since Thursday, the day Ethan left for D.C. Flipping through the pages, she saw that he'd scheduled a church council meeting for tonight. And there were various other meetings scheduled, among them one with Chuck Daniels for lunch tomorrow. Men's prayer breakfast Tuesday morning. Wednesday night meeting at church for Bible study. Thursday night choir. It looked as though most of the events he had scheduled here were of a personal nature. There was no reference to his meeting with Alex Jordan. She flipped the pages of the calendar back and noticed that the page for Sunday was missing.

She doubted Joe or one of the deputies would have removed a single page. They'd more than likely have taken the entire calendar. Did Ethan have another engagement scheduled after his dinner with Alex?

Opening the drawers, she found a file of correspondence from a law firm representing a Calfornia corporation wanting to build a shopping center in Bay Village. They had chosen a site but needed final approval. The letter was signed by their legal representative, Nathan Young. A copy of a letter from Ethan stated that the city council had denied their proposal. Then another letter from the lawyer threatened legal action against the city.

Helen had heard about plans for a shopping center, but she hadn't known the details. Though the land was mostly privately owned, part of it had been designated as a wildlife refuge, and Ethan was not about to let the new owners build anything that might disrupt the ecosystem there. But nothing in the letters indicated *who* the owners were. Too bad. Helen wanted to talk to them. She still harbored the idea that someone may have killed Ethan because of his environmental policies. Chuck fit this picture, and apparently so did whoever owned this property. Would they have a better chance with Ethan out of the way? Possibly. Helen made a mental note to check it out later— maybe call on the lawyer. Nathan Young, of Young & Associates in Lincoln City. She committed the name to memory, then shuffled through the rest of Ethan's papers.

She focused back on Chuck Daniels. He presented another part of the mystery. Was he actually missing, or had he killed Ethan and run? Then there was the matter of Rosie's letter opener. It seemed unlikely that Chuck Daniels would have used something like that. She saw him more as a gun man.

Helen replaced everything the way she'd found it and closed the desk drawers. Except for the shopping-center file, everything else had to do with the church and personal papers—warranties, bills, that sort of thing. There was also a copy of his will that indicated everything was left to his children, with the exception of a twenty-thousand-dollar bequest to the church for mission work. She suspected Brian and Nancy stood to inherit a great deal of money. It seemed strange that Ethan hadn't included a clause naming Eleanor as beneficiary. Not that it would matter to Eleanor. She'd come from a wealthy family and probably had more money than Ethan anyway. The will stipulated that Eleanor was to divide Ethan's estate equally between his children.

The distinct smell of chocolate drifted to her nostrils, reminding Helen of her intention to talk to Annie. She followed the aroma and found Annie up to her elbows in bread dough. Pots and pans and bowls and utensils of varying sizes filled the double stainless-steel sink, overflowing onto the white tile counter.

"Hi, Annie."

"Oh, Helen! What a surprise. What brings you here?"

"The luncheon, for one thing. I also stopped by to see if Eleanor needed anything."

"Well, you missed them. They're headed for the funeral home."

"Yes, I talked with them as they were leaving." The second the words left her mouth, Helen wished she could put them back. The family had been gone for a good ten minutes. "Something smells good," she added quickly, in case Annie discovered the time discrepancy.

Apparently she didn't. As busy as she'd obviously been, she probably wouldn't have noticed much of anything.

"Chocolate brownies." Annie winked at Helen and sent her a conspiratorial grin. "I just took them out of the oven. If you have a few minutes, I'll finish up here and have one with you. You can pour us some coffee while you wait."

"They smell absolutely wonderful, but I can't have any. I'm allergic to chocolate."

"Oh, that's right. I'd forgotten." She rounded up the bread and turned it into a large bowl. "How about one of my lemon squares? Made those this morning too."

"Wonderful." Helen poured the coffee into mugs she found on a rack above the opposite counter while Annie washed her hands and spread a towel over the dough. Setting the mugs on the kitchen table, Helen said, "I hope I'm not keeping you. I was hoping to talk to you about the women's luncheon."

"I'm glad you came by. I've been working nonstop since five this morning, so I needed a break." She wiped her hands and took out two dessert plates and forks. "Spent the night here last night, since they had a late dinner and I had so much to do today. There we go." Annie placed lemon bars on a platter and set it with the two plates and forks on the table in the breakfast nook. The table had already been laid with linen place mats and cloth napkins in different pastel colors. The bay window next to the table offered a terrific view of the ocean, which was probably another reason Annie hadn't noticed when the family left. She wouldn't have been able to see them, since the driveway and garage were on the street side of the house.

"Are you sure you'll have time to cater the luncheon?" Helen asked.

"Of course. Once the funeral is over and Brian is gone, things will be back to normal." She frowned. "Well, not normal, exactly. But the luncheon isn't for two weeks, so there'll be plenty of time."

Helen sliced into the delicate yellow-and-white dessert and put a small portion into her mouth, savoring the sweet, tangy taste. It reminded her of the lemon meringue pies she used to make when the children were small. They'd been Jason's favorite. She chased down the sweet with a swig of coffee. She hadn't baked a pie in ages.

"So, what would you like me to serve?"

"What?" Helen came back with a jolt.

"The luncheon. What would you like on the menu?"

"Um . . . why don't you choose? Can you do something for around ten dollars per person?"

"Sure—no problem." Helen listened as Annie developed a well-rounded menu of salad, two kinds of quiche—one with ham, cheese, and broccoli, the other vegetarian, assorted breads, and dessert. Dessert would be light, consisting of fruit— some plain and some chocolate-dipped.

Sitting there listening, eating, and drinking her coffee, Helen wished she hadn't taken on the responsibility. She'd never been one for serving on committees or heading up dinners. Though she could be as hospitable as the next person, it wasn't her thing.

"That should do it," Annie said at last. "I'll bring some things the night before and put them in the refrigerator. The rest I'll bring in the morning."

"Great."

"Helen?" Annie turned serious. "May I ask you something?"

"Sure."

"Well, it's probably nothing, but I couldn't help noticing." She leaned forward, resting her arms on the table. "You saw Brian this morning, didn't you?"

"Yes."

"Did you notice anything different or strange about him?"

"What do you mean?" Helen asked.

"Last night he and Nancy got into a nasty argument at dinner. She accused him of being glad their father was dead. He didn't deny it. Just shook his head and said she was crazy."

"She mentioned something like that to me as well. But men often keep their feelings hidden."

"I know. It's just that . . . later . . . see, I stayed here last night and was up late putting together the ingredients for a couple of casseroles. I thought I'd do some ahead and freeze them. Anyway, everyone had gone to bed except for Brian and me. When I came out of the kitchen, I saw him going through Ethan's desk. Said he was straightening things up. Well, it didn't need straightening. Eleanor had already seen to that.

"He muttered something about junk mail and tossed some papers in the fireplace. Now, why he had the fire going in Ethan's fireplace is a mystery, unless he started it specifically to burn the papers."

"That does seem odd," Helen said. "Could have been junk mail. Or he could be trying to hide something."

"My thoughts exactly. I was going to tell Joe this morning, but he got a call and we didn't have much time to talk."

"I can mention it to him if you'd like." Helen ate the last bite of her dessert and set the napkin on the plate.

"Thanks. I'm not sure when I'll get around to it." Annie leaned back and picked up her cup. In a strained voice, she added, "There's something about Brian that just isn't right."

Fifteen

Just what is it about Brian that upsets you?" Helen asked.

Annie circled the rim of her cup with her finger. "It's not a big thing. He's just so different than he was in school."

"I didn't realize you'd gone to school together."

"Yes, Nancy was two years behind us. Joe was in our class too. Anyway, Brian seems hard . . . bitter. I know he went through a divorce a couple years ago, but . . ." She glanced in both directions as if someone might be listening. "Don't tell Joe this, but Brian got really pushy last night. After he burned the papers, he asked me to sit up and talk with him for a few minutes. I did—figured he wanted to talk about his dad. Turns out that wasn't what he wanted at all."

"He made a pass at you?" Helen guessed.

"That's putting it mildly. He'd been drinking and . . ." She looked away. "I don't want to use the word *rape*, but he came awfully close. I managed to get away from him."

"That's terrible. Did you talk to Eleanor?"

Meeting Helen's gaze again, Annie said, "No. I think it was the alcohol. He was fine this morning. He even apologized. I don't think I need to say anything. Especially now."

Helen sighed. "I'm glad you told me. If it happens again . . ."

"I don't think it will. I shouldn't have mentioned it. It's so unlike him."

She made Annie promise to tell her if there were further problems and then Helen left. It was time she located Rosie. Things were getting far too complicated, and she needed to pull in some of the loose ends. She'd find Rosie, then come back and talk to Joe. And later, if there was time, she'd call Nathan Young and glean whatever information she could about the corporation he represented.

Minutes later she was back on Highway 101 in the northbound lane, appreciating the view. There was nothing quite like the Oregon coast on a clear day. Helen thought seriously of aborting her mission and hitting the beach instead, but she needed answers to her many questions. Why, for instance, would Rosie have a picture of a confessed murderer on her dresser?

Helen checked Rosie's sister's address again and turned up a narrow lane at the northern end of Lincoln City known as Road's End. The street went straight up the side of the hill, then curved around to the left. Adele's house was the second from the corner. Though Helen had seen Adele several times, she'd never been to her home. Like so many of the houses here, this one had an ocean view.

There was a white pickup truck parked in the driveway, with the logo *Feldman's Construction* lettered on its tailgate. So Adele's husband was a contractor too. Interesting. No sign of Rosie's car, but then she hadn't expected there would be. If Rosie didn't want to be found, she'd park it in the garage or somewhere inconspicuous.

On the drive up she'd thought about how best to approach Rosie and Adele. She'd decided on the straightforward method: Show up out of the blue and ask about Alex Jordan.

On the other hand, suppose Alex really had killed Ethan, and Rosie was an accomplice?

Rosie has nothing to do with Ethan's murder and you know it. Helen grabbed her backpack off the passenger seat and hurried to the front door before she could change her mind again.

Adele shared Rosie's talent for decorating. Flowerpots with variegated purple-and-white kale lined the small aggregate entry. The door, nearly all window, allowed her to see into the hallway and living room. Helen had never seen a house with so many windows. She rang the doorbell twice before someone answered.

A short, lean man with a beard and mustache opened it. "If you're selling, I'm not buying," he grumped before she could speak.

"I'm here to see Rosie." Helen smiled and extended her hand. "Helen Bradley. You must be Adele's husband."

His sky blue eyes lit up in recognition. He shook her hand. "Dave Feldman." Opening the door wider, he stepped aside to let her in. "I recognize your name. Rosie talks about you all the time."

"We're good friends." *Or were.* Helen followed him into the huge room with a high angular ceiling that served as a kitchen, dining room, and living room. She loved the open feel of the place. With all the windows, it was as light and bright as being outside. Her eyes were automatically drawn to the surf. While the oceanfront houses blocked parts of the beach, she could still see the ocean and the cape to the north. A telescope stood near one of the living room windows. She turned to Dave and said, "Lovely house. Did you build it?"

He nodded. "On spec. Once it was done, Adele wouldn't let me sell it. Might have to, though. Got too much money tied up in it."

"That's too bad. If you do decide to sell, let me know."

"Are you in the market? I could give you a good deal."

Helen grinned. "I wasn't until I saw this place. Now . . . well, I guess I am interested."

"Would you like a tour?"

"That would be great." Then remembering her mission, Helen added, "But I would like to see Rosie first. Is she here?"

"No. She and Adele went down to the factory outlet place." He shook his head. "Had some serious shopping to do." Glancing at his watch, he added, "They should be back pretty soon. Said they were only going to be a couple of hours. Guess Rosie had to pick up some clothes."

"Yes, I suppose she would. She left in a pretty big hurry yesterday."

"I wouldn't know about that. All I know is she's upset about Ethan Crane's death and seems to think the police are going to tie her to the crime." He went on without waiting for a response. "Told her the worst thing she could do was run from the police. Still not sure what happened. She showed up here babbling about needing a place to hide out for a few days."

"I tried to tell her the same thing. In fact, that's why I'm here. She didn't have to run at all. The police have a suspect in custody."

"That quick?" His grin revealed a straight slightly yellowed set of teeth. "Glad to hear that. Rosie's been driving us crazy— well, Adele anyway. I've pretty much stayed out of it."

Helen drew her heavy pack from her shoulders. Since Dave was being so helpful, she decided to question him about Alex. It might be easier to get answers from him than from Rosie. Before she could ask, the phone rang in another room.

"That's my business line. I'd better get it." He disappeared into a room on the other side of the kitchen. Through the open door she could hear him talking to some guy named Al.

"Yeah. Well, what did he say?" Dave didn't sound too happy. After several seconds, he swore. "All right. I'll be there in a few minutes." Mumbling expletives under his breath, he emerged from the room, pulling his jacket on.

"I'm sorry, Mrs. Bradley. Got some trouble at the construction site." He looked at his watch. "I'm sure Adele and Rosie will be back soon. You're welcome to stay. Um . . . just make yourself at home."

"Oh no, I couldn't. Don't worry about me. I can just wait in my car."

"Hey, it's not a problem. A friend of Rosie's is a friend of ours. Stay. Look around." He grinned again. "Who knows? Maybe you'll decide to buy the place."

"Thank you, Dave. I appreciate that." She nodded toward the kitchen. "Do you mind if I make myself some tea?"

"Help yourself. You don't even have to heat the water. I installed a hot-water tap." With another good-bye, he was out the door.

What a trusting man.

Helen rummaged around in the kitchen cupboard for a cup and tea. She found both in short order, and after dunking the peppermint tea bag into the water, she took her cup to the living room and settled into the thick cushions of a swivel rocker.

Helen waited for a while, then decided she could make better use of her time by visiting the lawyer who represented those wanting to build a mall and condos next to the wildlife refuge. After checking the phone book for Nathan Young, Helen left the house and headed south to downtown Lincoln City. The law office was sandwiched between a Realtor and a deli in one of the many strip malls that lined the main highway.

Helen noted that Nathan was the only lawyer working out of the office. "Can I help you?" An attractive brunette moved away from the computer she'd been working on and peered over the top of a curved oak counter. Helen suppressed a smile. The desk made her look like a child playing office.

She read the nameplate on the counter. *Gretchen Young.* "I hope so. Are you Gretchen?" Helen leaned on the counter, looking down at the second tier of the desk, which was surprisingly free of clutter.

A warm light glinted in the young woman's eyes. "Nathan is my husband." She flashed an expensive-looking diamond. "We've only been married a month. Of course, we went together for two years, but with Nathan still in law school, we decided to wait. He graduated this last June."

Helen quickly surveyed the small but nicely decorated room. "From the looks of things, he must be doing very well."

"Oh, he is. He landed a really big account. . . ." Her voice faded as if she'd been caught talking out of turn.

Helen introduced herself and then asked, "Is Mr. Young in?"

"Did you have an appointment?" Gretchen ran her fingers over the open spiral notebook.

"No. I was in town and thought I'd take a chance. You see, I've recently come into a large sum of money and was thinking of investing some of it in a project a friend told me about."

"Really?" Her smile faded. "You wouldn't be talking about Riverside Mall at Bay Village, would you?"

"Yes, that's the one. I'm hoping the developers will be interested in another partner."

Gretchen bounced to her feet. Though she had small features, she stood at about five-ten. "Tell you what. You wait here a minute and I'll ask Nathan—Mr. Young—if he can see you."

"Thanks." Helen retreated to one of four straight-backed cushioned chairs. She felt a twinge of guilt for leading them to believe she wanted to be a backer. But when seeking privileged information, one occasionally had to stretch the truth. And for her it wasn't that much of a stretch. She did have a great deal of money and was indeed looking for some investments.

Nathan Young emerged from his office. Helen, on the tall side herself, had to look up to meet his hazel eyes. A man in his late twenties, he was about J.B.'s height, only fifty pounds lighter. He appeared too thin for his over-six-foot frame that wore a gray suit and pale olive shirt with a speckled olive, gray, and pink tie. The result was an overall chic look. He shook her hand and invited her into his office. He'd spared no expense, it seemed, with the plush aqua carpeting and furnishings found in the most successful corporate offices. She sat in one of two chairs, identical to those in the waiting room.

Helen set her bag on the floor. "I understand you haven't been practicing law for long."

"Since June. I've been very fortunate in developing a strong clientele." He met her gaze and turned the conversation to her reason for coming. "I understand you're looking for an investment. Gretchen said you were asking about the Riverside mall complex."

"Yes. I've heard about the project and was wondering if there might be room for another backer."

He frowned. "I can't speak for them, but I can certainly inquire. How much are we talking about here?"

"Well, that depends on how secure it is. Two to three million perhaps."

His Adam's apple shifted up and down, though otherwise he appeared unruffled. "What did you mean by secure?"

"I heard they were having some problems getting permits because part of it will be built on what is currently a wildlife refuge. The city council and mayor seemed adamantly against it, and it's not very popular with the current nearby retailers."

"My sources tell me they're having a 'change of heart.' And I think when I present it to them again, they'll see the advantage."

Helen sat higher in her chair. "Does this change of heart have anything to do with Ethan Crane's death?"

He picked up a pen and rolled it between his hands. "I'd hate to think so. Ethan was coming around. The environmentalists opposed to the project haven't been completely honest and have exaggerated the problem. You see, the original owner wasn't interested in developing the land, so he just let it go. He encouraged the wildlife population, and people got used to seeing it as part of the wetlands area. When he died, his son inherited it and put it up for sale. The investment group I represent bought the land in good faith. They never anticipated any problems, since it was privately owned. Because the development takes out only ten acres of the refuge . . ." He paused and opened the top right-hand drawer. "It's easier to show you."

He pulled out a file and, after thumbing through it, laid a sketch on the desk between them. "The wildlife refuge covers about fifty acres." He ran his finger along the perimeter. "The land along this side is slotted for development. There's plenty of room left for the birds and animals. There will be some displacement, but the owners plan to leave a big hunk of the property in its natural state. There'll be trails and overlooks. Several ponds and a golf course."

"Sounds lovely. I heard the argument wasn't only about the land. There's the matter of disrupting the wildlife. The environmental groups have a strong voice. What happens if the government steps in and disallows the project?"

He bit his lower lip. "Then the backers lose their investment. But," he was quick to say, "that probably isn't going to happen."

"How much is tied up in the project so far?"

"About fifty million." He leaned back in his leather chair. "Like I said, the deal should go through. The development will provide hundreds of jobs and make Bay Village a destination resort. It'll bring in more revenue."

"Yes—and more tourists." Helen didn't mention that she preferred Bay Village just as it was, small and quaint.

"It may cause a few problems for the wildlife initially, but I believe pushing the development through will be beneficial to all of us."

Helen thanked him for the information and stood to leave. "I trust you'll talk to your clients and get back to me?"

"Of course. As I said, I can't speak for them, but I think they might welcome another investor."

With her hand on the door, she turned back around. "You know, I would feel more comfortable knowing who the investors are—maybe talk to a few. How many are there?"

He hedged. "I'm not at liberty to say."

"Well, could you at least give me a couple of names?"

"Not without talking with them first." He then shrugged.

"Why so secretive? The information on the buyers should be available through the courthouse."

"You're welcome to check, but I can save you the trouble."

"All right. Who signed the papers closing the real-estate deal?"

"I did. I'm acting as power of attorney." His pale cheeks flushed a deep rose. "The truth is, Mrs. Bradley, Riverside Development is a group of private individuals who want to remain anonymous."

"Why? Are they hiding something?"

"No. They're protecting their interests. Maybe they're afraid of what the opposition might do. I've heard some of these environmentalists will stop at nothing to protect the wildlife out there."

"Have you been representing this group all along? Are you the one who presented the proposal to the mayor and city council?"

"Yes."

"I'm curious about something, Mr. Young. How did you react when the council turned you down? How much do you stand to lose if the deal doesn't go through?"

He frowned. "I don't think that's any of your—"

"My business? That may be. But I'm wondering if the loss would be substantial enough that you'd do just about anything to push it through, despite Ethan's attempts to stop it."

The deep rose in his cheeks extended to his neck. "I don't know what you're getting at."

"Don't you?" Helen stood her ground. "Ethan Crane was murdered. I have a hunch it was because of his political stand on the Riverside project. That would make you a primary suspect."

"You're way out of line, Mrs. Bradley."

"Am I?" Helen opened the door and stepped into the waiting room. "Maybe *you* didn't kill Ethan, but one of your clients may have. I'd watch my back if I were you, Mr. Young. You could be representing a murderer."

Sixteen

After leaving the attorney's office, Helen drove back to Adele's place and parked where she had before, then walked back to the house. The empty driveway testified that Adele and Rosie still weren't home. Helen let herself in and, as Dave had suggested, made herself at home. She was still there an hour later, soaking in the view, drinking a second cup of tea, and leafing through a stack of magazines when she heard the door open.

"Dave must have left the door unlocked again," Adele said. "I keep having to remind him."

"If that's his worst vice, you are a very lucky woman. Guys don't come much better than Dave."

Adele chuckled. "Hey, don't get me started. I love the guy, but . . ." She stopped and stared openmouthed as Helen swiveled around to face the door. "How? Who? Helen Bradley. What are you doing here?"

Rosie dropped her armload of shopping bags and dove for the still-open door.

"Rosie, wait!" Helen ran after her. She leapt over the pile of plastic bags and clothes spilling out of them, then raced around the house and down the hill. Halfway down, she caught up with Rosie, who was having trouble running in her sandals. Helen grabbed her arm and pulled her to an abrupt halt. "Aren't you listening to me? They have a man in custody. But Joe still needs to talk to you."

Rosie bent over, hands on her thighs, trying to catch her breath. "They do?"

"Yes." Helen started to tell her about the break-in and Alex's arrest but decided to hold off. "You need to come back home, Rosie."

She straightened and held a hand on her chest. "Who? Who did it?"

"I'll tell you all about it, but first let's get you up the hill and into the house so you can sit down." Helen placed Rosie's arm around her neck and her own arm around Rosie's waist to help her walk.

"I'm . . . in terrible . . . shape." Despite Helen's attempts to keep her upright, Rosie sank onto the blacktop.

"So I see."

"Give me a minute . . . to catch . . . my breath."

"Take all the time you need." Helen frowned and then crouched down beside her friend. Rosie's face contorted in pain as she grasped the front of her T-shirt. "You don't look so good. Are you sure you're okay? Are you having chest pains?"

"I'm fine. Will be in a minute. Get these spells when I . . . exert myself. Been meaning to see . . . the doctor."

"Well, you should. What if it's your heart?" Helen bit into her lower lip. "Maybe I should get an ambulance."

She waved her hand in dismissal. "No. I . . . I just can't run. I knew that. Stupid of me . . . to try."

Helen sighed. "Oh, Rosie, what am I going to do with you?"

The pained look gradually left her face, and within a couple of minutes her breathing returned to normal. "I'm okay now. Help me up." Rosie extended a hand, and Helen pulled her to her feet.

Helen walked her back up the hill, stopping three times. Even after she'd gotten Rosie to the couch and lying down, Helen remained concerned. She wasn't sure she should talk to Rosie about Ethan or Alex. The last thing she wanted to do was get Rosie upset again.

Half an hour later, though, Rosie seemed like her old self and was anxious to hear about the man in police custody.

"First," Helen said, "I want you to tell me what you know about Alex Jordan."

Rosie's mouth dropped open. "Where . . . ? How . . . ?"

"He came over to fix my roof. And I saw his picture in your apartment. I broke in so I could feed your cats and try to figure out why you were acting so weird. Don't worry, I'll fix the window."

"My cats. Oh, I'd forgotten. Thank you. But what do you mean, you broke in? You have a key."

"I lost it." She waved her hand. "None of that matters. I want you to tell me who this guy is and why his photo was on your dresser."

Rosie leaned back against the cushions, her frantic gaze connecting with Adele's.

"You may as well tell her," Adele said. "She'll find out anyway."

Rosie glanced at Helen, then looked away. "I was going to tell you eventually. I would have right away, except that I'm not the only one involved." She closed her eyes. "Alex Jordan is my son."

"Your son? Oh, Rosie." The pieces fell together. Perhaps Alex Jordan had a motive after all. "Ethan is the father, isn't he?"

Rosie groaned. "How did you know? Ethan didn't even know until—"

"Until Alex met with him the night he was killed."

"But he didn't do it."

"That's why you ran, isn't it? When I told you that your letter opener was the murder weapon, you thought Alex had killed him. He had access to the letter opener and to Ethan."

She shook her head, sending her wild hair flying. "No!"

"Then why did you run?"

"Okay. I did think Alex might have done it at first, but only because I was in shock. I just wanted to find Alex and talk to him. He'd been sitting on my desk, playing with the opener some days before. I was afraid his prints would be on it. Once I had time to think about it, I knew he couldn't have killed Ethan. Alex isn't like that. He wouldn't hurt anyone. He's a sweet boy. He only wanted to meet his father."

"Rosie, there's something I need to tell you." Helen dreaded telling Rosie about her son's arrest, but delaying would only make matters worse. "I'm not the only one who broke into your place last night. Alex did too. He made quite a mess of your desk. He may have been removing evidence of his connection with you and Ethan."

Her teary eyes widened in disbelief. "Why would he do that?"

"You tell me." Helen then told her about the canceled check she'd found in the bushes. "I'm certain Alex dropped it as he was making his getaway."

Rosie paled and kept shaking her head.

"You don't have that kind of money," Helen went on. "Yet you made a deposit in that same amount just last week. Did you borrow it? Was Alex blackmailing you—or Ethan? If Ethan were still alive, I doubt he'd appreciate this kind of scandal. It would tear his family apart, not to mention his career."

"No-o-o." Rosie let out an exaggerated groan. "You don't understand."

"Okay, then, explain it. I want to help you, Rosie. Tell me what's going on."

"It's a long story."

"I have time."

"Go ahead and tell her, honey." Adele sat on the arm of the couch, her hands soothing her sister's flaming hair. "Like I said before, she'll find out one way or another. It's better if she hears it from you."

"You're right." Rosie offered her sister a small smile.

"Would you two like some coffee?" Adele asked.

Rosie nodded.

Helen handed her empty cup to Adele. "I'll have tea, if you don't mind." She then went over to sit on the sea-green leather couch beside Rosie.

"I don't know where to start." Rosie toyed with the button on the top she wore over a pale lavender T-shirt. Helen suspected the drab-colored clothes had come from Adele's closet. They were attractive: a pair of crinkled-cotton pants and large matching shirt in an off-white. Yet they hung on Rosie, making her look thin and pale.

"Why don't you start at the beginning," Helen suggested.

"But it was so long ago."

"The past might have a bearing on the present." To help Rosie into the subject, Helen said, "I heard a rumor that you and Ethan dated in high school."

"Dated?" Her melancholy smile nearly broke Helen's heart. "Yes, I guess you could say that, but it was so much more. We were planning to get married when we graduated from college. We were so in love and naive. I never thought to use birth control. We hadn't meant for anything to happen. The night of our prom, we got too involved and . . ."

"You got pregnant." Helen provided the words when Rosie couldn't seem to get them out.

"I was so ashamed. I didn't know what to do. I couldn't tell anyone at first—except Adele." Rosie looked up at her sister and leaned forward to accept the coffee.

"We were very close." Adele handed Helen her tea and sat in the chair Helen had vacated. "Still, Rosie never told me who the father was—until last night. She kept her secret all these years. No one else knew, not even Ethan."

"But if Rosie was dating Ethan, surely you must have put two and two together—"

"I told her I'd been raped." Rosie glanced away. "It seemed easier that way."

"Why didn't you tell Ethan?" Helen asked. "This sort of thing happens all the time. I'm sure he would have—"

"That's just it," Rosie said. "He would have married me. He'd have gotten a job right out of high school and forgotten about going to college. Ethan was like that. But I couldn't let him. I didn't want him to sacrifice his future for me. He was an A student and everyone was always saying what a wonderful career he would have. I couldn't destroy that." Rosie shook her head.

"What about *your* future, Rosie?" Helen ran a hand through her hair.

"That's one of the reasons I couldn't tell him. I wasn't just trying to protect him. I didn't want to get married. I wanted to finish school and become a librarian. It had been my dream for as long as I could remember. Ethan would have insisted on keeping the baby, and I didn't want to."

"Don't you think Ethan had a right to know—to at least have a choice in the matter?"

"There would have been no choice where Ethan was concerned. I knew from the start I couldn't involve him. I told Adele I was pregnant and didn't know who the father was. She encouraged me to talk to our folks." Rosie gave Helen a crooked smile.

"They were furious at first," Adele added, "and wanted to go to the police. Rosie refused. Said she didn't want anyone to know and insisted it wouldn't do any good, because she couldn't identify the guy who did it. Once they had time to think about it, they agreed not to subject the family to the humiliation. They became very supportive."

Rosie nodded. "Mom and Dad finally agreed to keep my secret. As you know, things weren't so open and aboveboard back then. None of us wanted me to bear the stigma of having a child out of wedlock. Abortion wasn't legal, but even if it had been, I could never have had one. The only real choice for me was to give the baby up for adoption. My parents were pretty adamant about that. They wanted me to have the baby, give him to a good family, and go on with my plans to finish school. At the time it seemed the perfect solution. I just didn't realize how totally devastating it would be to give up my child.

"It was so hard," Rosie went on. "There were times I thought about keeping the baby and letting Ethan know after he'd finished college. In some ways that's what kept me going. Since it was early in the pregnancy, I was able to graduate that June. I left town shortly after."

"What did you tell Ethan? He must have been heartbroken."

"I told him I was going to visit relatives for the summer, which was true. Mom and Dad sent me to Aunt Hattie's in Minnesota. I stayed with her until Alex was born. I told him I'd be back long before our college classes started. We'd both planned to go to the University of Oregon." Rosie paused to take several sips of coffee. "I hated lying to him that way. I knew at the time I might never see him again. My parents arranged for me to attend college in Minnesota." Fresh tears trailed down her cheeks.

"I'm sorry." Helen patted Rosie's hand. "If this is too painful for you . . . you don't have to go on."

"No. I want you to know everything. You need to understand what happened with Ethan and me—and Alex." Rosie set her cup on the coffee table. "By the end of the summer, I had to let Ethan know I wasn't coming back to Oregon. I wrote him a Dear John letter, saying I'd met a man and we'd gotten engaged. I didn't actually lie. I *had* met a man. A neighbor of Hattie's who would have married me if I'd agreed. I almost did, but I realized it wouldn't have been fair to him. I still loved Ethan."

"And you still do." Rosie's expression confirmed Helen's comment, even though she didn't admit it.

"I went through with the adoption and moved into a dorm on campus. Finished school and became a librarian. I decided never to go back to the Northwest, but I couldn't get Ethan or Oregon out of my mind. Finally, when my father died several years ago, I was forced to come home." She gave Helen a watery smile. "Once I got here, I couldn't leave."

After dabbing at her tears and blowing her nose, Rosie composed herself and told the rest of the story of how she used her savings to buy the Victorian and restore it. "It had always been a dream of mine to own a bookstore. I didn't know what to expect. Ethan was angry—especially when he learned I had never married. Not that it would have done any good. Six months after I broke up with him, he was engaged to Eleanor. I was hurt, but not surprised."

"Eleanor had always liked Ethan," Adele said. "She was more than happy to mend his broken heart."

"Sounds like you're not too fond of her." Helen wrapped both hands around the warm mug and stared into the steam curling above it.

Adele raised her eyebrows. "She's okay. It's my problem—not hers. I was jealous of her for years. Her parents were rich, and I thought she was spoiled rotten. I had mixed feelings about her marrying Ethan. I hated her for Rosie's sake, but in a way I was glad. Ethan deserved some happiness, and Eleanor gave him that. She was the best wife he could have had, considering his career in law and politics. Maybe it was fate that Rosie left."

"He never stopped loving me." Rosie's voice went soft.

Helen thought again about Eleanor's suspicions the day before. "Sounds as though you and Ethan took up where you left off. Were you having an affair?"

"Not in the way you're thinking."

"Come on, sugar," Adele urged, "be honest."

"I am." Rosie clasped her hands. "As much as we wanted to go back to the way things were, we couldn't. Ethan had a family. We decided to be friends—nothing more."

Helen wasn't sure she believed that. Adele apparently didn't either.

"Right." Adele pursed her lips. "You never did make much of a liar, sis."

"Okay," Rosie admitted, "we tried not to get involved. And we did fine until Alex showed up. Then it was as though a dam broke loose in both of us."

Helen and Adele waited while Rosie seemed to struggle to keep her emotions intact. When she finally spoke, it was in hushed tones and Helen had to lean forward to hear. "Alex came to me—about a month ago. He said he'd been able to track me down through a service on the Internet. I was thrilled. You can't imagine. It was like having that big empty hole in my heart filled up again. He was everything I'd dreamed he'd be and more. And he looks so much like Ethan. Oh, Helen—my heart was so full. I had my son back. I couldn't have been happier . . . until he asked about his father. He wanted me to tell him who his father was, and I refused."

"Why didn't he just track Ethan down? He'd found you."

"I hadn't put the father's name on the birth certificate."

"How did he react when you refused to tell him?"

"He wasn't too happy. In fact, he got rather angry. Insisted he had a right to know. We argued and he . . . he left. Said he'd find out with or without me."

He had apparently done just that. Helen's mind tumbled with possibilities. Could Alex have killed Ethan after all? "How did Alex find out?"

"It wasn't all that hard. Ethan came into the store one day while Alex was there. He'd learned that Ethan and I had gone steady in high school. . . ." Rosie sighed. "I guess I really didn't try that hard to hide the fact. When Alex told me he'd figured out who his father was, I pleaded with him not to contact Ethan. Alex seemed desperate to meet his father. I convinced him to wait. I wanted to think about it."

"And did Alex wait?" Helen could see the evidence piling up against Rosie's son. A man angry with the father who'd gotten his mother pregnant, then wanted nothing to do with her. Of course that wasn't true, but what did Alex believe?

"Yes, as a matter of fact, he did," Rosie said. "He was anxious to meet Ethan, of course, but I managed to convince him that Ethan would take the news better coming from me."

"And how did Ethan take it?"

Rosie bit the fleshy part of her thumb. "I'd never seen him more angry. He couldn't believe that I had kept it from him. When he finally calmed down, he insisted on seeing his son as soon as possible. He felt terrible that he hadn't been there for me. We cried together over the life we'd lost because of my selfish and foolish decisions. That night we fell in love all over again. It was wrong. I know. But . . ."

Helen rubbed at her forehead, marveling at how complicated people's lives could become, especially in the midst of lies and deceit. "What about the check? Why did you give Alex a check for a hundred thousand dollars?"

"Ethan wrote a check out to me that night. I'm not sure why, really. He wanted me to have it for all the trouble I'd been through. I didn't want it. He insisted. It made me angry. I felt like he was paying me off. He said it was a gesture of goodwill. I told him I was going to tear it up."

"But you didn't."

"No. I decided to give it to Alex. I deposited it and wrote Alex a check. Told him it was from his father."

"Could Alex have considered it hush money? A payoff?"

"Is that what you think? Alex isn't like that. He didn't even want the money. But I insisted."

Covering her face, Rosie rocked back and forth, her sobs

coming in agonizing moans. "Ethan is dead and it's my fault."

"Why would you say it's your fault, Rosie? Alex is in custody. . . ."

"Helen, please. No more questions." Adele grabbed a box of tissues from under an end table and stuffed a bunch in Rosie's hand. "She's been through enough already."

"You're right. I'm sorry." Helen put a hand on Rosie's slumped shoulder. "I shouldn't be pushing you this way. It's just that you've been a friend for a long time and you're in trouble here. I'd like to help."

Adele's sharp gaze fastened on Helen's. "Wait a minute. Did I hear you right? Did you say Alex was in jail?"

"Unfortunately, yes. He was arrested last night after he broke into your store."

Rosie wiped her eyes and blew her nose. "They had no business arresting him. He didn't break in—he had a key. Just like you did, Helen. If I refuse to press charges, they'll let him go, won't they?"

"It isn't that easy."

"But he hasn't done anything wrong. The money was from Ethan." She sniffed and blew her nose again. "Alex wasn't blackmailing us."

"Rosie." Helen took hold of her friend's hand and squeezed it. "Alex confessed. This morning he told Joe he killed Ethan."

Adele clutched her throat with one hand and gripped Rosie's shoulder with the other. "I told you to be careful." Looking at Helen, she added, "Rosie is so trusting. I mean, this guy pops into her life and announces he's her son. And she doesn't even do a background check."

"He had a birth certificate," Rosie sobbed. "Don't you think I'd recognize my own son?"

"Okay, so he looks a little like Ethan, so what?"

Helen followed Adele's train of thought. "Alex may or may not be your son, Rosie. Adele is right. This could be a scam. Alex may have used you to extort money from Ethan. Suppose Ethan had checked into his background and discovered the truth?"

"Please. You've got to believe me. I know Alex didn't have

anything to do with Ethan's death. You have to believe that."

Helen stood and took her cup to the sink. Part of her could see Alex Jordan as a thief and a killer, but her heart argued against it. "I hope you're right, Rosie. I do so hope you're right."

Seventeen

Rosie stared at the road through Helen's rain-spattered windshield. "I killed Ethan."

"Humph." Helen gave her passenger a quick glance and shook her head. "Right, and I'm Clint Eastwood. Forget it, Rosie. Nothing you say is going to convince me of that. You think you can protect Alex by confessing to the murder yourself, but you can't. If anything, you'll make matters worse. Joe will know you're protecting him, and that will only make him look more appealing as a suspect."

"Well, I have to do something. You and I both know that if there's enough evidence against him, the police aren't going to look elsewhere."

"I doubt that's the case. They'll keep investigating—at least for the next few days. They still need to look at the medical examiner's report and find Ethan's car. They may not go as far as we want, but they'll do the best they can to get at the truth."

"The truth is, Alex didn't kill Ethan."

"You can't be certain of that."

"Yes, I can."

Helen rubbed the back of her neck. "As I told you earlier, the best thing to do is tell Joe everything."

"No, and don't you tell him either. I told you the truth, and look where it got me. You think he did it."

"I'm not convinced he's guilty either, but you have to admit things are not looking good for him." The night before, looking into Alex Jordan's eyes, she'd believed him. After hearing

Rosie's story, she didn't know what to believe. "I need to see Alex again. Talk to him. Find out exactly what kind of evidence they have against him."

"You're going to tell Joe whether I do or not, aren't you?"

"I have to, Rosie. You know that."

"You'll help Alex, won't you?" Rosie was tearing up again. "Right now I feel like no one's on my side. I need you."

What could she say? Helen wanted to walk away from the entire mess, yet knew she had to see it through. At the same time, she wanted to pack up and head for Portland, find J.B., and demand he tell her exactly what was going on. "I'm not sure I'll be of much help."

"Of course you will. I'll work with you."

"Not a good idea. If Alex didn't kill Ethan, then the real killer is still out there."

"I already have an idea of who it might be."

"Really?"

"What if Eleanor found out about Ethan and me?"

Even though the thought had crossed her mind, hearing it aloud gave Helen pause to consider the idea more thoroughly. "Seems to me if she suspected you were having an affair with her husband, she'd kill *you*, not him."

"Not necessarily. She might be even more angry with Ethan."

Helen nodded. "You have a point. If J.B. were having an affair, I'd be tempted to kill him first, then the woman. But only tempted, mind you."

"But that's you, Helen. I couldn't actually kill anyone either."

"Eleanor probably feels the same way. Can you really see her knifing someone? If she did commit murder, Eleanor would do something less messy—like putting poison in his drink."

"I suppose you're right." Rosie smiled. "Now that I think about it, she couldn't have done it. The killer had to have access to the letter opener, and Eleanor hasn't been in the store for months."

Helen mulled over Rosie's comment. "What about Nancy or Brian? Did either of them have access to the letter opener?"

"Nancy was in last week sometime with Melissa—I don't remember the day." Rosie twisted in her seat. "You don't suppose Nancy could have taken it . . . ?"

"That would mean Ethan's death was premeditated."

"Well, it's possible."

Helen shook her head. "Nancy plotted to kill Ethan and lay the blame on you? I don't see it. What would her motive be?"

"Jealousy. Money. Ethan planned to change his will so Alex would get an equal share. That would have meant less money for Brian, Nancy, and Eleanor. Maybe they were in on it together."

"Not Eleanor. She won't get anything. She never needed Ethan's money. If it weren't for her, I doubt Ethan would have gone into politics. She's a wealthy and powerful woman in her own right."

"That's true enough." Rosie frowned.

"Eleanor loved Ethan. And I thought he loved her."

"He was torn. He loved both of us. That's why I didn't want him to know about Alex. It doesn't seem fair that the choices Ethan and I made as kids could so totally mess up our lives today."

"Choices have a way of doing that," Helen murmured. "Especially poor ones."

Rosie closed her eyes and rested her head against the seat, seeming to retreat into herself.

Helen felt an overwhelming sense of sadness for her friend. Losing Ethan. Finding her son and now facing the fear of losing him again. She concentrated on seeing the road through her fogged-up windshield. She had switched on the defroster earlier, but the glass hadn't completely cleared. A drop of water pooled in a small crack above the visor and dripped onto her leg. She didn't like driving her Thunderbird in the rain anymore. Maybe J.B. was right. She should retire the classic to the garage and get a newer, more reliable car. She could still drive the T-bird in the summer and show it off at antique car shows. Also, she was way overdue for a trip to her mechanic. Jeb had called many times to remind her. She smiled. He loved the car more than she did.

Helen scanned the gunmetal-gray sky. The day had turned on her. Helen's opportunity to walk in the sun had come and gone while she'd been learning about Rosie's relationship with Ethan and about the son their union had created. Not that she would've had time to walk anyway. It was already three in the afternoon, and she'd agreed to drive Rosie to her car, which was stashed at the Spirit Mountain Casino and Hotel located twenty minutes northeast of Lincoln City. First, however, she intended to connect with Joe. No way was she going to let her friend out of her sight until the sheriff had a chance to talk to her.

"Did you ever find out what happened to J.B.?" Rosie asked out of the blue.

"No. And I'm not sure I want to." The question uprooted the anger and hurt she'd been trying to repress most of the day.

"Uh-oh. What happened?"

Helen shrugged. "I'm not sure. He left a message on the answering machine. He apologized and said he'd be gone for a few days. I'm supposed to trust him." She went on to explain how she'd called the number he'd called from. She could barely get the words past the lump forming in her throat. "He had lunch yesterday with a woman."

"Oh, Helen. Do you think . . . ? No, he wouldn't."

"Like Ethan wouldn't."

"What do you mean?"

"Rosie, I know you loved the man, but the fact is, he cheated on his wife. No matter how much you whitewash it with romance, he was a jerk."

"He was . . ." Rosie turned to look out her window. "It wasn't like that."

"Because you're not a prostitute? Because you two were lovers in high school?"

"It was a mistake," Rosie lashed back. "I . . . I know it was wrong. I mean adultery is just . . . just that. I've asked God to forgive me a hundred times since it happened." Tears gathered in her eyes again. "But you know what? I don't think God can forgive me, because I'm glad it happened. I'm glad I had a chance to be with him before he . . ." She lowered her head. "Never mind. I don't expect you to understand."

Helen sighed. "I do understand, Rosie. More than you know. And I'm sorry. I had no business criticizing you like that. I shouldn't be taking my anger with J.B. out on you."

"Hey, it's okay. Really. I wish I could tell you not to worry about him." She pulled a soggy tissue out of her pocket and dabbed at her cheeks. "But I can't."

"I know. Which is why I'm thinking of driving into Portland after I drop you off. I can visit the family and—"

"Spy on J.B.?"

"Not spy exactly." It was a bad idea. Helen had already asked Kate to check the hospitals. Now she doubted she had much chance of locating him anyway.

"You can't do that, Helen. You can't leave me now. Besides, J.B. said he'd be back, didn't he?"

"You're right. J.B. asked me to trust him, and I suppose that will have to do for now."

"I think what you really need to do is trust God. No matter what happens, Helen, no matter how it works out. Even if J.B. isn't there for you, God will be."

Helen puzzled over Rosie's comment. She *did* trust God. Didn't she?

As they neared the bridge crossing the Siletz River, Helen spotted two sheriff's cars and a tow truck turning left onto the Siletz Highway, then driving on past Kernville Steak and Seafood House. The restaurant, one of Helen's favorites, offered great food and a terrific view of the river. But Helen doubted it was the food bringing out half the deputies in Lincoln County. An official truck was launching a patrol boat at the ramp to the west of the restaurant. And another patrol car was parked in the lot. A deputy leaning into his trunk pulled out scuba gear.

Rosie stretched around, craning her neck. "What's going on?"

"That's what I'd like to know." Helen drove on past the exit. "Hope it wasn't a boating accident." She considered turning around and going back. *It isn't really your business,* an inner voice said. *The last thing they need is another curious onlooker.* Curiosity and the knowledge that, with this much interest shown by the authorities, Joe would be there and she could hand-deliver

Rosie caused her to make a U-turn, cross the bridge, and turn right toward Kernville, following the curving two-lane road. When she reached a graveled turnout—where the tow truck, four patrol cars, and a couple of pickups were parked—Helen stopped about fifty yards from the activity so she wouldn't be in the way.

Joe, Stephanie, and Tom stood near the water's edge talking to a man in a khaki canvas vest, heavy flannel shirt, and jeans.

"M-maybe I should stay here." Rosie leaned forward, clasping her knees and ducking down. "I'm not sure I'm ready to see Joe right now. Besides, he's busy."

"Suit yourself." Helen grabbed her keys out of the ignition. "I'm going over for a closer look." She climbed out of the car, noting the black skid marks on the road and how they angled toward the river.

The tow-truck operator, a man built like a linebacker, was backing down the incline. Stopping a few feet from the water's edge, he jumped out of his truck and headed over to talk to Joe and the others.

The patrol boat she'd seen earlier came into view. The pilot cut the engines directly in front of them and dropped anchor. Two deputies in scuba gear disappeared into the water.

Stephanie spotted her and came up to meet her. "Hi, Mrs. Bradley. What are you doing out here?"

"I saw the tow truck turn in and the patrol boat. What's going on?"

"We're not sure just yet. A fisherman spotted what he thought might be a car in the water. We have a couple of divers checking it out now."

As if on cue, both divers surfaced at the same time. "It's a car, all right," one of them yelled. "Someone's inside."

"Oh no." Stephanie grimaced.

Helen's heart about stopped.

A reverent hush fell over the group of people standing nearby. Another death. A moment of silence.

"Any idea who it is?" Joe hunched his shoulders against a sudden onslaught of rain.

"Can't ID," the second diver shouted back. "Water's too stirred up."

"What about license plates?"

"Can't see them either. There's mud clear to the back window."

Joe gave orders to pull the vehicle out of the murky water and mark the area off as a crime scene. Within minutes the scuba divers had connected the winch hook from the tow truck onto the submerged vehicle.

"Probably some drunk taking the corner too fast," Stephanie said. "I hate this stuff."

"I know what you mean." Helen looked her way. "Too many senseless deaths."

They both turned their attention back to the water. The tow-truck operator came out from behind his vehicle. "All set," he called to Tom and Joe. "Should have 'er up in a couple minutes."

"I'd better get down there." Stephanie left Helen standing alone.

She shivered as much from the anticipation as the cold. Who would they find drowned in the muddy water?

"What's happening?" Rosie slipped up beside Helen. "I saw the skid marks."

"There's a car down there." She then gave Rosie a sidelong glare. "I'm not sure it's a good idea for you to be here. The scuba diver said the driver is still in the car."

"Oh no. Do they know who it is?"

Helen shook her head. Water dripped from her hair down her face. Standing out in the rain waiting for them to pull a vehicle out of the drink was the last thing Helen wanted to do at the moment, but she seemed rooted to the spot. Rosie apparently felt the same way.

The tow truck roared to life. The winch started turning and the submerged vehicle began its ascent from the river. Soon a dark green sports car emerged from the gloomy water.

Rosie gripped Helen's jacket and buried her head against her shoulder.

Helen didn't need an explanation for Rosie's behavior. She'd seen the car often enough. It was Ethan's Jaguar.

Eighteen

Rosie wailed against Helen's shoulder.

"I know." Helen held her, patting her back and offering words she hoped were comforting. Seeing the car come up like that set off an explosion of grief in Helen as well. It wasn't the car, but the implications. The reality that Ethan was gone forever.

As the turmoil in Helen's chest settled, she tried to make sense of it. She had no doubt the car belonged to the mayor. The green Jaguar wasn't the only one around, but the vanity license plates with the letters MAYOR-BV were one of a kind. But Ethan's body was in the morgue, so who was in the car? And why? What was the car doing here?

Joe, who was standing nearby, observed the two women. Irritation flooded his features. He spoke to one of his deputies. Helen was too far away to hear but had no doubt she and Rosie were the subject of their conversation. The grim-faced sheriff and his deputy strode toward them.

"I see you've found our runaway." Joe gave Rosie a none-too-friendly look.

"I was staying at my sister's." Rosie raised her head and turned to face him.

"I need to ask you some questions. But right now, we're tied up. I've asked Officer Grant here to take you to my office."

Grant took a step toward Rosie. She stepped away. "Am I under arrest?" she asked in a guarded tone.

"Not at this point," Joe said, "but I don't want to chance your running away again."

"I won't." She hauled in a ragged breath, sounding weary and defeated. "Can't I just go back to my store?"

He shook his head. "I'm sorry. You have a lot of questions to answer. Valuable information to contribute to our investigation."

Rosie turned to Helen, her eyes displaying fear. "Should I call a lawyer?"

Knowing the lawyer was more for Alex's sake than for hers, Helen said, "It might be a good idea."

Rosie nodded. "Why does *he* have to take me in? Can't you take me?"

"Go with Officer Grant," Helen counseled. "I'll be along in a few minutes."

"You'll stay with me when they talk to me about . . . ?"

It hurt to see Rosie so beat down. Helen wanted her vibrant, carefree friend back. The old Rosie seemed lost, and it looked as though the road back would take a long, long time. "I'll be with you all the way."

Rosie hugged her and whispered, "Don't tell them about Alex being my son yet. Please."

Helen squeezed her hand as she stepped back, giving her a nod of agreement. "I think it'll be best coming from you."

Joe and Helen watched the two figures walk up along the shoulder of the two-lane road until they disappeared behind the building. "What did you find out?" Joe asked.

"It's a long story. Best to let her tell it."

He looked irritated again. For a moment she thought he would press her for details. Water formed rivulets that dripped onto his highly polished black shoes. "How do you do it, Helen? Do you have some sort of built-in radar or something?"

"Do what?"

"You find Ethan's body. You already knew he was missing. You find Rosie while we've got people searching every nook and cranny, and now you're here. How did you figure out where Ethan's car would turn up?"

"I had no idea his car would be here. I was driving home

and spotted the patrol cars. I wasn't even going to stop, but when I saw the tow truck, I . . . well, I . . ." Helen turned back toward the car, now fully on shore. Water drained from the vehicle, settling in pools and running back into the river.

Apparently satisfied with Helen's answers, Joe's annoyance faded. He seemed more than willing to share information. "A fisherman snagged a good-sized salmon this morning. As he was reeling it in, his boat drifted over the car. He couldn't see much more than a shadow. He noticed the tire tracks on the bank and gave us a call." Joe started walking toward the river.

Helen fell into step beside him. "Do you know who the victim is?"

"Not yet, but it looks like we're about to find out."

One of the deputies pulled at the dead driver's door. "It's locked."

They then tried the passenger door. Also locked. So they went back to the driver's door and, using a short crowbar, jimmied it open. Water poured out of the car. The victim, a man, was still strapped into the seat. His head lolled to the side with the surging water. His medium-length dark hair swayed like seaweed in the tide. A blue cap swept past him and, following the course of the water, fell to the ground.

Helen's stomach lurched. She'd seen the cap dozens of times in the last few months.

Tom scooped up the soggy cap and brought it to Joe. "The guy's face is pretty distorted. Been in the water a couple of days."

"Probably since Sunday night." Helen turned away from the gruesome sight.

Joe cursed under his breath. "Stephanie, call Dr. Fisher. Find out what's keeping him. I don't want the body or anything else moved until he gets here."

"It's Chuck's cap, isn't it?" Helen murmured. "I rarely saw him without it."

"That's what I'm thinking." He stared down at the logo—a fisherman reeling in a salmon with a snowcapped mountain in the background. The white printing above the scene read *Woodruff Charters. Anchorage, Alaska.*

Joe turned the cap over. As if to verify their identification, the inside beige band bore the initials *CD*.

Nineteen

Helen shivered as a trickle of cold rain made its way down the back of her neck. Unasked questions hovered between her and Joe. Why had Chuck been driving Ethan's car? How had he ended up in the river? "Any ideas on what happened?" Helen ventured.

Joe removed his hat and flicked the water off. "Your guess is as good as mine. Looks like he took the corner too fast."

"But what was he doing in Ethan's car?"

Joe sighed. "The million-dollar question. You have any answers?"

"I suppose an obvious one is that he killed Ethan and wanted to get rid of Ethan's car—maybe to buy some time. Distract you. But that supposition creates even more questions: Why bring the car clear out here? What was he planning to do with it? How was Chuck planning to get home? Somehow I don't see him walking that far."

Joe stared out at the river, hands resting on his hips. "You got that right. He might have arranged to meet someone out here."

"Which means he had an accomplice."

Helen tried to imagine the scene. Chuck and an accomplice killing Ethan. Chuck driving Ethan's car to the river—running off the road. "If someone had followed him, wouldn't they have seen the accident and gotten Chuck out?" Something hit her. "Didn't I hear someone say the doors were locked? Somehow I can't see Chuck locking himself into a car—unless it had automatic locks."

"Good point. In which case we're looking at Chuck as a victim. We'll know soon enough." Joe pocketed his hands and hunched his shoulders. "Knowing Chuck, I'm thinking he was in the wrong place at the wrong time. Might've witnessed Ethan's murder. Ethan's killer had to get rid of Chuck too. Which brings me back to Jordan. Since he'd had dinner with him, he'd have motive for removing Ethan's car. He'd want to lead us away from the restaurant. He probably killed Chuck, stashed his body in the car, and once he got out here, he put Chuck behind the wheel, set the car in drive, and sent it down the embankment."

Helen felt deflated. She glanced up at the heavy cloud layers. The rain showed no sign of letting up. "So Alex kills Ethan, then runs Ethan's car into the river with Chuck's body in it? Why bring the car clear up here? It's a long way back to where Ethan's body was found. And Jordan is new to the area."

"Rosie isn't."

"Come on, Joe." Helen was about to argue in her friend's defense when another vehicle pulled up.

"Excuse me." Joe hurried over to where George Fisher had parked his car.

Helen frowned at Joe's retreating figure. He seemed bent on nailing Alex, regardless of whether or not it made sense. Of course, he had good reason. A man doesn't admit to murder without just cause. If Rosie was right and Ethan had changed his will to include Alex, it meant their son stood to inherit a great deal of money. Resentment and money could easily add up to murder.

"What's going on around here?" George shook Joe's hand, and the two of them started walking toward the Jaguar. "I thought I was moving into a peaceful resort area. You have more crime out here than they do in Portland."

"It's not quite that bad," Helen told him as they neared her.

He greeted Helen with a smile that lit up his face. "We meet again, dear lady."

"Only briefly. I'm leaving. Not much I can do here."

"Oh, I don't know about that. Have you had a chance to investigate the scene?" He'd aimed the question at Helen.

"Joe's the authority on that." Helen answered quickly, sensing Joe's annoyance. As much as she would have liked working beside her old friend, Helen thought it best to stay in the background. For some reason—maybe because George was still treating her as a colleague—Joe seemed threatened. She took a step back. "I was just leaving."

"By the way," George said, "did you get my call?"

"No. I haven't been home."

"Well, then, I may as well ask you now. Would you like to have dinner with me tonight? Give us a chance to catch up."

"I'd love to."

"Where's a good place? I haven't had much time to do any restaurant hunting."

"How about we meet at Tidal Raves in Depoe Bay?"

"Ahh. That one I know. Good choice."

Joe cleared his throat. "I hate to rush you, Dr. Fisher . . ."

George apologized and turned back to Helen. "I'll see you tonight, then—about seven?"

Helen promised to make reservations, then trudged back to her car. Before going to see Rosie, she would stop at the house to change clothes, dry her hair, check her messages, and grab a bite to eat.

Once at home, she placed a quick call to the restaurant, then checked the answering machine. Four messages: Kate, Eleanor, George, and Annie. Nothing from J.B.

She called Kate first, skipped their usual greeting, and plunged right in with, "Have you heard from J.B.?"

"Hi to you too. And no, I haven't. None of the hospitals have him on their patient list. His doctor's office won't tell me a thing. You know how they are with confidentiality. I got Jason working on the FBI, but they're saying they haven't talked to him. They must be telling the truth. Your friend there, Tom Chambers, called me and wanted to know if we'd heard from him."

"I see." Helen sank onto the couch, her heart as heavy as the blown-glass paperweight she picked up off the coffee table.

"Apparently J.B. doesn't want to be found."

"I'm really upset with him right now, Mom, and I think you should be too. I don't care what he's doing—he shouldn't be worrying you like this."

"I'm sure there's a good reason."

"Good reason, nothing. You sound like Jason. All this secret-agent business. It's crazy."

"Jason thinks he might be on an assignment?" Helen ran her hand over the smooth surface of the glass ball. If he were, she could accept his strange behavior. It might even explain the fact that he'd had lunch with a woman. And maybe she was just fooling herself.

"Jason is engaging in wishful thinking. There's nothing to suggest that J.B. is on assignment. Jason checked all the flights going out of Portland, and J.B. wasn't on any of them. He even flashed a picture of J.B. around the airport, but no one remembered seeing him. I think you were right the first time in thinking it had something to do with his health. Maybe he checked into the hospital under an assumed name."

Or left town using an alias. The lump in her throat made talking next to impossible. She didn't want to tell Kate that J.B. had a third reason for disappearing. One she'd have never thought possible until she'd phoned the restaurant. One she still couldn't quite believe.

"Mom?"

Helen swallowed back her tears. "I'm here."

"Do you want us to keep looking?"

"No. There doesn't seem to be much point. I imagine he'll come back when he's ready."

"Well, when he does, I plan to give him a piece of my mind."

If he comes back, you mean. The words stayed in her head while Helen made her apologies for cutting the conversation short and hung up.

If he comes back. She closed her eyes and imagined J.B. on their wedding day. Everything had been perfect. He'd looked straight into her eyes when they'd exchanged vows. He'd never hesitated or wavered. *"You are my one true love,"* he'd said time and again.

Helen thought back over the short time they'd been married. Had she insisted too much on maintaining her independence? Had she pushed J.B. into the arms of another woman by leaving him alone too often while she left home to visit family and work on her writing assignments?

He will come back, she insisted. Still she wondered if he ever would.

The phone rang. Helen pushed herself up and grabbed it before it could ring again. It was Rosie.

"Helen, is . . . is that you?"

Helen released the breath she'd been holding. "Yes, Rosie. It's me."

"You don't sound like yourself."

Small wonder. "I just stopped by the house to change. I should be there in a few minutes."

"Please hurry. I'm worried about Alex. He won't talk to me. He keeps insisting he killed his father and that I should accept the fact and go home."

"Maybe you should, Rosie. I'm not sure there's much I can do—"

"Helen, how can you say that? I know he didn't kill Ethan. Please come and talk to him. Maybe he'll listen to you."

Helen doubted it but didn't say so. "Have you hired an attorney yet?"

"Yes. She's meeting me at the jail in a few minutes. You're coming, aren't you?"

"I'll be there."

❖   ❖   ❖

Fifteen minutes later, Helen walked into the room where Alex Jordan waited on the other side of a glass partition. He was handcuffed and badly in need of a shave. His brown hair curled over his collar, giving him a bad-boy look. Helen could easily have revised her former opinion of him.

His dull blue eyes didn't lift to meet hers when she greeted him. "Did Rosie send you?" he asked as Helen sat down.

"Yes and no. She asked me to talk some sense into you, but I'd have come even if she hadn't asked."

"Why?"

"Last night, when you were arrested, you told me you were innocent." Helen crossed her arms and leaned forward. "Now I understand you've confessed to Ethan's murder."

"So I lied."

"What made you change your mind?"

He shrugged. "Nothing special. I just realized I couldn't get away with it."

"You are lying now, Mr. Jordan." Helen looked him straight in the face.

"You don't know that." His eyes darted from hers to the table.

"I can read it in your face. It was the letter opener, wasn't it? When the sheriff showed it to you, you changed your story."

He didn't admit it, but Helen knew she'd hit a nerve.

"You knew where it had come from and were afraid Rosie might become a suspect. You changed your story to protect her. Though I can't fathom why. You barely know her. You haven't had time to build much of a relationship."

He continued staring at the table, hands clasped.

"Alex, listen to me. Rosie didn't kill Ethan. You don't have to lie to protect her."

He frowned. "I . . . know she didn't, because I did. I took the letter opener and used it to kill Ethan."

"No, you didn't."

"You're crazy, lady," he burst out. "Why would I admit to killing someone if I didn't do it?"

"You don't have to do this, Alex. Think about it. Rosie's devastated over losing Ethan. Do you want her to lose you too? Have you any idea what this is doing to her?"

"Like you said, we haven't known each other long enough to build a relationship."

"Hogwash. Rosie's loved you since the day you were born. She held you in her heart all the time you were growing up. You've apparently been thinking a lot about her too. It must have taken a great deal of effort, time, and money to find her.

When you walked back into her life, she . . ." Helen heaved a sigh and leaned back. "This is getting us nowhere."

"I told you, I did it."

The idea was preposterous. Why couldn't Joe see through it? Helen had to think of a way to trip Jordan up. After a few moments, she said, "Rosie's letter opener disappeared over a week ago."

"Yeah, like I said, I took it."

"Hmm. You took it to use as a murder weapon to kill Ethan, whom, if memory serves correctly, you hadn't even met yet?"

"That's right. But I knew who he was."

"So you're saying you took Rosie's letter opener and used it to kill Ethan. Why would you use a weapon that would lead directly back to Rosie and eventually to you? Why not use a gun or a kitchen knife? Or even a piece of wood? No one setting out to commit a crime purposely implicates himself. If what you say is true, you deliberately set out to pin the murder on Rosie or yourself, since you two had easiest access to the murder weapon."

"I didn't think about it."

"All right." Helen decided to take another route. "Say you did kill him. I'd just like to know one thing."

"What's that?"

"Why did you kill Chuck Daniels?"

He jerked his head up. The look on his face was one of genuine surprise.

Helen finally had his attention. "Your boss. Chuck Daniels."

"I—"

"You didn't know about him, did you?" Helen pushed on. "His body was found this morning. I strongly suspect Ethan and Chuck were killed by the same person."

His shoulders sagged. "How did he die?"

"You'll find out soon enough. I'm not going to give you information you can feed back to the sheriff. He might actually believe you."

His defeated gaze rose to meet hers. "Okay. You win. I didn't kill my father. But I've already confessed. What if the sheriff doesn't believe me?"

"I think he will, eventually. In the meantime, you can help me find out who did kill him."

Alex pulled his chair closer and seemed to relax. "How?"

"Tell me what you were doing in Rosie's store last night."

"I . . . I was scared. There were some things that could have linked me to Ethan, and I wanted to get rid of anything that might look suspicious."

"Like the check for a hundred grand?"

He frowned. "How do you know all this stuff?"

"I was upstairs feeding the cats while you were digging through Rosie's desk." Helen saw no reason to elaborate.

"You're the one who called the cops?"

"No. But I'm the reason they were there."

"I don't understand."

"I lost my key and had to break in. While the officer and I were talking, we heard you and Joe downstairs. I saw you running away."

His Adam's apple floated up and down. "It was a stupid thing to do. Going there, I mean. I'd heard about the murder at work Monday afternoon. I was afraid the cops would find out about him being my father and about the meeting we had—and the money."

"Yes. I can see where a check like that would be incriminating. Did you know about Ethan before you contacted Rosie?"

"All I had was my mother's name. I did some digging and started asking questions. Just put two and two together."

"When you found out who your father was, did you ask him for money?"

"What are you getting at?" Alex unclasped his hands and balled them into fists. "You think I was blackmailing him?"

"You have to admit, it looks suspicious."

"I wasn't. Anyway, he gave it to Rosie—not to me. She was upset that he'd even offered. He apologized to me that night. Said he just wanted to do something. He hadn't expected Rosie to take his offer as an insult."

That sounded like something a man might do, Helen thought. All too often they had a propensity for trying to fix things in what they felt was a logical and practical way.

"Would you have taken the money if he'd offered it to you?"

"I . . . I don't know how to answer that. Ethan wanted to include me in his family. He wanted to make sure I got a share of his estate when he died. I probably wouldn't have turned him down." He glanced up at her and then looked away. "I didn't go looking for money. I just wanted to know who my real parents were."

"I'm sorry you won't have a chance to know him better," Helen said.

"Yeah, but at least I got to meet him. He was a good man." He folded his arms on the table and rested his head on them.

"I need to go." Helen stood. "I trust you're going to tell the sheriff the truth."

He nodded. "I hope it's not too late."

"I suggest you see the lawyer your mother is bringing. You're going to need one."

On the way out, Helen bumped into Rosie and the attorney, a woman named Marcia Davidson.

"Marcia," Helen nodded in acknowledgment. Although Helen had never worked with her in the business sense, they had met socially. "Nice to see you again."

"Likewise." In her pinstriped suit she looked like a feminine candidate for *Gentlemen's Quarterly*. The only thing missing was the tie. Marcia was a seasoned lawyer with a reputable law firm.

"Have you talked to him?" Rosie held Helen's arm in a vise grip.

"Yes." Helen gave them a quick recap of the conversation she'd had with Alex.

Rosie tipped her head back and raised her hands in prayer position. "Thank you."

"He's willing to admit he didn't do it, but we've still got some big hurdles." Helen turned to Marcia. "Did Rosie tell you about the check Ethan wrote?"

Marcia nodded. "Have you told the sheriff about it?"

"He knows." Helen then shifted to Rosie and, before she could protest, said, "You need to tell him everything, Rosie."

"Helen's right." Marcia placed a hand in her pocket and extracted a card. "Call me if you learn anything that might help us. The prosecuting attorney feels they have a solid case against Mr. Jordan. I haven't had a chance to review the evidence."

Half an hour later Helen sat across the desk from Joe Adams's empty chair, staring at his gold nameplate and waiting for him to come in. He'd just talked with Rosie and Alex, and she wanted to know the outcome.

"Well?" She watched Joe walk to his old wooden swivel chair and settle himself into it.

He shrugged. "I still think Jordan is guilty."

Helen pinched the bridge of her nose. "I can't believe you're saying that. Alex Jordan did not kill Ethan or Chuck."

"Well, that's where you're wrong."

Helen glared at him. "I can't believe you're being so stubborn about this. The man just admitted he lied to protect Rosie. It makes no sense whatsoever that he'd use her letter opener as a murder weapon. He wouldn't want to implicate his own mother."

"Are you sure about that? Maybe you're the one who's reading him wrong. Maybe he deliberately set Rosie up as a suspect so he could play the hero."

Helen leaned back and folded her arms. "I've never heard of anything so ridiculous—except maybe in a twisted plot in a mystery novel."

"Maybe he's read a few. He knew Rosie would jump in and save him. And she has. She's got you and Marcia helping her. Three women at his beck and call. No, make that four. Lynn Daniels is sticking up for him as well. She told me he was just too nice a guy to commit murder."

Joe tossed her a patronizing look. "I'm surprised at you, Helen. I might have expected something like this from Rosie and Lynn, but not you. How can you be so gullible?"

"I'm not gullible! I think he's innocent."

"Because he told you so?"

"Because my instincts tell me so."

"As much as I respect your instincts, I'm afraid you're off the mark on this one. Jordan is a con. He had a set of Ethan's car keys on him when he was arrested. He went back to Rosie's to remove evidence that linked him to Ethan. He had motive, means, and opportunity. I'm not closing the books, but it's going to take a lot more than intuition to convince me he didn't do it."

Twenty

Helen entered the restaurant at seven-fifteen. She spotted George right away, sitting at the corner table on the lower level overlooking the bay. His attention was focused on something out in the water. A surge of yearning swelled in her chest. Not for George, but for J.B.

George was seated at the table she and J.B. usually reserved. Helen and J.B. loved this place and had eaten many romantic dinners as they enjoyed the glorious sunsets. They'd spent hours watching the waters of Depoe Bay ebb and flow. Teeming with life, the water swirled around the golden brown rocks it had sculpted into a myriad of fascinating shapes.

She wondered for a moment at the wisdom of having dinner with her former colleague. Normally, she wouldn't have given it a second thought, but J.B.'s luncheon with a woman raised questions about her own behavior. Someone seeing her and George might get the wrong idea. A smidgeon of guilt kneaded its way into her mind.

Nonsense, Helen told herself as she moved toward the corner table. *Whatever J.B. is up to has nothing to do with my having dinner with George.* If anything, she should take it as a sign that J.B. may have been doing the same thing. Having lunch with a colleague. For all she knew, it was strictly business. Which was more than she could say for herself. With George she was looking forward to the easy camaraderie they'd once shared. She also hoped he'd share his findings with regard to Ethan and Chuck.

"There you are." George's narrow face split into a wide grin when he saw her. "I was about to call out the guards."

"Sorry I'm late." Helen accepted a peck on the cheek from George, then hung her jacket on the back of the chair he'd pulled out for her and sat down.

"Rough day?"

"You might say that." She set her bag on the floor beside her and picked up a menu. The server came to take their order for drinks. Helen selected mango iced tea. "If you know what you want, we can go ahead and order."

"You haven't had a chance to look at the menu."

"I know it by heart. This is one of my favorite haunts." Looking up at the server, a young girl with burgundy hair and a Russian accent, she said, "I'll have the sautéed oysters with rice and salad. Ranch dressing on the side."

George ordered the salmon in a lemon-caper butter sauce. When the girl left, he focused his attention back on Helen. "I can't believe my luck in finding you here. I have to admit you've crossed my mind more than once over the years."

Helen smiled. She couldn't make the same claim. "So, George, tell me what you've been up to for the past decade."

"Besides work, I've gotten into golf." His easy grin came back. "Say, do you golf? I've been looking for someone to join me Saturday mornings."

"No, I don't. But J.B. might be interested."

"J.B.?"

"My husband."

Disappointment flitted across his face. "I didn't realize you'd remarried."

"J.B. and I got married last June—in Paris." She smiled at the thought. J.B. had always been a romantic. "At any rate, you were talking about golf. J.B. used to go quite often. He hasn't played much lately. . . ." She let her voice trail off. Somehow she got the feeling George wasn't the least bit interested in J.B. or golf. Apparently she'd given him the wrong idea. "How is your family?" she asked. "As I recall, you and Mary had several children."

"Four. Two boys and two girls. All married."

"Grandchildren?"

"Eight. And they are all doing fine." George chuckled. "I'm making you uncomfortable, aren't I?"

Helen shrugged. "A bit." It had been a long time since anyone besides J.B. had looked at her with such open admiration. While Helen found the attention flattering, she also found it disconcerting. "Um . . . I'm wondering if this was a mistake."

"I'm sorry. It's just that I've always admired you. I guess I was hoping . . ." He sighed. "Well, you know what they say—a day late and a dollar short." He took hold of her hand and squeezed it. "I hope this J.B. fellow is making you happy."

Helen pulled back her hand and fiddled with her napkin. *Happy? Not at the moment.* She avoided the comment and gave him the brightest smile she could muster. "He's a hero, you know—my husband." Helen told George about J.B.'s recent assignment to free hostages in the Middle East. As she talked she began to relax. Somewhere along the way, George slipped out of his flirtatious mode and seemed more like her old friend.

"You know, I think I read about that," he said when she'd finished her tale.

"He's been commissioned to write a book on his life."

"I'm impressed. A real spy. Have you known him long?"

"We met in Ireland while I was still in college. He came back into my life after Ian died."

"Sounds like an exceptional man. You're very much in love with him."

Was it that obvious? "Yes, I guess I am."

"He's a lucky man. I'd like to meet him. In fact, you should have asked him to join us."

"He's on a . . . business trip."

George's gaze bored into hers. "I gather all is not well between the two of you."

"I miss him." Helen hoped that would suffice. She didn't want to talk about J.B. anymore and gratefully accepted the server's interruption.

When she'd gone, George seemed to sense Helen's reluctance to talk about J.B. and asked her about the investigation. "Joe tells me he has a promising suspect with a confession."

"Alex Jordan. He didn't do it."

"Really. How can you be so certain?"

Helen told him about Alex and his connection with Rosie and Ethan, and how Alex had confessed in order to protect his mother.

"What a tangled web." He leaned back when the server brought their salads. "The past does come back to haunt us, doesn't it?"

"Hmm." Helen broke apart a sourdough roll. "Poor Rosie. I can't imagine how she must be feeling. Seeing her son after all these years and then having him arrested for Ethan's murder. I hope for her sake that Alex is innocent."

"You don't sound as certain of his innocence as you did a few minutes ago."

Buttering her bread, Helen considered his question. "There's always room for doubt. We don't know all that much about Alex. Though he denies it, there is still the possibility that he found out about his father's status and wanted money to keep quiet. Rosie insists that's not the case. Supposedly, Ethan welcomed him as a son and planned to change his will, making Alex a rightful heir."

George leaned forward. "Did he?"

"Not that I know of."

"I don't expect Ethan's family would be too happy about a will change."

"You're right about that." Helen remembered what Annie had said about Brian burning papers in the fireplace. After telling George, she added, "Somehow I can't see either of them opening their hearts or pocketbooks to a half brother. Apparently they had alibis. Brian was in Portland, and Nancy was at home with Melissa—her daughter."

"What about Ethan's wife? Wouldn't she have a lot to lose as well?"

"I've considered that. She was at church that evening." Helen speared a shrimp and some greens.

"I assume Joe checked that out."

"I'm sure. Joe is very thorough. Why do you ask? Is there something I should know?"

George frowned. "She seemed a little cool and reluctant

when I talked to her about the autopsy. Her biggest concern was how soon I'd be able to release the body to the funeral home."

"Eleanor is like that. Cool, stiff upper lip. She's efficient—which is what makes her so great at heading up projects. I think she's trying to maintain a good front. Focusing on details. Taking care of others. She's still numb."

He nodded. "Now that I think about it, I was pretty much the same way when Mary died. I went on autopilot. It didn't hit me until about a month later that she wasn't coming back." He sighed heavily. "All this talk about death. This isn't exactly what I had in mind when I asked you to dinner."

"It's hard not to think about it."

"As I recall, you were always taking your work home with you," he said.

"And you didn't."

He grinned. "Touché."

They ate for several minutes in silence. Helen reflected on Eleanor's demeanor, then tried to imagine her stealing Rosie's letter opener, planning out every detail of Ethan's death, and framing Rosie. Could Eleanor have gotten angry enough over the affair to kill Ethan? Helen couldn't see it. Besides, Eleanor had an alibi. Rosie didn't.

"Joe may be right," she said. "I may be letting my friendships color my perception of the case."

"You're not losing faith in yourself, I hope. Joe isn't exactly objective either at the moment."

"Really. And why is that?"

"He seems a little too eager to wrap things up. He's upset about something. Grumpy as all get out. I asked him about it today, but he insisted it wasn't anything he couldn't handle."

Helen took a sip of her iced tea and asked what he'd learned so far about Ethan's and Chuck's deaths.

George winced. "I was hoping you wouldn't ask. I wanted this to be a relaxing evening—for both of us."

"I'm sorry. It's my nature. Can't rest until I ferret out every detail. Tell me what you've got so far, and I promise for the rest of dinner we won't mention work again."

He shook his head and offered her a forgiving smile. "What would you like to know?"

"Let's start with Ethan. Cause of death?"

He raised his eyebrows. "You didn't know? I'm surprised Joe didn't tell you."

"I haven't talked to him since earlier this afternoon."

George glanced toward the restaurant entrance. "I'll be happy to tell you what I know, but maybe we'd better save it for later. Mrs. Crane and her family just came in."

Helen's gaze met Eleanor's as she stepped down to the lower level. Her hand fluttered up and down in greeting. She revealed a brief expression of curiosity and disapproval when she noticed Helen's dining companion. Nancy and Brian acknowledged her as well. Melissa lagged behind, her arms folded in a stubborn pose, clearly wishing she were somewhere else. Helen suppressed a smile. Having two teenaged granddaughters, she could read the behavior quite well. The difference, however, was that Jennie and Lisa still loved being included in family outings.

The server seated them three tables away.

Eleanor set her purse on a chair and hurried over to Helen and George's table. "Helen? Dr. Fisher?" She said it as though she couldn't quite believe the two of them were there—together.

He stood and shook her hand. "Mrs. Crane. Nice to see you again."

"George and I used to work together when I was with the police bureau in Portland," Helen explained.

"Oh, well . . . how nice." Eleanor shifted back to Helen. "I'm glad I ran into you. Didn't you get my message?"

"Yes. I was going to stop by after dinner. Unless you'd like to talk to me now?"

"No. It's a personal matter. Later tonight will be fine." She looked at her watch. "Say around nine-thirty?"

Helen agreed and Eleanor went back to her family. The entrées arrived. Helen dug into her oysters. Excellent as usual. During the rest of their meal, they talked about their grandchildren and travel plans. George warmed to the idea of meeting J.B. and possibly finding a golf and fishing partner.

⁜   ⁜   ⁜

"This was a bad idea." Their conversation came to an abrupt halt when Brian Crane shoved his chair back and stood.

"Brian, please!" Eleanor glanced around the room. "You're making a scene."

"Good. It's about time someone did." Grabbing his jacket, he stepped away from the table.

Melissa looked as though she wanted to disappear into the woodwork. Nancy rolled her eyes and took a drink of wine. "You tell her, Brian."

He flung a disgusted look his sister's way and walked out.

Eleanor's embarrassed gaze met Helen's. Turning to Nancy, she said, "We'd better go."

"Why? We haven't eaten yet. I'm hungry."

"I'll fix you something at home."

"That's what I wanted in the first place." Melissa shrugged into her jacket. "I'll meet you in the car."

Nancy drained her glass and followed her daughter outside.

Eleanor gathered her things and signaled the server. "I'm sorry about this."

"Don't worry. Guess he just didn't like the food." She set the check on the table.

"I think it was the company." Eleanor pulled some bills out of her purse and placed them on the check. "Keep the change."

She hesitated near Helen's table. "You're still coming?"

"Of course."

Eleanor nodded. She then turned and, lifting her chin in dignitary fashion, walked away.

"Wonder what that was all about." George pulled his gaze from her retreating figure.

Helen shrugged. "Maybe Eleanor will enlighten me when I visit. While I'm at it, I think I'll have a talk with her son."

"Be careful. He seems rather volatile."

"Seems?" Helen glimpsed over her shoulder at the green Mercedes backing out of the lot. Brian wasn't in the car.

158

❖   ❖   ❖

Helen and George left the restaurant at eight-thirty. When George suggested a walk along the waterfront, Helen agreed. She still had a lot of unanswered questions. They drove separate cars to the south end of the seawall. Grabbing a pair of gloves and a hat from her trunk, Helen joined George on the sidewalk.

Helen pulled on her winter hat, a plain gray felt with a brim and a six-inch band of material on either side that served as a scarf. She brought the ties down to cover her ears, then crossed them under her chin and flipped the ends back over her shoulders.

George hauled in a deep breath. "Lovely night, isn't it?" He exhaled vapor puffs as he spoke. "Nothing like fresh sea air. I am so glad I moved here."

"I love it. Don't even mind the rain most days." Helen pulled up her collar against the wind and pushed her gloved hands into the pockets of her jacket. "Brrr. Winter is definitely on its way."

"Maybe it'll be nice tomorrow. Look." He pointed skyward. "We can see a few stars."

Helen stargazed for a moment, then zeroed in on the questions George had left unanswered. "So tell me about Ethan."

They fell into step, matching each other stride for stride. He hunched his shoulders. "I suppose the most crucial thing is that the letter opener didn't kill him as we'd originally thought."

"Oh?" Helen's questions tumbled over themselves like the water below them, scrambling forward in an effort to be asked first. "What did?"

"From what I can determine, he was stabbed first. He may have tried to run or move away from his attacker. My hunch is that when the knife attack failed, the killer went for the first available weapon. A rock or piece of concrete. Hit him on the back of the head about here." George brushed the back of his head just above the hairline.

"Any ideas on *where* the murder took place?"

"A lot of ideas. Without physical evidence, all we can do is speculate. We know he'd been in the restaurant. The most likely scenario is that he went for a walk on the beach. Or he may have been attacked near the parking lot and dragged out to the beach."

"That's a long way to drag a body—unless the killer dumped it into the river in front of the restaurant. What with the currents, it could have drifted down and come back in on the tide."

"I don't think so. There's another problem—if he'd been brought in on a wave, the letter opener would have been dislodged. I think Ethan was murdered on the beach. Probably close to where you found him."

"That makes the most sense."

"Something else. Whoever killed Ethan wanted to make certain the body was found with the knife in it."

"I'm not sure I follow you," Helen said.

"There were two knife wounds. My guess is that with the first strike, the knife came out. Now it's anyone's guess as to what happened next, but that knife wound didn't kill him. Once he was dead, though, I think the killer tried to reinsert the knife into the old wound to make it look like he'd been stabbed only once. Went in at almost the same place but at a slightly different angle. There was sand in the second track."

Helen shuddered. "How gruesome."

"Deliberate, premeditated murder."

"One meant to frame Rosie." Helen stopped at the seawall and sat on its concrete surface. Below them the sea churned and foamed in a cauldron, pounding the rocks and shooting huge plumes of water into the air. The spray stung her face like tiny needles, but she didn't turn away.

Helen mulled over her theory of Alex confessing and playing the role of a protective son. Perhaps he'd planned this from the moment he discovered who his father was. Or maybe he'd planned it before he came to Bay Village. He'd take Ethan for as much as he could get, then kill him, making it look like Rosie did it. Still, he seemed genuinely sad over Ethan's death. He could have been faking it. "Maybe Alex isn't who he says he is."

"What's that?" George asked.

"Just thinking out loud." Helen heard an engine rev up. A white pickup backed out of a parking space at the north end of the seawall. It had some sort of logo on the side and looked similar to the one she'd seen in the driveway at Adele and Dave's house, but she couldn't be sure.

The truck moved toward them and slowed. Helen recognized the Feldman's Construction logo and waved.

The driver's arm came up. Helen caught sight of the weapon just as it went off.

Twenty-one

L ook out!" George yelled.

Helen dove to the concrete. George landed on top of her. Gunshots. Two. Three. The bullets hit, then ricocheted off the stone wall.

After a few long excruciating moments, the gunfire stopped. Tires screeched as the driver spun around and drove away.

"Are you all right?" George rasped as he rolled off Helen.

"Not exactly." Helen gasped for air. "What about you?"

"Been hit." He grimaced and tried to sit up.

Helen forgot her own injuries and cranked herself up onto her knees. "Lie still, George. Where did they get you?"

"Hip." He gritted his teeth. "It'll be okay. Just need to put some pressure on it."

Helen turned him so the wounded hip faced upward, then whipped off her hat and bunched up the material. Straightening her arms, she leaned forward, pressing the hat against his hip, and began calling for help. Blood seeped onto her pants as she knelt beside him. Helen prayed the bullet hadn't severed an artery. They needed help fast. Most of the buildings across the way were businesses. The street was deserted except for their cars, which might as well have been in another country. Her cell phone was in her bag in the trunk.

A man came out of one of the buildings on the opposite side of the street. "What's going on? I heard shots."

Thankfully, the man had already called 9-1-1, and within minutes a rescue vehicle from the local fire department had

George on a stretcher. One of the EMTs checked Helen over and wanted to take her in as well, but she declined. She'd survived the fall better than expected. While she'd probably be sore for a few days, her heavier clothing and gloves had protected everything except one knee. For the moment her scraped and bloodied knee had adhered to her pants leg. Helen fought against the draining adrenaline and impending shock. She had to hold it together long enough to figure out why Dave Feldman would want to shoot her or George.

Helen couldn't imagine the friendly contractor risking everything by using his own truck in a drive-by shooting. She hadn't actually seen the driver's face, but who else would be beyind that wheel? Unless it had been stolen.

"Are you sure you won't come along, Helen?" George asked, interrupting her thoughts.

"No, I'm okay. I'll see you in the hospital later."

He asked the EMTs to hold off on putting him into the back of the ambulance. Reaching for Helen, he said, "I don't feel comfortable about leaving you alone. Not after what just happened."

She took his hand and held it in a firm grip. "Nonsense. Whoever shot at us is long gone. Besides, I'm hardly alone. In case you hadn't noticed, the place is crawling with cops." She gave him a reassuring smile. "I need to go home and change before I do anything else."

"Not by yourself." He lifted his head off the stretcher to emphasize his concern. "Have one of the officers check the house out first."

"George, that really isn't—"

"Sounds like a good idea to me, Mrs. Bradley."

Helen spun around. "Stephanie. When did you get here?"

"A couple of minutes ago. I was heading home when I heard the report. Thought I'd come down and check things out."

"Helen, promise me you'll be careful," George urged as the stretcher slid inside the ambulance.

Helen turned back to him. "All right—I'll have one of the deputies escort me to the house. Now relax. I'll see you soon."

The doors closed and the ambulance sped off for the hospital in Lincoln City. Helen swung her gaze back to Stephanie. "Have you talked to the officer in charge?"

Stephanie nodded. "He's calling it a drive-by, but we'll check out your claim that it was Dave Feldman's truck."

"My claim? It was his pickup."

"No offense, Mrs. Bradley, but the guys are saying Dave Feldman isn't exactly the kind of guy who'd do something like this."

"I didn't think so either, but it *was* his pickup."

"Deputy Perry said that if it was Dave's truck, someone stole it. Might have been some kids out for a joyride."

"And a little down-home shooting spree? Right." Helen felt light-headed. Her hand shook when she brushed it through her hair.

"You sure you don't want to see a doctor?" Stephanie grabbed hold of her arm and eased her to the sidewalk.

"Just give me a minute." Helen hung her head down between her knees and took several deep breaths.

When she regained her composure, she straightened. "If Deputy Perry is finished with me, I'd like a lift back to my car." The steadiness in her voice surprised her.

"Are you sure you should be driving?"

"I'm okay now." She patted Stephanie's arm. "There's no way I'm going to leave my car out here all night."

Stephanie insisted on driving Helen to the house after enlisting the help of another officer to follow. Once they'd seen Helen safely home, he'd drive Stephanie back to her patrol car.

The arrangement annoyed Helen, but she complied. Not doing so would have taken more time. Since she had to ride with Stephanie, she decided to make the best of it.

"Have you learned any more about Chuck's death?" Helen buckled herself in and handed Stephanie the keys.

"Chuck? Oh, you mean the guy we found in the mayor's car. Still waiting for the ME's report. Joe thinks Jordan killed him and took him out to the river, then set it up to make it look like Chuck was driving." Stephanie plugged the key into the ignition and turned it, pumping the gas as Helen instructed. She smiled as the car came to life.

"Runs good," Stephanie said. "It's a great car. If you ever decide to sell it . . ."

"I don't think that will be anytime soon." Helen waited until Stephanie had backed out, then brought their conversation back to Chuck.

"You were telling me about the investigation into Chuck's death. What's your take on it?"

"Like I told you earlier, I don't think Alex is guilty. Maybe Daniels killed himself."

"I doubt it." Helen dismissed the idea.

"It's possible. He was in the mayor's car. He could have killed the mayor and was afraid of getting caught. Remember the doors were locked and the windows closed. It doesn't look like he tried to get out."

"I wouldn't figure Chuck as the suicidal type." Helen thought about the arrogant contractor and the way he'd handled problems. "His solution to just about anything was to go fishing."

"Still, don't you think it's possible he killed Ethan and the guilt of what he'd done put him over the edge?"

Helen shook her head. "Even if he did kill himself, wouldn't you think running the car in a closed garage would be preferable to driving into the river and drowning? I doubt he had a choice."

"I suppose you're right." Stephanie glanced at Helen. "Maybe he didn't mean to do it. Maybe he was hurt and couldn't get the doors or windows open."

Helen's thoughts skittered back in time to when she and her granddaughter Jennie had been forced off a bridge near Sanibel Island in Florida. The car had been a convertible, yet had bobbed on the water for a short time before sinking. They'd both been able to swim away. True, Chuck may have been injured and unable to get out, but he had been wearing a seat belt. "Except for the muck, the car didn't look badly damaged," Helen said.

"It wasn't."

"Judging from how far it had drifted from the bank and

with it closed up, I suspect it floated for several minutes before it sank."

Pulling into the driveway, Stephanie said, "Did I tell you his alcohol level was over the limit?" She turned off the car and handed the keys to Helen.

"No, you didn't. I'm not surprised—about the alcohol, I mean." Helen dug a tissue out of her pocket to wipe her nose, then got out of the car.

"He went to a bar to have a few drinks when he got off work. The bartender knows him. Said he left a little before eight. By then his wife had already gone home. Chuck was there about the same time Ethan and Alex supposedly left. Chuck and Ethan may have gotten into an argument over that land deal . . . remember you told me about that?"

Helen rubbed her forehead. "So you're suggesting that Chuck got into a discussion with Ethan and the two men decided to take a walk on the beach? Chuck knifes Ethan with Rosie's letter opener. Only he doesn't kill him, so he grabs a piece of driftwood and uses Ethan's head as a baseball. Then puts the knife back in the wound, goes back to the parking lot, and drives Ethan's car all the way to the Siletz River. How was he planning to get back to his own car? And what happened to Alex?"

Stephanie cast her a surprised look. "How did you know the mayor was stabbed twice?"

"George—Dr. Fisher told me."

"Oh."

"Now, as I was saying, the idea of Chuck using Rosie's letter opener as a murder weapon and taking off in Ethan's car is too farfetched." Helen massaged the back of her neck. "By the way, did you ever find Chuck's truck?"

"It turned up in his garage. Mrs. Daniels didn't know how it got there. He usually parks outside. The keys were in it, so she figured Chuck had brought it back and was too scared to come in. No one seems to know anything about that. You know, Mrs. Bradley, it's possible Daniels didn't know what he was doing. A drunk can do some pretty irrational things. We found an empty bottle of whiskey under the front seat. He could have missed the curve and gone into the river and been too drunk to get out."

"I don't know. . . ." Helen mused. "I can certainly see Chuck getting into an altercation with Ethan. Especially if he'd been drinking, but how would he have gotten hold of Rosie's letter opener? Maybe the bigger question is why would he? He'd have no reason to implicate Rosie."

"That we know of." Stephanie sighed. "You're right. No matter how I try to piece it together, it doesn't come out right. Much as I hate to admit it, Joe might be right."

"You mean in thinking Alex is the killer?"

"It's looking really bad for him, Mrs. Bradley. Did Joe tell you we found Alex's jacket in the backseat of the mayor's Jag?"

Twenty-two

Alex Jordan's jacket. *In the back of Ethan's Jaguar.* Helen was stunned. Another attempt at framing him? Or more evidence that he killed Ethan?

"Here's my ride," Stephanie said.

The other deputy pulled in behind the Thunderbird, and the three met at the sidewalk. Helen started to follow them into the house, but Stephanie placed a restraining hand on her arm. "Stay here while Bill and I have a look around."

Helen didn't argue. Normally she'd have felt perfectly capable of taking care of herself. At the moment, however, she wasn't sure she could walk to the front door. Her shoulder had begun a major protest and her knee pulsed in pain. Her legs felt like leftover spaghetti squash. She went slowly back to the car and leaned against it, then dutifully waited while the deputies checked the house.

With nothing amiss, she thanked them, told Stephanie she'd see her later, and limped inside. Though Helen had promised George she'd meet him at the hospital, she had other things to attend to first and wasn't sure where to begin. Helen went into her bathroom to clean up for what seemed like the umpteenth time that day.

"If you had two ounces of common sense," she growled at her reflection in the mirror, "you'd go to bed and let Joe handle this."

But she couldn't. Especially not now. She and George had almost been the next victims. It all had turned excruciatingly personal. Was the shooting related to the two previous murders? Helen felt certain it was, simply because the shooter had used Dave Feldman's pickup.

What Stephanie had said about Alex's jacket being in the trunk of Ethan's car hit Helen full force. Why had it been there? What had happened in that parking lot? Witnesses had put Chuck, Alex, and Ethan there around the same time. Ethan and Chuck were dead. Alex was alive. The driver who shot at them was using Feldman's pickup. *Dave. Adele's husband. Rosie's brother-in-law. Alex's uncle.*

Alex couldn't have stolen Dave's truck. He was still in jail. So who was driving? Maybe Helen was again letting her friendship cloud the issue. Rosie could easily have gotten ahold of Dave's truck. She could have killed Ethan.

"No way." She folded her arms and tipped her head back. "Rosie is not a killer."

She had a gun. She used it to force you into the closet.

Helen shook her head to dismiss the idea. Rosie would never have shot her. Even if by some remote chance she did kill Ethan, she wouldn't then be dumb enough to use her brother-in-law's pickup in a drive-by shooting.

She sagged against the wall. Maybe the deputies were right. She and George had been victims of a random drive-by. It happened far too often these days with guns being so readily available to anyone with the cash to buy them. But why would car thieves go clear up the hill to the Feldmans' place to get a pickup? There had to be plenty of vehicles that were more accessible. And why take one with an identifiable logo?

"It wasn't a random drive-by and you know it," Helen muttered. Whoever used that pickup wanted them to recognize it and come to the conclusion that someone in Dave's family was responsible for the shooting.

Confusion dragged her into another scenario. Helen hadn't considered the possibility before, but when Dave invited her into his house, he later admitted to being financially strapped. Strapped enough to kill Ethan to give them a better chance of pushing the Riverside development through? Was Dave one of the owners?

She thought back to her conversation with the lawyer. Nathan refused to or couldn't come up with the names of his investors on the Riverside project. Until she saw that list, all she could do was speculate, and so far that had gotten her nowhere.

Helen temporarily shelved the questions and rooted around in her linen closet until she found her first-aid kit. With it at her side, Helen sat on the edge of the bathtub and gritted her teeth as she pulled her pants leg free of the wound. The scrape was only about an inch in diameter, but the pain ripped through her entire body. She stopped the bleeding and ran water over her knee, dug out particles of dirt, then dressed it with an ointment and applied a bandage.

Ignoring the rest of her protesting muscles, Helen pulled on a fresh pair of jeans, another sweater, and sneakers. She threw her dirty sweater into the laundry hamper and her slacks and nylons in the trash, then painstakingly made her way down the stairs to the phone. No messages.

Her thoughts drifted again to J.B. She wanted his arms around her, holding her, kissing away her concerns.

"Stop it. Just stop it!" She jumped at the sound of her own voice. For whatever reason, J.B. had taken himself out of her life. Maybe it was only temporary. Maybe it was forever. Either way, Helen didn't want to deal with it just now. She mentally placed J.B. and her heart in God's hands. To continue ruminating over where he was or what he might be doing served no purpose at all. All she could do about him for the moment was to pray that God would keep him safe.

Instead of worrying about him, she needed to focus on finding Ethan's killer. She had to keep moving. But in which direction?

With so many questions and so many routes to take, Helen felt scattered. First things first. She crossed her legs and dropped to the floor. Closing her eyes, she said another prayer for J.B., then prayed for clarity and peace. She concentrated on clearing her mind of the chaos that had been building up since finding Ethan's body. Taking a deep breath, she placed her list of things to do in priority and then sat still for a while with her eyes closed, calling on God's help to discover the truth.

When she felt more calm and controlled, Helen called the hospital to check on George. The nurse in emergency told her he'd been taken into surgery. She glanced at her watch, thanked her, and hung up. It was going to be a long night.

She'd promised to meet Eleanor around nine-thirty. It was already nine-fifty-five. She called to apologize for being detained but didn't go into details.

"It's not a problem, Helen. I'll probably be up all night anyway. I'll put the hot water on for tea."

Helen's sore knee and aching joints pleaded for mercy. The more rational side of her brain insisted on telling Eleanor she couldn't come until morning, then going straight to bed. She wouldn't, of course. And she needed something to occupy her time while she waited for George to come out of surgery. That gave her an hour or two.

"I'll be there in a few minutes," she heard herself saying.

While Helen headed over to see Eleanor, she puzzled over the shooting incident. If it wasn't a random act, then it had to have been someone who knew where she and George were. Joe knew, of course. And the few people who'd been in the restaurant. The Cranes.

Brian had walked out. Had she and George been the cause of his anger? But why? And how? He would have had to follow them, drive to Lincoln City, steal Dave Feldman's pickup, then come back and shoot them.

"Now, that makes a lot of sense," she mumbled sarcastically.

Still, he had been upset and left the restaurant. But how could he have known they'd be at the seawall? If he'd been following her, he'd know. He could have taken the pickup earlier and already had it at his disposal. But wouldn't Dave have missed it? She shook her head. It made no sense at all.

Helen drove on to the Crane home. She'd try to find out where each of them had been while she and George were being attacked.

Eleanor opened the door before Helen had a chance to ring the bell. "Come in. Please." Eleanor stepped aside. Her grief was reflected in the stoop of her shoulders and a weariness in her eyes.

"I almost didn't come," Helen said.

"Well, I'm glad you did. The water's hot. Did you still want some tea?"

"Yes." Helen followed her through the entry. "In fact I can't think of anything I'd like better. Earl Grey, if you have it."

"I'm sure I do. Why don't you come with me into the kitchen. We can talk in there without anyone disturbing us."

Helen settled into the straight-backed wooden chair with woven seat at the kitchen table and watched Eleanor pour the already-hot water into cups.

"Where are Brian and Nancy?" Helen asked.

"I suspect Nancy's in her room. She and Melissa were going to play Scrabble. Brian hasn't been home." Her tone indicated disapproval.

"I take it you're not too happy with him."

She brought the cups to the table, then went back to get a wooden tea chest. "Disappointed."

Helen chose her tea from a wide assortment and ripped off the wrapper. "He seemed quite angry at the restaurant."

Eleanor scowled. "He got in a huff over something I said. I can't remember what. It was my fault. I thought going out might cheer us up. I guess no one, especially Brian, wanted to be cheered. I'm sure he's upset about losing his father. They didn't see eye to eye on a lot of things. In fact, the last time Brian was here, they had argued over something. I'm not sure what it was. Ethan was disappointed in Brian's life-style. When I spoke with the pastor earlier today, he suggested that maybe Brian is feeling some guilt over that last visit. There had been no time for them to reconcile."

"How sad," Helen mused.

"At any rate, I didn't ask you here to talk about Brian." Eleanor reached into her jacket pocket and pulled out a white standard-sized envelope. Setting it on the table, she rested her hand on it. The stones in her rings sparkled under the artificial light. "I wanted to ask your advice."

"My advice?" Helen dunked the bag into the water several times.

"You see, it's rather a delicate situation. I was going through some of Ethan's things looking for... burial clothes when I found this." She pushed it across the table. "I'm still not sure what to make of it. Do you think it's real?"

Helen examined the envelope. There was no address or postmark. Only Ethan's name, handwritten in the center and, at the right edge, a logo depicting a pastel drawing of Rosie's Victorian house and the caption *Past Times* with the address. Helen pulled out the contents and unfolded the papers. A photo of Alex fell out, identical to the one Helen had found on Rosie's dresser. On top was a letter with no date. *To Ethan from Alex.* The second paper was a copy of Alex's birth certificate. Helen turned her attention back to the letter. In it Alex explained how he'd come to find Rosie. He then wrote:

> *I've been searching for a long time and couldn't believe my luck in finally locating Rosie and now you. I don't expect anything from you. I just want you to know that you are my birth father. I know you already have a family, and I will understand if you don't want me in your life. I only hope you'll agree to meet me. All I ask is that we have a chance to meet. Your son, Alex.*

Helen looked up at Eleanor and said, "This must have come as quite a shock."

"Quite." Eleanor closed her eyes. "You were close to Rosie. Did you know?"

"Not until today."

"He's the one who's been arrested for Ethan's death, isn't he?"

"Yes." Helen sipped at her tea.

"Do you believe Alex is really Ethan's son?"

"I'm not sure how to answer that. If the birth certificate is authentic, then yes, Rosie and Ethan are his parents. Rosie says the dates are right."

"Is she sure it's Ethan's child? She didn't list a birth father."

"She's sure. They dated in high school."

"I know." Eleanor picked up the photo and examined it more closely. "He does favor Ethan, doesn't he?"

"Yes, I noticed it right off." Helen puzzled over Eleanor's calm. "Do Nancy and Brian know?"

"I haven't told them." Eleanor set the photo down and concentrated on the contents of the tea box, then made a selection. "I thought it might upset them too much."

"You'll have to tell them eventually. Rosie indicated that Ethan planned to tell you and them."

"Did he? That's good to know. I'll tell them after the funeral." Eleanor folded her arms around her waist and stared at a spot on the table.

"You don't seem too upset about the news."

"I've had time to process it. I couldn't believe it at first. I was furious and felt certain it was some sort of con. Now that I've had some time to adjust, I think it's probably true. Rosie and Ethan were very much in love back then. It's just—I wish Ethan had told me. He never said a word. Not one word."

"Ethan didn't know until a day or so before his trip. Perhaps he meant to tell you when he returned," Helen said.

"But he didn't get the chance. I suppose he was afraid of what my reaction might be. But I would've understood. I knew he and Rosie dated in high school. When she left, he was heartbroken. I never dreamed she left because she was pregnant. If I'd known that, I'd . . . well, I doubt things would have worked out the way they did. Ethan would have married her. I knew he loved Rosie. But after she left and he realized she wasn't coming back, he decided to get on with his life." Eleanor looked away. "He eventually grew to love me too."

"I'm sure he did." Helen blew ripples across the surface of her tea, wondering whether or not to bring up the issue of Rosie and Ethan's affair.

"Well." Eleanor straightened and seemed to gather strength as she inhaled. "We can't relive the past, can we? It's best to pick up the pieces and move on."

"That's not as easy as it sounds."

"Helen." Eleanor leaned forward. "I would like your advice. I'm not sure what to do about Alex."

"What do you mean?" Helen set her cup down.

"As Ethan's son, Alex has a right to part of his father's estate. I know Ethan would have wanted to include him in his will."

Had she heard right? Helen had expected outrage or denial,

but not acceptance. Certainly not acceptance. "Eleanor, I can't believe I'm having this conversation with you. Are you serious about giving Alex a portion of the inheritance? The man is being held as a suspect in a double homicide."

"Apparently they have the wrong man. I went to see him today, you know."

"No," Helen gasped. "I didn't know."

"After I found the letter. I felt I should meet him. We talked for a long time and . . . Helen, that young man did not kill Ethan."

Helen couldn't help it. Her jaw dropped. And it took several seconds before she could engage it again. "You actually went to see him?"

"Well, he is my stepson. I wanted to see for myself. To be sure. He told me he'd lied about killing Ethan because he wanted to protect Rosie. I believe him."

"If you already knew, why did you ask me about him?"

"I wanted another opinion." Eleanor reached across the table to take the envelope and papers back.

"Mine? Wouldn't it be better to talk to Brian and Nancy about it? They have a right to know."

"And what do you think their response would be?" Eleanor shook her head. "No, I'm doing the right thing. Of course, I've asked the medical examiner to do a paternity test, to find out if Alex really is Ethan's son. And if he is, there's only one thing to do."

She offered a half smile. "I've made up my mind. Brian and Nancy are not going to be happy about my decision. I know it's terrible for a mother to say negative things about her own children, but they are both too selfish and spoiled. It's my fault as much as Ethan's. We gave them everything. Unfortunately, we didn't teach them enough about getting through life's problems. Not that they're bad, you understand. Neither of them was ever into drugs or illegal activity of any kind." She glanced at Helen, then focused on her cup. "Though Nancy has been drinking too much of late. At any rate, I don't intend to tell them about Alex until I've taken care of the details. They'll find out when the will is read. They won't be happy, but by that time it will be too late."

"Too late?" Helen echoed. "Are you planning to change Ethan's will?"

"Oh, goodness, no. Ethan's estate was to be divided equally between his children. I'm going to see to it that Alex is included."

"That's very generous of you."

"Not generous, Helen. I'm not doing this out of a kind heart. It's more a matter of doing what's right. It's what Ethan would have wanted." Eleanor's right hand fluttered, obviously dismissing the subject. "There's something else I want to discuss with you."

Helen didn't know if she could take any more surprises. "It's getting quite late . . . maybe we could save it—"

"Nonsense. You need to finish your tea. Besides, this won't take but a minute."

Helen lifted her cup and drew in a long swallow of the lukewarm brew in a salute. "All right."

"Good." Eleanor scooted her chair closer to the table. "I don't want you to take this the wrong way, but . . ." She paused and settled a concerned expression on Helen. "It's about Rosie."

Helen tensed. "What about Rosie?"

"I know she's a good friend, but . . . you see, after talking to Alex and Joe, I wonder if you haven't developed a blind spot."

"Look, Eleanor, I think I know where you're going with this. You think because Alex confessed in order to protect his mother that Rosie actually might have—"

"Killed Ethan," Eleanor finished. "Yes, I do."

"That's crazy. Rosie would never hurt anyone."

"Joe told me she pulled a gun on you yesterday when you went to tell her about Ethan. Now I ask you, why would she do that?"

"She was afraid Alex might have been involved. She needed time to sort things out."

"Doesn't that seem like a strange reaction to you? I'm sorry, Helen, but I just don't buy it. If I had been in her shoes, I certainly wouldn't have pulled a gun on my best friend and run away. Not if I were innocent. Would you?"

"No, but Rosie wasn't thinking clearly. And in her mind, I probably posed a threat."

"In what way? You certainly weren't going to arrest her. You're no longer a police officer. But you *are* her friend. How could she behave so outrageously toward you?"

"She was frightened. When I told her about the murder weapon being her letter opener, she panicked." Helen had no idea why she was so adamantly defending Rosie.

"Of course she panicked—because she'd been found out. If she were innocent, why would she be afraid? And why would she automatically suspect her own son? I know the authorities look closely at the family in these cases, but never for a moment have I questioned whether or not Nancy or Brian had anything to do with their father's death. I wouldn't even consider such a thing."

Why *had* Rosie been so quick to suspect Alex? Helen wondered. Anyone could have walked off with the letter opener.

"Then there's the money," Eleanor continued. "Doesn't it seem strange to you that Ethan would pay her such a large amount? He certainly didn't buy that many books. And as far as I know, he wasn't planning to purchase her store."

"Joe told you about the money?" That seemed odd. Joe wasn't ordinarily so free with information—especially not during an investigation.

Eleanor sighed impatiently, like one might do when explaining a math problem to a difficult student. "No, Alex did. He said Rosie didn't want the money and tried to give it back. I don't believe that. After all, she deposited it."

"Rosie explained all that to me. When Ethan refused to take the check back, she deposited it and wrote a check to Alex for the same amount." As Helen spoke, she wondered about Rosie's motives, her thoughts echoing Eleanor's next question.

"But if Rosie really didn't want the money, why didn't she just tear up the check?"

"Maybe she thought, as you do, that Alex was entitled to a share of Ethan's estate."

"I could understand that. But there's more. You see, Helen,

I found something else while I was going through Ethan's things."

I don't think I want to hear this. Aloud, she said, "I'm listening."

"Ethan had a personal checkbook. One that's separate from the account we have together and the one for his business. He used it for miscellaneous expenses. There were *two* checks written out to Rosie. The first for one hundred thousand, written a little over a week ago. The second was written last Thursday, the day he left on his trip. Helen, it was for five hundred thousand dollars."

Helen's insides bunched into a gigantic knot. "Are you sure?"

"Absolutely. I'd show you the check register, but Joe insisted on keeping it as evidence."

"Both made out to Rosie?" Helen moved her eyes across the table, onto the doily, and up to Eleanor's face. She'd expected to see a smug look—an I-told-you-so look. She found neither. If anything, Eleanor seemed as disturbed as Helen felt.

"I couldn't believe it either," Eleanor went on, "but there it was in black and white. Now, Ethan may have felt remorse and guilt over what happened to Rosie, but I doubt he'd have parted with that much money. As much as I hate to say it, I'm afraid Rosie may have been blackmailing my husband."

Twenty-three

There was no point in arguing with Eleanor. She'd made up her mind. Rosie was an adulteress, a blackmailer, and a cold-blooded killer. There was simply no other explanation. And no reason to look further for the murderer.

Helen couldn't entirely dispute Eleanor's logic. Not that Eleanor noticed Helen's lack of support. She said her piece, then dropped the matter as though she'd suddenly run out of steam. Eleanor closed her eyes for a moment and, in the time it would take to change a CD, began talking about the arrangements for the funeral.

"I'm anxious to have it over with." She ran her fingers over the beige-and-pink place mat. "I suppose that sounds brash and uncaring—at least that's what Nancy accuses me of being. I feel as though I'm in some kind of twilight zone."

"I can understand that." Helen had experienced a similar feeling with Ian's death. "What with the investigation into the bombing and getting the officials in Beirut to release his body, Ian's funeral was delayed for six weeks after we learned of his death."

"Six weeks! That must have been unbearable."

"Unsettling. Somehow I kept thinking there had been a mistake—that he'd walk through the door at any moment. He didn't, of course. When a loved one dies, it's important to have closure. I couldn't really accept his death. Even now, there are times . . ."

"Yes. That's how I feel. Like it can't be true. And it's all been a terrible nightmare." Eleanor rubbed her forehead. "I hate having to wait like this."

When she raised her head, there were tears in her eyes. "Have you any idea how long it will be before Dr. Fisher can release Ethan's body for burial?"

"I'm not sure." Helen shoved her chair back. "I should go. I promised George I'd see him at the hospital."

Eleanor frowned. "Hospital? This time of night? Whatever for?"

"He was shot."

Eleanor stiffened and made a shrill, chirping sound. "How . . . ?"

"After we left the restaurant, we went for a walk along the seawall. Someone driving by in a pickup tried to gun us down. George took a bullet in the hip."

"Oh, how awful. You should have said something sooner. I'd never have expected you to come by tonight."

"It seemed important to you." Helen shrugged. "At any rate, I'm sure it'll still be a while before I can see him. He's in surgery."

Eleanor clicked her tongue. "A drive-by shooting, of all things. I can't believe something like that could happen here at the coast." Walking Helen to the door, she added, "I suppose I shouldn't be surprised. We've had two murders here in Bay Village in less than four months. A person isn't safe anywhere these days."

Brian came in before Helen could respond. Judging by the scowl on his face, his anger hadn't abated much. "What are you doing here?"

"Brian, please. I asked her to come. I don't know what your problem is, but as long as you're staying here, I expect you to be civil to my guests."

"Fine. I'll get my things."

"Brian!" Eleanor started to follow him. She stopped at the stairs, then turned back to Helen. "I'm sorry. I don't know what's gotten into him."

"Go ahead." Helen glanced at the stairs. "I'll let myself out."

Helen had no sooner reached her car than Brian slammed

out of the front door. He came to an abrupt halt beside her. "You still here?" He sounded more civil.

She held up her hands and examined her palms. "Apparently."

He smiled at that. "Look, I'm sorry I was so rude. I've been blowing up a lot lately. Mom was right, I had no business being angry with you."

"You just lost your father. I suppose you have a right to be angry at the world."

He shook his head. "I am pretty bummed out about that. It wasn't just losing Dad, though—it was gaining a brother."

"Alex?"

"You know about him?" Brian hoisted his duffel bag over his shoulder.

"Yes, but I'm surprised you do. Your mother just told me she didn't plan to tell you until after the funeral."

"I didn't realize she knew."

"She says she found the information on Alex in one of your father's desk drawers." Helen opened her car door. "How did you find out?"

He gave her a lopsided grin. "I . . . ah. . . . Don't suppose you'd give me a ride down to the Bay View Hotel, would you? I could tell you on the way."

Helen shrugged. "Sure, hop in." As soon as the words were out she wondered at the wisdom of going off alone with him.

"Thanks." He settled his lengthy frame into the passenger seat of her car. His hostility seemed to have melted, and while she didn't feel a sense of immediate danger from him, she still didn't trust him. Also, she reminded herself, the ride into town would provide an excellent opportunity to hear his side of things.

Once they'd buckled up and backed out of the driveway, Helen asked him again about Alex.

"Dad called me from the airport in Portland when he got in."

"Sunday? What time?"

"Around three in the afternoon. Said he had something important to tell me and wanted me to meet him down here that night."

"And did you?"

"No. He'd been leaning on me pretty hard lately, so I told him no way was I driving clear to the coast. If he had something to say to me, he could say it over the phone."

"So did he?" Helen stopped at the highway junction and waited for several cars to pass before making a left.

"Yeah. You got that right. Hey, don't get me wrong. I'm not mad about him messing around in high school or having another kid."

"Then what?"

"This so-called son killed my dad, and I let it happen."

Helen glanced over at him, wishing they were talking face-to-face rather than in a shadowy car. "I don't understand."

"I should have come home like he asked. Instead I told him to take a hike."

"And you think you're responsible for his death because you didn't meet him?"

"Aren't I? If I'd been here, I might have gone with my father to see the guy. That's what Dad wanted. For me to meet Alex first. Then he was going to tell Nancy and Mom."

Helen braked at the 35-mph sign as they headed into the main part of town. "Does Nancy know?"

"I called her right after I talked to Dad."

"And what was her reaction?"

"She was too drunk to care. Too many problems of her own, I guess. We talked about telling Mom but decided Dad should do that himself."

Helen pulled into the drive in front of the hotel lobby and turned to look at Brian. "Did either you or Nancy talk to your mother about Rosie and Alex?"

"I didn't, and I don't think Nancy did either. Dad being killed was hard enough on her. I didn't think she'd be able to handle anything else. Guess I was wrong."

"Your mother is a strong woman."

"Apparently." He started to get out of the car.

"Brian, wait. I need to ask you something."

"Sure."

Helen told him about the drive-by shooting. He seemed surprised. "Whoa. You think it's related to my dad's death?"

"I'm sure it is. When you left the restaurant, did you happen to see anyone suspicious or notice a white pickup?"

He wagged his head back and forth. "If it is related, then Alex might not have killed Dad after all." The idea seemed to please him. "I mean he's still in jail, right?"

"As far as I know."

He nodded. "So if Alex didn't kill my old man, who did?"

You? Though Helen hadn't said the word aloud, Brian must have picked up on her thoughts.

"Hey, wait a minute." He leaned back and raised his hands. "You don't think *I* had anything to do with it? Man, like I told the cops, I wasn't even here."

"Do you have proof of that?"

"No . . ." He leaned forward, elbows on his knees, head almost touching the dashboard.

"When did you leave Portland?"

"Monday—early."

"Did you stop to get gas or eat on the way?"

He raised his head and frowned. "Yeah, both. Why?"

"Did you use a credit card?"

He tilted his head back against the seat and hit his hand on the dash.

"Your receipt has Sunday's date on it, doesn't it? Along with the time. The police are going to be able to tell exactly where you were when you used your card and estimate your time of arrival."

"I'm a dead man." He moaned but made no move to run.

"Not necessarily. Why don't you tell me what happened?"

"When Joe started asking me questions about where I was when Dad died, I got scared. Figured it was easier to say I hadn't come down until Monday."

"Did you see your father Sunday night?"

"No. Well, I saw his Jag parked about a block from Rosie's. Figured he had to be seeing her, as all the businesses in town were closed. He was there, all right. I caught them making out in the upstairs window before they got wise and pulled the curtains."

"Are you sure that's what you saw?"

He gave her an incredulous look and didn't bother to answer. "I got mad all over again. I mean it was one thing to get a girl pregnant in high school, but to cheat on my mom . . ." He hesitated. "I felt like going up there and killing both of them. But I didn't," he added quickly. "I just drove down by the seawall and parked till I could figure out what to do."

"How long were you there?"

He rubbed his forehead. "About an hour and a half. I walked around for a while. It took that long for me to cool down and work things out. I wasn't about to let him get away with that kind of stuff. I knew what it would do to Mom. After a while, I decided to go back to Rosie's and tell them exactly what I thought. When I got there, his car was gone and the lights were out. I remembered he was going to the restaurant, so I went there."

"What time was that?"

He shrugged. "I don't know. Around eight-thirty, I guess."

"Ethan had asked you to meet him at seven, right? He must have left Rosie's right after you saw him."

"I guess."

"You went to the restaurant to look for him." Helen wasn't sure what to make of the now-docile Brian Crane. Though he wasn't acting much like a cold, calculating killer, she still had her doubts.

"I went by but didn't go inside. I didn't see his car out front, so I left. Figured I'd talk to him later. Only he never came home." He cradled his head in his hands. "I should have been there to help him."

Helen looked over his muscular torso, trying to get a take on him. Brian had motive and opportunity. He'd admitted to being angry enough to kill his father. He'd lied before and could be lying again. Brian also admitted to being at the restaurant. Could he have waited for his father in the parking lot? Perhaps Ethan had suggested they walk on the beach. Helen imagined him confronting Ethan. Ethan walking away. Brian could become angry. She'd experienced that fury firsthand. It wasn't hard to picture him grabbing a piece of driftwood and hitting his father over the head.

No, that didn't work. Unless George was wrong about the knife wound. According to him, the killer stabbed Ethan first, then hit him in the back of the head. The letter opener had apparently fallen out of the body and was reinserted later, purposely framing Rosie. Could Brian have done that?

He was angry enough to kill them both.

"Do you know how your father died?"

"Joe told us he was stabbed. Later we found out about the weapon being Rosie's letter opener. Seemed weird to me."

"Weird? In what way?"

"Well, if you were going to use a letter opener to waste somebody, you'd have to know exactly where to stick it. Otherwise it wouldn't do all that much damage. Must have been a long one."

"Have you ever been in Rosie's store, Brian?"

"Sure, a few times—for coffee. I don't read much so . . ."

"What about mysteries? Did you ever go upstairs to her mystery room?"

He shook his head and frowned. "No. Why are you asking?"

"Just wondering if you'd ever seen it."

"Not that I recall."

"She kept the letter opener up there."

"So?"

"It's not your average letter opener. It had a blade about an inch across and about eight inches long."

"Whatever. Look, Mrs. Bradley, it's been nice, but I gotta go."

"I have one more question for you, if you don't mind."

"Why not? It's not like I have a hot date. I'd just like to get checked in. I haven't gotten much sleep the last few nights."

"I was wondering why you left the restaurant in such a hurry tonight."

"Why?" He turned to look out the window. "Because my mother was driving me nuts with all that funeral talk. I couldn't stand it anymore."

"I asked you this earlier, but I'd really like you to think

about it again. When you left the restaurant, did you happen to see a white pickup with a Feldman's Construction logo?"

"You mean the guy who shot at you?"

"I'm thinking whoever was driving it must have been watching us when we left the restaurant, then followed us."

"I can't help you there. I walked from the restaurant straight to Annie's place."

"Annie's?" After what Annie had told her about Brian's advances, Helen's stomach knotted with concern.

"I had to apologize to her. Got a little carried away the other night."

"Yes, she told me." Helen made a mental note to call Annie. Had his visit been partly to blame for his anger?

"Well, we worked it out."

Helen hoped so.

"Um, speaking of Annie," Helen ventured, "she said you'd burned something in the fireplace that night. Care to tell me what it was?"

"Humph. Guy can't get away with anything."

"I noticed a page missing on his calendar. . . ."

"Dad had written my name down for dinner with him and Alex Sunday night. I didn't want the police to see it."

"Annie indicated there was more."

"Some notes. Dad had written out a preliminary will naming Alex as a beneficiary. I was upset so I tossed it."

Helen nodded. "I won't keep you. If I were you, though, I'd go to the sheriff's office and tell them the truth about Sunday night."

He told her he would, then shut the car door and jogged into the hotel.

Helen headed for Annie's place and pulled up at the curb. Joe's car was parked out front. Was it a social visit, or had Annie borne the brunt of Brian's anger? Maybe Helen was being foolish, but she couldn't help worrying. Annie's comment about Brian's behavior gave reason enough for concern.

Going up the walk, Helen had second thoughts. Joe was with her. Annie would be safe. The lights were on, but she had no idea how far Joe and Annie's relationship had progressed.

She didn't relish the idea of interrupting whatever they might be doing.

The drapes parted. Annie's welcoming wave saved Helen from making the decision. The door opened, and Annie, seeming almost relieved, pulled her inside. "Come in. I'm surprised to see you. Joe was just telling me about the drive-by shooting. We thought you'd be at the hospital with George."

"I am heading that direction. I've been at Eleanor's, and I just had an interesting conversation with Brian. He said he'd been here and . . ."

She smiled. "You wanted to make sure I was okay. That was sweet of you, but I can hold my own with these guys. Brian came to apologize again for . . . making a pass at me."

Joe, looking none too happy, joined them at the door. "Um . . . look, Annie, I'd just as soon not hear this again." To Helen he said, "I was just leaving." And he did.

Looking at the closed door, Helen asked, "What was all that about?"

Annie ran a hand through her springy blond curls. "Joe asked me to marry him yesterday. I said no."

"That certainly explains his foul mood. I thought you and Joe were getting serious."

"We were—are. It's just that I'm not ready for marriage. My business is in jeopardy, and, well, to be honest, I think the proposal is Joe's way of bailing me out."

"I'm sure it's more than that. He loves you."

"I know, but I don't think he's ready for marriage yet either. He came by tonight to try to convince me it was for the best." She shook her head. "He just doesn't understand. I need to concentrate on building up my business now. Besides, I'm not sure how I feel about him. Brian asked me to go out to dinner."

"Whoa." Helen moved over to the recliner and sat down. "Yesterday you told me Brian came close to raping you, and now you're thinking of dating him?"

"That was Joe's reaction." Annie winced. "I overreacted. Brian apologized for coming on so strong. He assured me he would never hurt me. He was very sweet and . . . well, he's going through a hard time right now. I dated him for a while in high school, and I'm just not sure how I feel about him. I told him I was dating Joe, only now I'm not sure."

"Oh, Annie." Helen leaned back into the cushions. "I can't tell you what to do here, but . . ."

"But you're going to anyway."

"Not if you don't want me to."

Annie plopped onto the sofa and clasped her hands. "Go ahead. I could use some motherly advice."

"It's not advice. Just an observation." Helen picked a piece of fuzz off the arm of the chair. How could she say it? Since Brian had an alibi for when she and George were being fired at, Helen could probably cross him off her suspect list. "Brian seems likeable in some ways. I admit I don't really know him, but from what I've seen, he seems . . . volatile. Maybe even abusive."

"I led you to believe that, didn't I? It wasn't fair of me. He'd been hitting the bottle pretty hard that night."

"Yes, but drinking isn't an excuse for unacceptable behavior, just as grief or guilt or whatever he was experiencing is no excuse for drinking too much. He and Nancy both seem to have a problem with alcohol." An idea came to mind. "Listen, Annie, do me a favor. Before you consider going out with Brian, go to an AA meeting. Monday night at the church."

"But I don't drink."

"No, but you know someone who does." Talking about the AA program turned Helen's thoughts to Lynn Daniels. She'd have to pay the young woman a visit and see how she was doing.

Annie sighed deeply, bringing Helen's thoughts back to their conversation. "You think I should forget about Brian and marry Joe, don't you?"

"I think highly of Joe, but I certainly can't advise you one way or the other when it comes to dating or marriage. If you're not sure, maybe it would be best to wait." Helen smiled. "I will tell you one thing about Joe. If you'll talk to him about your concerns, I think you'll discover that his reason for asking you to marry him has little to do with your business and a lot to do with how much he loves you."

,"Then why would he include taking care of me financially on his list of reasons we should get married?"

"Who knows? Maybe he thought that's what you needed or wanted to hear."

"Hmm. So you think I ought to talk to him and find out what his motives really are?"

"That would be a step in the right direction."

They talked briefly about Brian, and Helen asked if he'd said anything about his father or Alex.

Though they'd talked about Ethan's death, Annie couldn't remember anything specific. Only that Brian was feeling guilty and upset. Nothing Helen didn't already know.

On her way to the hospital, Helen passed by Rosie's. Lights were on in her upstairs apartment. It was getting very late, but Helen wanted to talk with her, if for no other reason than to assure herself that Rosie was indeed innocent. Eleanor's accusations had become a burr under her proverbial saddle, and Helen couldn't seem to shake the idea that she might have been wrong about Rosie all along. The discussion with Brian hadn't helped. If he was telling the truth about Rosie's lights being out when he had come back to confront her and Ethan, then she either would have left or gone to bed. Rosie never went to bed until after the eleven-o'clock news. So where had she been?

Pulling into the parking lot, Helen cut the engine and looked around. Rosie's car wasn't parked in its usual place. Nor was it in the garage. If she wasn't home, then why were her lights on? An intruder? She stepped out of her car and carefully pushed the door closed until it clicked. There were no other cars in the parking area that bordered Main Street. Helen moved closer to the house and crept around to the back. Her heart hammered against her chest. Sitting in the far corner of the parking lot, where it wouldn't be noticed from the main road, was Dave Feldman's pickup.

Twenty-four

The window on the passenger side was still down. Helen didn't need much light or imagination to see inside. The keys were still in the ignition. A gun, looking far too much like Rosie's, lay in the open tote bag on the floor of the passenger side. Not wanting to disturb the evidence, Helen backed away.

What's going on, Rosie? She jogged back to her own car and slipped inside, then picked up her cell phone, intending to call Joe. Something almost tangible stopped her.

You can't. Not yet. Rosie is innocent. She has to be, an inner voice insisted.

But the evidence . . .

There's too much of it. You've always trusted Rosie. You've shared your most intimate thoughts with each other.

Not all of them. She never told you about Ethan. Or Alex—at least not until she was forced to.

Rosie hadn't told her a lot of things. Could she have been wrong about her all this time? And what about the checks Ethan had written to her? Rosie told her about the first one but hadn't bothered to mention a second. If she'd really told Ethan she didn't want his money, why would he give her a second check for even more? And as Eleanor had pointed out, why hadn't Rosie just torn up the checks?

Rosie loved Ethan. At least that's what she claimed. Why then would she kill him?

She wouldn't. She certainly wouldn't want to implicate herself by using such an identifiable weapon.

She might. What if she'd lied and Ethan wanted nothing to do with Alex? What if Rosie had expected Ethan to leave Eleanor, and when he wouldn't, she killed him? Or maybe Alex and Rosie were working together to extort Ethan.

Could Eleanor be right in thinking that Rosie was blackmailing Ethan?

Helen closed her eyes and leaned her head against the steering wheel. Joe had accused her of not being objective. If it had been anyone other than Rosie, would she feel so protective?

No. You would not, she answered without hesitation.

If Dave's pickup had been anywhere else but in Rosie's parking lot, would you call it in? Absolutely.

Then why don't you call Joe right now?

Helen couldn't answer. She wanted Rosie to be innocent. More than that, her intuition wouldn't allow her to believe anything else. Or *was* it her intuition? Calling Joe would result in Rosie's arrest. Helen didn't want that. At least not yet. She needed time to sort things out. Helen shook her head to dispel the barrage of inner voices.

A few minutes later she punched in Joe's cell phone number and reported her findings.

"Amazing. She just parked it right there in her lot?"

"Someone did." Helen peered up at the illuminated windows. "Do me a favor. Hold off for half an hour or so. Give me a chance to talk to Rosie. The truck may be here, but I doubt Rosie used it in the drive-by."

"Just like she didn't—"

"Pull a gun on me, I know. I have to trust my instincts on this one. By the way, Eleanor told me about the second check Ethan wrote to Rosie. Did you question her about that?"

"Haven't had a chance," Joe said. "Since you're there, why don't you see what you can find out? I'll be there as soon as I can get away. Call if you run into any trouble."

"Of course."

Helen hurried around to the entrance of Rosie's apartment and was about to ring the bell, then stopped, hand poised in midair. If, by some remote possibility, Rosie really was the shooter, seeing her now might not be such a good idea. Helen's next thought wasn't a great idea either, but she needed to know the truth.

She wanted to have a look at Rosie's desk and files. Joe had searched through everything on Monday night. There had been no sign of a second check. Rosie kept her books—both personal and business—in the store. According to Eleanor, Ethan had made the check out on Thursday, before his trip to Washington. Had he given the check to Rosie before he left town? He must have. It made no sense that he'd take it with him. Even if he had, wouldn't he have given it to her on Sunday when he returned? Brian had seen him in Rosie's apartment. Rosie would have had plenty of time to deposit it. Unless she was waiting until things cooled down or had it in another account somewhere.

One thing Helen knew for certain. The authorities hadn't found the check on Ethan's body or in his car. The only things in his pockets were his billfold with credit cards, receipts, a little over a hundred dollars cash, and some change. His car keys were gone, but they had shown up in his car along with Chuck's body. And there had been another set in Alex Jordan's jacket. That second set of keys bugged her. Where had it come from?

Maybe Ethan carried a second set of keys in case he lost the first. That wasn't unheard of. He could have had another set at home—accessible to Nancy, Brian, and Eleanor. Ethan might have had a set in the office, which was accessible to any number of people.

Helen dragged her scattered thoughts back to Rosie and the money she'd received from Ethan. She needed to find out what had happened to that check. If Rosie had gotten it, there would be a record of deposit. She went around to the store entrance and used a credit card to slide open the lock.

Rosie needed a dead bolt and maybe a security system. It was much too easy to break in. Helen had mentioned the lack of security more than once. Though Rosie owned a few rare books and a number of autographed first editions, she didn't seem all that concerned about losing them. Rosie would brush away Helen's suggestion with the wave of a hand and say, *"I'm not worried. If someone wants something bad enough to steal from me, then they must need it more than I do. Besides, nobody breaks into a bookstore."*

Except maybe your son or your best friend. Helen felt anew the conviction that Rosie was innocent. Rosie was being set up, pure and simple.

Objectivity. She had to set her personal feelings for Rosie aside. Once she'd unlocked the door, Helen pushed it open just enough to allow her to slip inside without letting the wind set off the chimes. She quickly closed the door again, then leaned against it and waited for her eyes to adjust. From Rosie's apartment came a familiar television advertisement for an insurance company. The streetlight gave her enough light to find her way around. Hearing a soft thud, she snapped to attention.

Buttermilk wrapped herself around Helen's legs. "You little scamp," she whispered. "You about gave me a heart attack." She reached down to scratch the cat's neck, then straightened and made her way to Rosie's desk. Pulling out her keys, Helen clicked on her penlight and went to work methodically, looking over the stacks of papers on the desk's surface, then sliding open the drawers. She started with the one in the center, the one in which Rosie had kept her gun. It wasn't there and Helen felt a stab of disappointment. She proceeded with her task, rooting through the various papers and supplies. The check wasn't there, nor could she find where it had been deposited in Rosie's personal or business checkbooks.

After thoroughly searching the desk, she snapped off the light again and leaned back in the chair. No deposit for five hundred thousand. Nothing anywhere close. Helen recalled Alex's attempt to clear Rosie by removing any sign of himself from her store. She'd found the one check, but suppose he'd taken the other as well? The deputies hadn't found it on him, but he could have stashed it and whatever else he'd taken into the woods. Or maybe it had escaped his pocket and, like the first one, flown off in another direction.

Then again, Rosie might still have the check upstairs or in her wallet. Helen thought about the bag sitting in Dave's pickup. Was her wallet in there too?

Helen found herself frustrated, confused. How had Rosie's

tote bag gotten there? Rosie would never leave her bag in a ve-hicle with the window down. Especially if she'd just used the vehicle in a drive-by shooting! And the gun sitting there in plain view? Rosie could be forgetful at times and a bit scatter-brained. No, someone had set her up. That was the only an-swer. Someone had left her bag in the truck for the authorities to find.

If that's the case, she asked herself, *how could they have gotten ahold of Rosie's bag and keys? How could they have known about her gun? And why use Dave's pickup?*

She really needed to talk to Rosie.

Helen massaged the stiff muscles in her shoulders. The cat jumped onto her lap, turned around three times, and curled into a ball.

"Sorry, Buttermilk." Helen picked her up and set her on the desk. "No naps tonight. At least not on my lap."

Buttermilk meowed, then batted at a pen, which rolled off and hit the floor.

She then heard a creak on the stairs. Light flooded the room. Helen raised a hand to her forehead to shield her eyes.

"Hold it right there," Rosie ordered. "One move and I'll shoot."

Half expecting Rosie to whip around the corner with gun blazing, Helen ducked under the desk. "Rosie," she called. "Put the gun away. It's just me."

"Helen?" Rosie stepped into the room.

Helen peered over the edge of the desk. Rosie had on flan-nel pajamas and a bathrobe and looked as though she'd been asleep. Pulling her weaponless right hand out of her pocket, she shuffled toward Helen.

"What are you doing here?" Rosie yawned and settled a hip on the desk.

"Looking for evidence." Placing a hand on the desktop, Helen pulled herself up and sat in the desk chair. "Don't you know better than to sneak up on a burglar?"

"You're not a burglar . . . are you?"

"No, but that's beside the point. I could have been." Helen eyed the right pocket of Rosie's bathrobe. "Where's your gun?"

She shrugged. "I don't know. Um . . . it's probably still in my car. Why do you want to know?"

"Where's your car?"

"Up at Dave and Adele's. I had dinner there tonight, and when I went to leave, it wouldn't start. Dave loaned me his pickup and said he'd take a look at my car in the morning."

"Dave loaned you his pickup?" Helen dragged a hand through her hair. She had told Joe the pickup was at Rosie's. "When did you get home?"

"Around seven, seven-thirty." Rosie eyed her suspiciously. "Why all the questions?"

"I'll tell you in a minute. Just bear with me, okay?"

Rosie moved away from the desk and started pacing. "Something else has happened, hasn't it? Another murder?"

Helen shook her head. "Are you sure you were home by seven-thirty?"

"I was. I remember. I started watching *Wheel of Fortune*."

"Did you go out after that?"

"Um . . . no." She stopped at the espresso bar. "Want a cup?"

"No—yes." Helen pushed out of the chair and joined Rosie in the coffee nook. "Are you sure?"

"Sure of what?"

"That you didn't go anywhere." Helen glanced out the window, wondering what was keeping Joe.

Rosie glanced at her, then focused on opening the bag of coffee. "Too tired. I brought in my groceries and put away the yogurt. Then I watched television and read the paper for about ten minutes and fell asleep. I just woke up a few minutes ago and realized the cats were still downstairs." She set the coffee bag back in the cupboard. "What's going on? Why all the questions?"

"I wish I knew. Someone driving Dave's truck slowed down by the seawall where George and I were walking and tried to pump us full of bullets."

Rosie's eyes flashed. "Dave's truck . . . ?" Her hand flew to her chest. "Oh . . ." Her mouth flopped opened and closed again, but nothing came out. She staggered to the nearest chair and collapsed. "You think I . . . ?"

"I've been trying very hard not to."

"Is that why you were down here snooping around? You were looking for evidence to prove I did it?"

"More to prove you didn't. I'm really trying to believe you didn't have anything to do with this, Rosie, but it's getting harder all the time."

Frown lines creased her forehead. "You said someone shot at you and George. But you're okay. You didn't get hurt? Is he . . . ?"

"He'll be okay." Helen explained what had happened.

"What about Dave's truck? If anything happens to it, he'll have a fit."

"It's here, parked in back with the keys still in it."

"Keys . . . oh no. I had my house keys on another chain. I forgot all about those."

"Your gun is there too—along with your bag."

Rosie bounced to her feet. "But how . . . ?" Her hands flew to her face. "Oh no . . . Helen, I forgot to bring my bag in. I brought in the groceries and was going to make a second trip. I can't believe I did that."

Helen placed both hands on Rosie's shoulders. "Sit. I'll finish the coffee and we'll talk about it. Just calm down."

"But we have to get it. I can't leave that stuff out there. It might get stol—"

"Too late for that. At this point, it's evidence. Maybe there are prints other than yours and Dave's in the truck. It's better if we don't touch anything."

"Did you call Joe?"

"Yes. He should be here any minute. I'm surprised they haven't been here already. Someone from the department should have had someone questioning Dave right after the shooting."

"He's not home. He and Adele went to the casino. They were having a jazz concert there tonight."

"Still, you'd think if your car was there, they'd make an obvious connection."

"It wasn't parked by the house. I got about a block away before it conked out."

"How convenient," Helen murmured. "Once they find out you have that pickup, they're sure to arrest you."

"But I didn't do anything." Rosie folded her arms on her desk and rested her head on them.

Helen put the coffee on, then borrowed a note pad and pen from Rosie's desk. She pulled a chair out from one of the tables and started making notes. She had to get things in some sort of order, and often writing the events and suspects down helped put things into perspective.

"Okay," Helen said, "let's start with the checks Ethan gave you."

"I told you about that." Rosie wrapped her arms around herself. "And it was only one."

"Ethan wrote you a check dated last Thursday for five hundred thousand. Are you saying he never gave it to you?"

"No." She frowned. "Why would he give me that kind of money?"

"Blackmail?"

"That's ridiculous!" Rosie began pacing, rubbing her arms. "To blackmail someone you need dirt from someone's past. Ethan didn't have any secrets."

"He didn't?"

"He wasn't ashamed of Alex."

"Is it possible that Ethan planned to offer you more money to keep quiet? You were having an affair with him. Maybe he thought it over and decided he didn't want people to know about your relationship or about Alex."

"He was excited about meeting Alex," Rosie insisted. "He seemed a little worried Sunday night, but he didn't say anything about keeping it quiet."

"What about your affair?"

"It wasn't an affair. We made a mistake. We decided that night not to see each other privately anymore. He came by Sunday night to tell me that he had no intention of leaving Eleanor or breaking up his family."

Helen shuddered. Rosie had motive after all. "That must have hurt you—losing Ethan twice like that."

"Of course it did, but I knew from the start that we couldn't be together. I never intended to break up their marriage."

"I find that hard to believe. Brian Crane said he saw you and Ethan Sunday night. 'Making out' were his exact words."

"Oh no." Rosie covered her face.

"Were you lying to me about breaking it off with Ethan?"

"No." Fresh tears streamed down her cheeks. "He—we were saying good-bye. That's all. Just a kiss good-bye. If Brian saw us . . . oh, Helen. Do you think he could have killed Ethan?"

"He says he didn't. He admitted to wanting to kill both of you but says he went for a walk instead. When he came back by here, the lights were out. He drove by the restaurant, but his dad's car was already gone."

"And you believe him?"

"I don't know. He wasn't lying about being at Annie's tonight, so he wasn't involved in the shooting."

"M-maybe they're not related."

"They have to be." Helen got up to get their coffee while Rosie set out mugs and a plate of biscotti.

"Maybe Brian has someone working with him—his sister . . ." Rosie sat down again and clasped her hands. "Eleanor could be in on it with him. If she knew about Ethan and me, it's no telling what she'd do."

"She did know. She's known for a long time. I really think if she wanted revenge, she'd have done it when she first found out."

"She must hate me."

"She probably does. And I don't blame her. You had an affair with her husband. Anyway, we've already been over that ground. If she did kill Ethan, how would she have gotten the letter opener? You said yourself she never comes into the store."

"She could have broken in."

"Not likely." Helen told Rosie about Eleanor's generosity toward Alex. "She doesn't seem to resent him."

"I don't know what to say. I didn't expect any of them to accept Alex, certainly not Eleanor." Rosie smiled. "Shows how wrong you can be about people. I guess I shouldn't be surprised. Ethan told me they would all come around."

"Maybe he was right. It's entirely possible we're too focused on the family to see the other players." Helen flipped to a fresh piece of paper and began jotting down events on the yellow note pad.

> 1.. *Sunday night—Ethan murdered. Killer drives Ethan's car to Kernville Road and ditches it into the river with Chuck's body inside. Walks back or has someone pick him up.*
> 2. *Monday—Ethan's body found. Family told. Rosie panics and runs.*
> 3. *Lynn reports Chuck missing.*

"What are you doing?"

"Making a time line. Once I do that, I'll place people into slots. That way I can see who might have had opportunity, the method, and the means to commit the crimes. I'm missing something important. And this may help."

> 4. *Monday night—Alex breaks into Past Times and is arrested.*
> 5. *Tuesday—Chuck's body found in Ethan's car.*
> 6. *Tuesday night—drive-by shooting.*

"You got home around seven-thirty tonight, right?"

Rosie nodded.

"George and I were at the restaurant then. We left shortly after eight-thirty and parked at the seawall so we could talk privately about the investigation. We'd only been walking a short time when I noticed Dave's truck. I assumed it was Dave, but before I could get a good look, the driver started firing at us. A guy from one of the apartments heard the shots and called the sheriff's office."

"Who knew you were there besides me?" Rosie broke a cookie in half and dipped a portion into her coffee.

Helen frowned. "You knew we were there? How?" Rosie had already left the scene at the river when Helen and George had agreed to eat dinner together.

"I saw your car parked at Tidal Raves on my way home from the grocery store." Rosie paused with her biscotti an inch from her open mouth. "I didn't do it, Helen. You're my best friend."

Helen tapped the pen on the pad. "George asked me to dinner when we were watching them pull Ethan's car out of the river. So whoever was there heard us talking. Stephanie, Joe, Tom. While we were at the restaurant, Eleanor and her family came in—and left."

"Could one of them have done it?"

"They left early enough, I suppose, but Brian went straight to Annie's. She backed up his alibi," Helen added before Rosie could comment.

"Brian and Annie? What happened to Joe?"

"Don't ask." Helen waved her biscotti in the air and steered the conversation back on track. "Eleanor and the girls left the restaurant right after Brian did."

Rosie chewed on her lip. "What about Nancy?"

"I went to the Cranes' place shortly after the shooting, and Eleanor told me they'd come home and made a light dinner there. I don't think either Nancy or Eleanor would have had time to go home to drop the others off, come back here, steal Dave's truck, then go back to the seawall to shoot at us." She shook her head. "Makes no sense."

"Well . . ." Rosie bit her lower lip. "Someone did take my letter opener so it would look like I killed Ethan. They must have wanted to implicate me in this too."

Helen sighed. "So they steal your brother-in-law's truck and try to kill George and me. There's no way the authorities are going to buy your story. I don't even buy it."

"What do you mean? They have to. I'm not a killer—you know that. Neither is Alex. And this proves it, doesn't it? Alex is still in jail. So he couldn't have been the one who shot at you, which means he couldn't have killed Ethan."

But you could have. Helen breathed a sigh of relief as she caught a glimpse of blue flashing lights.

Twenty-five

W e have to talk." Helen spoke to Joe when one of his deputies led Rosie outside. It almost made Helen cry to see Rosie so subdued and giving up without a fight.

"I'll say." Joe shot her another disappointed look.

Helen sighed. "She didn't do it, Joe. Can't you see that?"

"What I see is some pretty compelling evidence saying she did. Now my job is to put it all together. I like Rosie, but you gotta look at the facts."

"If Rosie were going to kill someone, do you honestly think she'd use her own letter opener? Or her gun? Or her brother-in-law's pickup? My goodness, the path to her door couldn't have been better marked if it had been done by Girl Scouts on a camping trip."

"Not every bad guy is a brain surgeon. You have to admit Rosie hasn't been running on a full tank of gas lately. Pulling her gun on you the other day is proof enough of that. And this business of forgetting her bag and keys in the pickup is just plain nonsense. That gun has recently been fired. There was a check in her wallet for five hundred thousand. No way would she forget about that. She's either lying or developing Alzheimer's."

"Or she's telling the truth, and someone is going to great lengths to frame her."

"Who?" He snorted. "One of the Cranes? I don't think so."

"What about Nancy?"

"All Nancy cares about is herself. I don't think she's been

sober enough to add two and two together since she got to Bay Village."

"Are you sure about that? Maybe we've underestimated Nancy's abilities."

Joe shook his head. "She's got an alibi for Sunday night. She was in her room drinking and watching television."

"She could have sneaked out."

"Melissa corroborated her mother's story."

Helen decided not to argue the point. "There are other suspects. I talked to the attorney representing the developers for the Riverside Mall."

"You mean Nathan Young?"

"You talked to him?" Helen was surprised. But then why shouldn't he have interviewed the lawyer? Joe had always been thorough.

"Of course. Not long after you did."

"Did he give you the names of the investors?"

"No. Client confidentiality. When I pressed him and threatened a subpoena, he gave me the three names he had in his file. Only one was local, but I haven't had a chance to talk to her yet."

"Are you going to tell me who she is?"

"Lynn Daniels."

"Chuck's wife? Doesn't that strike you as odd?" Helen's heart beat a little faster. Could Lynn be their killer?

"Not really. The attorney told me that to register as a corporation, they needed to list three officers—the CEO, secretary, and the treasurer."

"Who were the others?"

"The secretary was a woman named Elsie Turner from Portland. Lynn was listed as the treasurer. Can't remember the name of the CEO. I've got it in my notes if you want it."

"Please."

Joe took a small note pad out of his left front shirt pocket and flipped back a few pages. "Here it is . . . Jonathan Meyers." His gaze narrowed as it moved to her. "If you're thinking Lynn might be involved in the murders, you're wrong. I've already talked to her."

"And she has an alibi?"

Joe gave her a withering look. "Sunday night, she left the restaurant about the time Ethan and Alex came in. Went straight home. Her kids corroborated her statement. Told me their mom made popcorn and watched *Touched by an Angel* with them."

"And after that? We don't have the exact time of death, do we?"

"Not exactly. Ethan left the restaurant around eight. No one remembers seeing him after that. Chuck's watch stopped at nine-forty-five. We figure Ethan and Alex took a walk on the beach. Sunday night was pretty balmy, as you recall."

She did recall—quite well, actually. She and J.B. had walked along the beach at Foggarty Creek State Park. Though she wouldn't have called it balmy, it had been nice: clear sky, around sixty degrees, and a light breeze. J.B.'s kisses had made it feel like a night in the tropics. Helen blinked away the intrusive thoughts and focused back on Joe.

"They argued," Joe went on. "Alex killed him and left his body lying in the sand. I'm thinking he might have run into Chuck when he started to take off in Ethan's car. Chuck tried to stop him, so Alex had to kill him too. Took him up the river and pushed the car into the water, then walked back to get his car."

"That's a long way. Wouldn't someone have seen him?"

"Maybe, but no one responded to our requests for information. It's possible he cut through the woods, but a lot of that area is marshland. That's where Rosie comes in. Alex denies it, but I'm thinking he asked her to meet him out there. That would explain why she panicked when you told her about Ethan. She may not have known about the murders."

"It's hard to believe she'd go to such lengths to protect a man she'd only just met."

"He's her son. If it makes you feel any better, I don't think she was in on killing Ethan or Chuck. I think Alex did that. She might have pulled that drive-by to take suspicion off Alex."

"And frame herself?"

Joe rubbed his eyes. He looked beat. "I don't have time for

guessing games. All I can do is assure you that I'm not going to stop looking until I have all the holes filled with the right pegs. Okay?"

Helen nodded. "I guess it has to be."

"Good. Now get out of here. You look terrible."

"Thanks."

When she reached the door, Joe called out, "Tell J.B. I said hello."

Helen didn't bother to respond.

Exhausted, she climbed into her car. George would be out of surgery by now. Though the cold air and coffee had revived her some, by the time she got to the outskirts of Bay Village, she could hardly keep her eyes open. The hospital visit would have to wait until morning.

She pulled into her driveway at two A.M., narrowly missing the back end of J.B.'s car.

"I do not want to deal with him tonight," she muttered between clenched teeth. Maybe he'd be upstairs asleep. She'd go in quietly and sleep on the couch. Better to have it out with him in the morning. Considering the foul mood she was in at the moment, she might say things they'd both regret.

With a prayer for courage and strength, she let herself in.

"It's late." Though he had said it softly, his baritone voice filled the room. Without turning on the light, he rose from the couch and came toward her. "Where have you been?"

"I might ask you the same question." She hung her keys on the peg by the door. When he reached for her, she moved aside to set her bag in the closet and hang up her coat.

"You're not still angry with me, are you, luv?" he crooned in that lovely voice of his.

"Shouldn't I be?" Though her body ached to feel his arms around her, she stepped around him and headed for the kitchen.

He followed her. "You know how it is. In my line of work—"

"Work? Don't give me that. You're retired. You had lunch with a woman. An attractive young woman who seemed to think you were fair game."

She switched on the light and captured the shocked look on his face. Good.

Then he had the audacity to smile as if he appreciated her detecting skills. "How did you find out about that?"

"It doesn't matter." She went to the cupboard to retrieve a glass of water. "What matters is that you lied to me."

"I've never lied to you."

"No, I suppose that's true enough. You just don't bother to tell me anything."

"You're jealous." The idea seemed to please him.

Helen ran the water, watching it drain into the black hole.

He came up behind her, enveloping her in his arms. Her legs melted like wax left in the sun. "Don't touch me." She concentrated on filling her glass.

He pressed his lips against the back of her neck. "Come now, luv. You can't mean it."

Helen slammed the glass on the counter and jabbed her elbow into his stomach. "I said don't touch me."

Clutching his stomach, he groaned and staggered backward, nearly knocking over a chair. He managed to right it, then leaned over the kitchen table, trying to catch his breath.

Helen rushed to his side. What had she done? He looked as though he were having another heart attack. "Oh, J.B., I'm so sorry. I didn't mean . . ."

Red-faced, he sucked in a breath and lowered himself onto a chair. "I can't . . . believe you . . . did that," he managed to say.

"Are you all right?"

He nodded. "Give me a minute."

J.B. became a blur as her eyes filled with tears. She moved away so he couldn't see. With her back to him, she dabbed at the tears with a napkin, then drank the entire glass of water.

When she'd gathered herself together and trusted herself to speak, she turned back to him. "I need answers, J.B. You can't leave me in the lurch like this and expect me to simply fall into your arms when you come back home."

"She was an agent." J.B.'s tone hinted at anger.

"Who?"

"The woman I was with."

"An agent? You . . . you went back to work? Without telling me?"

"Not exactly. I don't know what you're so upset about. I phoned you."

"Which told me nothing. I had visions of you going through surgery, being diagnosed with some dreaded disease. You were so secretive."

"My health is fine. The doctor said I could resume my activities."

"How was I to know that? All I knew was that you got a phone call and it changed everything. You shut me out, J.B. All I could think about was that your doctor had called with results of your tests. Then I find out you're having lunch with a younger woman. You should have told me something—anything to let me know what you were up to."

"Not then. I had no choice. I still can't tell you what it was all about. You know how it is."

"Not anymore. You're retired. You had a heart attack, remember? There was no reason for me to think you'd gone back to work. I admit that was my immediate reaction, but I figured there's no way they'd put you back in the field. They shouldn't have—"

"I didn't go back to work as an agent, Helen. I wouldn't have done that without talking to you first."

"Then what?"

"I'm on call as a consultant." He stood and held his hand out to her. "That's all I can tell you at the moment. You trusted me once. Why can't you do that now?"

His compelling blue eyes with their loving gaze shattered her defenses. "Consultant to whom and for what? Can't you at least tell me that?"

"Not yet."

"She was an agent?"

He nodded.

Again Helen looked him in the eyes. God help her, she did trust him. Implicitly. She'd never liked the secrecy his job often demanded, but she understood the need for it. Helen put her hand in his. "Let's go to bed."

He released her hand and gathered her into his arms. "I thought you'd never ask."

✢   ✢   ✢

Helen waited until morning to call George. He was doing fine and would be released in a couple of days. While she and J.B. ate breakfast, she told him about Ethan and Chuck. He listened sympathetically, occasionally asking for clarification.

When she'd finished, he remained silent for a while, then said, "Sounds as though this son of Rosie's—if that's what he is—has a way with the women, eh?"

"What do you mean?"

"Rosie was completely taken in. You tell me you think he's innocent. This new deputy—"

"Stephanie."

"Right. She's sympathetic to him as well. And Eleanor and Lynn . . ."

"Are you suggesting I let the man's charm color my thinking?"

"Not at all. I'm merely making an observation. Did Joe tell you whether or not his prints turned up anything?"

"He didn't mention it."

"Tell you what. I'll get one of the FBI agents in Portland to check him out. Send his photo around if Joe hasn't already done it. We should be able to find out in short order whether or not he's a phony."

"Don't you think Joe has already done that?"

"To some extent, yes. I would imagine he's gotten the process started, but with the department's limited resources, they won't have the manpower or the time to run a thorough check."

Helen and J.B. stopped by the sheriff's department on their way to see Rosie.

Joe welcomed the FBI's involvement in the investigation. "He's apparently had no prior arrests, and we haven't been able to match up his prints. I sent out a photo to law-enforcement agencies in Portland but haven't heard anything back yet."

Stephanie tapped on Joe's office door. "Sorry to bother you,

Joe, but I think you might want to see this." She handed Joe a manila folder.

While Joe looked over the contents of the file, Helen introduced Stephanie to J.B. Stephanie shook hands with him, then turned to Helen. "Looks like we were wrong about Jordan, Mrs. Bradley. He's not Rosie's son."

Twenty-six

The news wasn't a total surprise. Helen had wondered about Alex Jordan's authenticity from the start. Still, the man had charmed her and she resented it. "Does Rosie know?"

"Not yet."

"If you don't mind," Helen said, "I'd like to tell her."

Joe nodded. "Thanks. I wasn't relishing the task."

"I'll need the details."

"No problem." Joe leaned forward, resting his arms on the desk. "I thought it might be a good idea to check out Jordan's claim, so I asked Stephanie to do a search on the Internet. As you know, I've had doubts about him all along."

Stephanie closed the office door and leaned against it. "I accessed birth records and found that the birth certificate Alex gave Rosie is legitimate. Even the name is right. The baby Rosie gave up for adoption went to Charles and Evelyn Jordan. I called them, and they assured me that their son has not been searching for his birth mother. Doesn't even know he was adopted. He's happily married with three kids and living in Tucson."

"How did you locate them so quickly?" Helen asked.

"I went through the agencies who link people up to their birth parents. One of the agencies, Adoption Link, had already tracked them down. They said they'd gotten an inquiry from the birth mother about two months ago. The agency contacted the Jordans, who asked that no one try to contact their son. The agency said Rosie thanked them for trying and agreed not to pursue the matter. Here's the kicker. Rosie says she never tried to find her son."

"Which means Alex went on-line posing as Rosie."

"Looks that way." Stephanie unfolded her arms. "We e-mailed the Jordans a photo of our Alex. They said he definitely wasn't their son and had never seen him before."

"You're certain you have the right people?" Helen asked.

"I'm sure," Stephanie said.

"I have a feeling Rosie isn't the first person he's conned." Joe handed Helen the file. "Proving it may not be that easy." He nodded at the folder. "You'll want to show this to Rosie. There's a picture of her real son in there. Funny, Alex looks more like Ethan's kid than he does."

J.B. looked at the report over Helen's shoulder. "Helen tells me you have this Jordan fellow pegged as your killer."

"I did." Joe pulled a file from the side of his desk to the center and opened it. "After reading the reports this morning, I'm not so sure. Unfortunately, we don't have the kind of evidence that will stand up in trial. We can't prove he was the last person to see Ethan alive. Nor can we prove he had Rosie's letter opener. Jordan says he left the restaurant while Ethan was still inside paying the bill. The waitress confirms that. As it stands now, we can't even charge him with breaking and entering. Rosie told us he had a key and refused to press charges."

"How did Alex's jacket get into Ethan's car?" Helen took a small spiral notebook and pen from her bag and began making notes.

"Jordan claimed their jackets got switched at the restaurant. They were both a brown leather. He didn't realize he had Ethan's jacket until he got home. He drove back to the restaurant. Says when he got there Ethan's car was still parked in the same place. He figured Ethan must have called someone and gotten a ride home. Jordan went back home and called Ethan to tell him he had the jacket, but no one answered the phone."

"We know Eleanor was in church. Where were Nancy and Melissa?"

"Melissa says she had her earphones in and was listening to her CDs and hanging out in her room. Nancy claims she was in her room reading and didn't hear it ring."

Helen wrote both names and entered their alibis. "I'm sorry, you were telling us about Ethan's jacket."

"Alex told us he decided to wait until morning and take the jacket to Ethan at his office. Claims he didn't go out again that night—just watched some television and went to bed. We can't prove or disprove his statement. We do know that he showed up at the mayor's office Monday morning and left Ethan's jacket with the secretary. It was there when we searched the place, but nobody paid much attention to it at the time. We didn't pick up the jacket until yesterday."

"Which means Ethan must have called someone to pick him up at the restaurant."

"Or Alex is lying. I'm still not ruling him out as a suspect. Ethan did make a couple of phone calls. We were able to access the calls he made on his cell phone that night. At 8:50 he made a call to Rosie. At 8:53 he called a locksmith."

"He didn't call home?" J.B. asked.

"It was Sunday night," Joe answered. "He probably knew Eleanor would be in church—which she was."

"If he called a locksmith, Rosie must not have been home." Helen tapped the tip of the pen against the pad.

"She wasn't. My guess is that she had already gone to the restaurant. I still haven't ruled out the possibility that she and Alex were working together in this. She was under the impression that Alex was her son. We have to consider the money involved here as well."

Over the next couple of days, J.B.'s sources located six women who identified Alex as the son they'd given up at birth. In each case he'd provided a copy of what looked like an original birth certificate and claimed to want nothing other than to get to know them. Each of the women, like Rosie, was unmarried. The women were fifty-five and older, and in each case, at least one of the birth parents had a substantial income. The "son" showed up wanting nothing but eventually ending up with large sums of money through inheritances. None of the cases involved murder, but as Joe said, there's always a first time.

After his initial contact, Alex would stay in town for several months, then move on, promising to keep in touch. Which he did with phone calls and letters until one or both of the "birth parents" died. He'd then be notified, go to the funeral, and come out with an inheritance—some small, others substantial.

"People like me provide a service," Alex had admitted. *"I'm not doing anything wrong—just putting some happiness into their lives."*

So far they had found none of his mothers willing to press charges.

⚜   ⚜   ⚜

Rosie was anything but happy when Helen visited her in jail later that day.

"Are you sure he's not my son?" Rosie had already gone through a dozen tissues and was working her way through a new box. "He looks so much like Ethan."

"Maybe that's because you wanted him to." Helen put a comforting arm around Rosie's shoulders. "He's very good at what he does, Rosie. He's a patient man and very convincing. A number of people were taken in by him, and we've probably just skimmed the tip of the iceberg. We're fortunate to have learned the truth about him when we did. Who knows how much he'd have gotten away with? Eleanor was ready to give him close to a million dollars."

"I . . . I suppose you're right." Rosie blew her nose. "It's just . . . I loved having a son. Now I find out my real son doesn't want to see me."

"He doesn't know you exist. Maybe that will change."

"I feel so used, Helen. I put my life on the line for Alex. He asked me if I would help prove his innocence. That if I didn't do something, he'd be sent to prison for life. He thought if there was another incident, they'd know he couldn't have done it and they'd have to let him go."

Helen's mind raced over Rosie's words as she bounced to her feet. "What are you saying? The drive-by? You did that?"

"Nobody was supposed to get hurt. I aimed clear away from

you. The bullets were supposed to go over your heads."

"Then you are one lousy shot, lady!" Helen fumed.

"Um . . . I was going to do it when you came out of the restaurant. I was waiting across the street, but . . . I couldn't. I was so scared. I was afraid I'd hit the windows or one of the cars in the parking lot. I followed you far enough to see what you were doing and . . . and finally worked up enough nerve to . . ." She winced.

"I can't believe this!" Helen paced back and forth across Rosie's cell. "How could you do something so . . . so . . . crazy?"

"I don't know. All I wanted to do was help my son. It sounded so simple when Alex told me what to do. It would have been fine if I hadn't been driving that dumb truck. The shocks are horrible. I really wasn't shooting at you."

"You could have fooled me." Helen stopped pacing and, with arms folded, stood in front of Rosie. "George was seriously injured. And didn't it occur to you that we might be able to identify Dave's pickup? Or that the evidence would lead back to you? That would probably have happened even if you *hadn't* forgotten to take your bag in with you. What were you thinking?"

Rosie pressed her hands to her eyes. "Apparently I wasn't."

"You've got that right!" Helen forced herself to take a long, steady breath.

"I'm sorry. I'm so sorry."

"What about the check, Rosie? The one for five hundred thousand that was in your wallet? Were you lying about that too?"

She looked up briefly, clasping and unclasping her hands. "I don't know how it got there. I honestly don't. Ethan may have put it in there Sunday night. He knew I wouldn't take it. But it wouldn't be unlike him to try. Maybe he meant for Alex to have it."

"Maybe he did. I guess we'll never know for certain." Helen signaled for the guard to let her out. "Have you called your attorney yet?"

Rosie nodded. "I talked to her last night."

"Then I suggest you talk to her again. This time you'd better tell her the truth."

"I would never purposely hurt you, Helen. Or George either." She held out her hand. "I'm sorry."

Helen didn't know whether to hug Rosie or hit her. She looked so pathetic that Helen relented and took hold of Rosie's proffered hand. "I'm sorry too, Rosie."

"You'll still be my friend, won't you?"

"I have to go. J.B.'s waiting for me."

Rosie gave Helen a teary smile. "He came back, then. I knew he would."

"I guess deep down I knew it too."

After promising Rosie she'd come back the next day, Helen joined J.B. in the waiting area. He took one look at her and wrapped her in his arms. Several moments later she stepped away. "Thank you."

He raised an eyebrow in question.

"For not saying I told you so."

"Ah, lass. The man's a pro. Smooth as silk, he is. After talking to him, I can understand why you'd think him innocent. He's a con man, but I'm with ye all the way about the killing. His MO doesn't fit. Joe's right in saying there could be a first time. But I don't think so. Far as we can tell, he's never physically harmed anyone. Nor is he likely to. He's still swearing he had nothing to do with those two deaths, and I believe him."

Helen squeezed his hand. "I'm not sure I do. I don't even know about Rosie. I should talk to him again."

"He's gone. Released on bail."

Helen didn't know how she felt about that. For the moment she'd had enough of the entire affair. When J.B. suggested they take a walk on the beach and then have dinner in Lincoln City, Helen couldn't have been more pleased.

⚜   ⚜   ⚜

The next morning, the phone rang while Helen and J.B. were eating breakfast. Helen answered. It was Joe.

"Thought you two would want to know. There's been another murder."

"Oh no. I'm almost afraid to ask."

"Alex Jordan. A hiker found his body this morning up by Drift Creek Trail."

Twenty-seven

A shes to ashes. Dust to dust."

Helen only half listened to the pastor's words. This was her third funeral in as many days. Ethan, Chuck, and now Alex, or whoever he was. So far they hadn't been able to come up with his real name.

About twenty people had gathered around the gravesite. Helen recognized some of them as co-workers from Chuck's construction company. They'd come to know Alex as a hard worker, a man they could depend on. Even though the news media had exposed him as a fraud, the people who had met and worked with him felt a deep loss at his passing. While most came because he had touched their lives in some way, others were there out of curiosity. Eleanor hadn't come, nor had Nancy or Brian, but Helen would have been surprised if they'd shown up. When Eleanor found out about Alex's duplicity, she dismissed him. She would, however, set aside a portion of Ethan's estate for Ethan and Rosie's real son if and when the Jordans decided to reveal his past to him.

Helen recognized most of the people there. But there was one who stood off by herself.

Joe had been eyeing her as well. He'd undoubtedly catch up with her when the funeral ended.

"What a waste," Lynn Daniels whispered to Helen after the pastor had offered the final prayer, and they had all responded with an *amen*. "He was such a likeable man."

"Yes, he was," Helen agreed. *Con artists often are.*

"And dependable." Lynn's red-rimmed eyes filled with fresh tears. She dabbed at the corner of her left eye. "As soon as he got out of jail, he called me and said he'd be able to work the next day if I still wanted him."

"Really?"

"I told him I did, only he never got the chance." Her watery gaze drifted downward to Rosie who was sitting in the only chair. She'd been released on bail shortly after Helen's visit. "Rosie, honey, I'm so sorry. He was a good person."

Helen didn't comment. She was still angry at Alex for duping all of them. For that matter, she was still pretty upset with Rosie. Rosie's actions had damaged a good friendship. Helen doubted it would ever be the same. Still, with Rosie being so distraught, Helen couldn't abandon her. She'd see her through the upcoming trial for her part in the drive-by shooting and see what happened.

Helen backed away from the mourners and looked around for the woman she'd seen earlier. There was no sign of her or Joe.

J.B. put an arm around her. "Are you ready to go home, luv?"

She nodded. The two of them half carried Rosie to J.B.'s car and tucked her into the backseat. She would spend the day at Helen's house. Hers, she'd said, was too big and empty.

On the way home, Helen leaned her head back against the headrest and closed her eyes.

❖   ❖   ❖

Despite efforts to determine his true identity, the man who had just been buried as Alex Jordan remained a mystery. The woman at the funeral, Joe told them later, was just a curious onlooker. No link that he could see.

Alex had come to Bay Village with little more than a phony driver's license, the birth certificate he'd claimed as his own, and a few articles of clothing. Nothing to link him to the past. He'd purchased his van in Portland with cash. In fact, he'd paid cash for everything, including the rent on his small furnished bungalow at the south end of Lincoln City.

Circulating his photo on television and the Internet hadn't

produced a single lead as to who the man really was. They'd only turned up two more people identifying him as the man they'd come to know as a son or half brother. In each case, the victims of his scam were surprised to learn he'd lied to them. J.B. assured Helen that his department would be able to trace him eventually. She believed they would, but not soon enough to suit her.

Not knowing who he was or where he'd come from didn't bother Helen half as much as not knowing who killed him and why. He'd been shot, a single bullet through the head. Close range. The shooter had been sitting in the passenger seat of his van. Which meant he probably knew his assailant.

According to the police report, Alex had received a large sum of money over the last few weeks. His weekly paycheck, which he always cashed at the grocery store, had provided more than enough to live on. A teller at a local bank remembered him cashing the hundred-thousand-dollar check from Rosie and had even called Rosie for verification. The teller paid him in thousand-dollar bills, which he'd placed in a battered brown leather briefcase and then put in the back of his van. It was money the authorities had yet to locate.

Though he'd had no checking account, he kept detailed records of his income and expenditures in a long, narrow journal, beginning at the first of the year. There were no names to indicate the source of income. The expense side of the journal varied, except for two items. One was the five hundred dollars for rent. Another, which simply read "payment" for twenty-two hundred dollars, went out the first of each month.

His last entry, dated November thirteenth, was for ten thousand dollars, listed under income. That was on Monday—the day Helen found Ethan's body. With it, he had a balance of over a quarter of a million dollars.

J.B. looked at a Xerox copy of the logbook Joe handed him and whistled. "That's a lot of cash to be carrying around."

"He had a stash somewhere." Joe took a piece of garlic bread from the basket and passed it on to Rosie. "We just haven't been able to find it."

Annie had invited Joe, Rosie, Helen, and J.B. to dinner following Alex's funeral. She offered to cook the dinner if Helen would provide the house. They'd gathered in the formal dining room, and the conversation had naturally drifted to the investigation.

"Personally," Joe went on, "I think he had a partner. They'd planned to meet and split the take. Only his partner didn't want to share."

"Or," J.B. added, "this partner got spooked and feared Alex might talk."

Helen had other ideas. "He may have hidden it somewhere—maybe a storage shed or locker or some such thing. I doubt he'd carry it around with him."

Joe shook his head. "There would have been a key or a rental agreement. We didn't find anything like that in either his house or his van."

Helen considered that for a moment. "Rosie, did Alex say anything about a special account or what he might be going to do with the check you gave him?"

Rosie didn't answer at first. She looked up at Helen with a dazed expression. Helen repeated the question.

"I can't think of anything. Maybe he gave the money to someone," Rosie said. "He struck me as that sort of person. He lived so frugally. Maybe he sent the money to a wife—or a mother . . . or sister. Someone who . . . who needed a lot of medical care. He wouldn't have resorted to conning people if he'd had another choice."

Joe jabbed his knife into the butter. "I wish you'd quit trying to defend him, Rosie. The man was a crook."

"I can't help it. There was something good about him. I sensed it. He had a secret side, but . . ."

"He had a secret side all right—a dark one," Joe grumped.

"Maybe he buried the money somewhere." Annie set a bowl of hot, steaming pasta on the table, then turned to go back to the kitchen for the sauce. "It's kind of exciting when you think about it. Maybe he'll become a legend like D. B. Cooper. Remember, he's the guy who hijacked a plane and bailed out somewhere over Lake Merwin."

"Let's hope not." Joe speared a few lettuce leaves. "We'll have fortune hunters crawling all over the place."

"He had a checkbook." Rosie stared at her water glass. "I saw it once. When I gave him the hundred thousand, he took the checkbook out of his shirt pocket and set the check inside. He was so thankful and seemed relieved. As if he had some sort of large debt. He hugged me and said, 'Thanks, Mom. You don't know how much this means to me.'"

"I'll bet." Joe stuffed another bite of salad into his mouth.

"Joe," Annie said, with a warning in her voice. "Be nice. You can't expect Rosie to turn her feelings around just like that. She thought he was her son."

Helen and J.B. exchanged glances. Neither of them had been especially anxious to host the dinner. Helen thought it might be good for Rosie to be around friends. She'd tried to steer their conversation to safer ground a number of times, but it always shifted back to the murder investigations.

"You're right, honey," Joe said. "I'm sorry, Rosie. I just hate to see you taken advantage of."

"Excuse me." Tears filled Rosie's eyes. She pushed back her chair and left the room.

"I'd better check on her." Helen got up and followed Rosie out. She'd been on the edge for days. Too many losses. Too much grief.

The bathroom door was ajar so Helen eased it open. Rosie sat on the closed toilet lid, mopping up her tears. "I'm sorry, Helen. I can't seem to stop crying."

"That's understandable."

"I'm ruining your dinner party."

"Not much of a party. Anyway, that's the least of my worries. I just wish there was something I could do to help you through this."

"There isn't." She sniffled and blew her nose. "Well, finding the real killer would help. And maybe finding out who Alex really was. I need to know."

"So do I, Rosie." She settled a hand on Rosie's shoulder. "Can I get you anything?"

"No. Just let me sit here for a few minutes. I need to pull myself together."

Helen took a washcloth out of the linen closet and set it beside the sink. "In case you want to wash your face."

"Thank you." Rosie lowered her hands and looked up at her friend. "And thanks for sticking by me. I know I'm acting like a baby, but . . ."

"You don't have to explain. Grief is what it is. You've been through a lot lately."

"It might be best if I just go home."

"I wish you wouldn't . . . I hate for you to be alone. Why don't you go upstairs and lie down in the guest room for a few minutes?"

"M-maybe I will."

Helen closed the door and then joined the others at the table. They ate in uncomfortable silence for several minutes. At least the others ate. Helen just moved the food around on her plate.

J.B. spooned Annie's marinara-mushroom sauce over his noodles. "Just wish we had more to go on."

"The dental records should show us something," Joe said as he sprinkled freshly grated Parmesan on his spaghetti. "Dr. Sperling said his teeth had been worked on recently."

Dr. Sperling had come in to replace George, who'd gone to a rehab facility in Portland. Sperling had completed the autopsy report of the three victims, concurring with George on Ethan's stab wound. It turned out that Chuck had died from a cocaine overdose; he was dead before the Jaguar plunged into the river. There were traces of the drug in the empty liquor bottle. Helen felt certain he hadn't put it there himself.

"Possibly," J.B. said with regard to the dental records. "If he used his real name."

"I'm glad the FBI is in on this investigation," Joe said. "We just don't have the resources. It's all I can do to get a handle on the crimes happening in our own county."

"You need more funds." Annie swirled several strands of spaghetti around her fork.

"I've been saying that for years," agreed Joe. "Things should be getting better, though. With the new shopping mall going in, we'll get a fair amount of revenue from the new businesses."

Helen folded her napkin and set it on the table. "The proposal went through?"

"Passed city council by a landslide. The attorney for the corporation managed to convince everyone that the wildlife area was not in jeopardy and that the benefits far outweighed the negatives."

"I should have been there," Helen said. "I missed the notice in the paper."

"It's no wonder, luv, with all you've been doing these past few days. I'm not at all surprised. Last I talked to Ethan, he was saying most of the locals wanted the mall to go in, including his wife. She'd been after him for weeks to change his mind."

"Mmm. Eleanor told me the same thing. Said she'd rather shop than bird-watch."

Joe wiped his mouth on the napkin. "I'd sure like to know who's behind that development. Those names didn't turn up anything. Lynn didn't even know she was listed, but in checking over the books, she discovered that Chuck had invested heavily in it."

"Are we sure it was Chuck and not Lynn?" Helen asked.

"Yah. Nathan admitted that Chuck was one of the investors. He still says he doesn't know who the others are."

Helen turned to J.B. "When did you talk to Ethan about the development?"

"Thursday morning—we were at the men's breakfast."

"Was he thinking of backing down then?"

"Didn't say. I encouraged him to stick to his guns. There are still a lot of residents opposing it."

Helen heard the back door close. "Rosie's leaving." She excused herself and hurried into the kitchen. Their eyes met as Rosie was opening her car door. There was something in her expression—determination, anger? Helen couldn't be sure. Whatever it was set off an alarm in Helen's head. Rosie was up to something.

Helen walked back into the dining room. "She's leaving. I'd better follow her."

"I'll go with you," J.B. offered.

"No. You should stay with our guests. I'll be fine. I just want to make certain she's all right. She's been so depressed." While Helen talked, she had pulled on her jacket and retrieved her purse. "I have to hurry."

J.B. joined her in the entryway, then, opening the door for her, gave her a quick kiss.

"I'll be back soon," Helen promised. Seconds later she was on the road heading into Bay Village. Rosie's taillights were several blocks ahead.

When Rosie pulled into her place, Helen slowed and stayed out of sight. Something Rosie had said or reacted to during their conversation niggled at the back of Helen's mind. Rosie knew something. Maybe she knew about the money Alex had stashed away, or the murders—or both.

Twenty-eight

Helen parked a short distance away. The lights went on in the living room, then the kitchen. The door to the apartment was unlocked. Helen went inside, staying close to the wall to lessen the chance of Rosie hearing a creak in the stairs. From the living room she could see Rosie frantically pulling out kitchen drawers. Helen had been through those same drawers only a couple of nights before.

Helen eased forward and leaned against the doorjamb separating the kitchen from the living room. "Looking for anything special?"

"Oh!" Rosie whipped around to face her. "Helen, you scared me to death. What—how?"

Helen pushed herself away from the doorway. "I was worried about you. You didn't say good-bye."

"Uh . . . I have a headache. I was looking for some aspirin."

"I don't think so. At dinner, when we were talking about Alex's money, you remembered something, didn't you?"

Rosie looked away. "He—Alex—came to see me Sunday night. He was scared and said if anything happened to him, I should give the police his key." She backed against the counter. "I put it in this drawer, but I can't find it."

"What did it look like?"

"Just a key. Silver, kind of a *V* shape on the end where you hold it. There was a tag on it with a number. Fifteen, I think. Or maybe twenty-five."

Helen frowned. "It was there Monday night. I saw it."

"You . . . oh, right, when you fed my cats."

Helen rummaged through the drawer herself. "It's gone. Could Alex have come back here to get it when he got out of jail?"

"He might have." Rosie sighed. "That must be it."

"Next question—why didn't you tell us at the table? Why sneak around about it?"

"I wanted to be sure."

"You wanted the money."

"Well, maybe some of it."

"Rosie . . ."

"Stop!" She raised her hands. "I know it was wrong to even think it. It's just that when you started talking about storage buildings, I remembered the key and wanted to see for myself. Who knows? Maybe he left a letter or something telling us who he really is."

"Maybe he did. Could you have put the key somewhere else? The bedroom, maybe. Or the utility room."

"I don't think so, but it wouldn't hurt to look. As forgetful as I am these days, it could be anywhere. Of course, one of the cats could have found it, the way they bat things around." Rosie dropped to her knees and looked under the table.

"While you're doing that," Helen said, "I'll check the utility—"

Before she could get the rest of her sentence out, the utility room door flew open, smashing against her face.

A masked figure in black shoved past her, pushed Rosie aside, and raced down the stairs and out the door. Helen saw stars. Hundreds of them. She staggered after the intruder, then dropped to the floor when she nearly blacked out. Blood spurted from her battered nose.

She stumbled back to the kitchen counter and grabbed a towel to press against her face. At least now she had a pretty good idea of what had happened to the key.

Twenty-nine

I can't believe we let him get away." Rosie gunned the motor and pulled out onto the main highway. "I was so shocked, all I could do was sit there."

Helen held her nose with one hand and pressed against the dash with the other. "I'm the one who should have done something. All that training and I couldn't even get my hand up in time to stop the door."

"Do you have any idea who it was?" Rosie peered through the windshield and side windows, looking for their intruder.

"No. I saw the eyes. Something familiar about them. That's about it." There had been an odd scent as well. A woman's perfume.

"We were this close." Rosie held her thumb and forefinger about an inch apart.

Helen tossed the blood-soaked tissue aside and grabbed another one from the box on her lap. She looked a mess but hadn't wanted to take the time to clean up. Since the key was gone, they hoped the culprit would head straight for the storage unit. They had no idea which ones, but Rosie remembered seeing some just off the main highway not far from where Alex lived. It was their best shot.

When they reached the storage units, Rosie turned into the brightly lit area.

"Cut the lights," Helen ordered.

"Right."

The storage units had been built between the main highway

and a steep hill. The doors to all the units faced south and were set in four long rows. The streetlights lit up the units close to the road. Those near the hill were shadowed.

"I don't see any cars." Helen gripped the door handle. "Let's park out here by the road. I'll walk the rest of the way in."

"What do you mean, *you?*" Rosie braked and turned off the ignition. "I'm going with you."

"It isn't safe." Helen drew the tissue away from her nose. There were only a few red smudges. She stuffed some clean tissues in her pocket and opened the door. "Stay here. If I don't come back in fifteen minutes, you'll need to go for help."

Helen didn't hear Rosie's reply. She was already out and moving past the second row of units. Number fifteen was in the middle of the row. When she neared the next row, she crouched down and peered around the corner.

"Doesn't look like anyone has been here."

Helen's heart nearly jumped to her throat. She straightened and spun around in one smooth motion, clipping Rosie in the chin.

"Ouch!"

She grabbed Rosie's shoulders, pinning her against the shed. "I told you to stay in the car," she seethed.

"I'm sorry. I thought I could help."

Helen shook her head and stepped back. "Well, we're either too early or too late." She glanced at the hillside on her left and the scrub brush alongside the single-lane road that ran adjacent to the units.

"Do you think we have the right one?"

Helen stuffed her hands into her pockets. "I don't know." She turned and began backtracking. "Let's go back to the car and do what we should've done in the first place."

"What's that?"

"Call Joe."

They began the trek back to the car and were rounding the first building when Helen noticed headlights bouncing against the hilly backdrop. "Wait." Helen put out her arm to stop Rosie. The lights kept coming. Helen pulled Rosie into the bushes. Staying down, they watched the car make a left turn not more than twenty yards from where they were crouched. It was a dark car. Helen couldn't tell the make, only that she'd seen it at the Cranes' house on Monday.

They couldn't see the driver either, but Helen didn't need to. The pieces started coming together as her imagination constructed a face to match the eyes. The taillights turned down the third row.

Helen pushed Rosie forward. "Go to the car. Call the sheriff's office. Tell them to have Joe meet us here."

"But—"

"Hurry! Unless I miss my guess, the person driving that car is our killer. And she just made her first major mistake."

"She?"

"I think so."

"Who?"

"I'll tell you when I know for sure. Now go."

Rosie hurried toward the car, while Helen crept along the side of the buildings. The Lincoln was parked in front of unit twenty-five. The driver stepped out of the car and glanced around and then, with pantherlike movements, crept over to the door and inserted a key.

Helen jogged across to the next row of units. Once she'd reached the safety of the shadows, she hunkered down and began inching her way forward. She heard the door open, then waited a few seconds before rounding the corner. Helen wished now she were wearing dark colors so she'd blend into the shadows. But she hadn't left the house with the idea of prowling. The door closed as Helen approached. Did she dare risk opening it and confronting the killer?

Not a good idea.

She could, however, lie in wait for the thief to come out. Helen didn't much like being out in the open, so she went around to the other side of the car. Their mystery person undoubtedly had a gun, which he or she had used to kill Alex. While she waited, Helen tried to piece everything together in her mind. She suspected Alex had been killed because he knew too much. Perhaps Chuck had met his fate for the same reason.

Ethan had stayed in the restaurant to pay his bill. He'd

come out and didn't have his keys, because he had the wrong jacket, so he'd called a tow truck. Only when the tow-truck operator showed up, Ethan and his car were gone. Someone Ethan knew had come by, and for some reason they'd walked on the beach. Who? Helen thought she might know the answer to that one. Who else did a man walk on the beach with but his girlfriend, wife, or daughter? But which one? Eleanor had been in church. Nancy had been home. Of course, either of them might have been lying. Had Eleanor left the church early enough Sunday night to get to the restaurant around eight? Had Ethan seen her and hailed her down? Or had she known about his meeting with Alex? Had Eleanor been planning to kill him all along? If so, how had she gotten Rosie's dagger?

Helen noticed a brown briefcase lying on the backseat. Alex's? Unable to resist a quick look, she opened the car door and slipped inside, pulling the door closed to shut off the dome light.

She immediately recognized the scent permeating the car as the same one she'd smelled in Rosie's apartment. Eleanor's Calix perfume. The kind she bought at Nordstrom's in Portland.

Another piece of the puzzle slipped into place as Helen remembered her conversation with Eleanor the night Rosie decided to become a pistol-packing mama. Eleanor, of course, hadn't known anything about the shooting. But she did know about Alex. She had the birth certificate.

Ethan hadn't gone back home at all after he'd stopped by Rosie's Thursday night. That was the night Rosie gave him the birth certificate and letter from Alex. The envelope had come from her store, because Alex had asked her to give it to him prior to their meeting.

Eleanor couldn't have found the letter in his drawer. She'd taken it from his car or off his body. She had seen him Sunday night and she'd killed him.

Helen snapped open the briefcase and shuffled hurriedly through the papers. So that was it, Helen mused. Eleanor Crane had gone into partnership with Chuck Daniels. Daniels would build the Riverside development, while she supplied the bulk of the money.

The door to the storage unit slid open. Helen dove to the floor behind the driver's seat, closing the briefcase as she went down.

Seconds later the driver's-side door opened. The back of the seat brushed her shoulder as Eleanor got in, threw a box on the passenger seat, and started the car.

"Great." Eleanor muttered a few choice words and gave the car much more gas than was necessary. The car lunged forward.

Helen raised her head in time to see the headlights aimed straight at Rosie. Eleanor then saw Helen in her rearview mirror and screamed.

Helen shot forward and grabbed the steering wheel, yanking it to the right and praying that Rosie had gotten out of the way.

The car careened into the last storage unit. Helen felt herself being thrown forward, then back. The last thing she heard as she lost consciousness was the sheriff's blessed sirens.

Thirty

Helen came to as the paramedics were pulling her from the wreckage. "Eleanor . . ."

"She's alive." Joe's voice filtered through the commotion.

"Joe, she killed Ethan." Helen winced when she touched her nose. "She was going to run Rosie down . . . I . . ."

"So Rosie says. Look, don't talk right now. I'll get a statement from you later." He grimaced. "You'd better rest. You don't look so good."

"Thanks a lot."

"Where is she?" J.B. bulldozed his way to her side. "Helen, what happened?"

Helen moaned. Nothing more would come out.

J.B. followed her into the ambulance. "I'll stay with her, Joe. See that my car gets to the hospital, will you, lad?" He climbed inside and held her hand, refusing to leave her side until the next day when he took her home. She'd been discharged from the hospital with minor injuries. Minor! She supposed that was the case, yet she felt majorly damaged. Her face felt as if she'd spent eight hours in the ring with Mike Tyson.

⁂　⁂　⁂

Once at home, Helen settled on the couch and asked J.B. to make them some tea, which he was doing when the doorbell rang.

"Joe," Helen heard J.B. say. "Come on in."

231

Joe lumbered in and sank into the easy chair. He looked at Helen and winced. "How are you doing?"

"Better than I look." She tried to smile but didn't have the energy to complete it. Helen set her ice bag on the coffee table, then pushed herself up and fluffed her pillows so she could get a better look at him. "Did you find the briefcase and whatever Eleanor took out of the storage unit?"

"Sure did. Turns out he didn't have all that much cash in there. Eleanor came out with about fifty thousand dollars, a couple checkbooks, and some kind of journal. Rosie was right about the guy on that count—he did have a checkbook."

J.B. had gone back to the kitchen and now returned with two mugs. "Brought you a cup as well, Joe. Figured you could use it."

"Thanks. Been up all night. I was just heading home and thought I'd better stop and fill you in on what's been going on." Joe reached for the steaming cup and set it on the end table. "Turns out our con man lived in Des Moines. Name's Derek Matthews. He was adopted as a baby and a few years ago found his birth mother."

Helen eyed him skeptically. Or as skeptically as she could with a bump the size of a plum between her eyes and a nose swollen to twice its normal size. Her face was one huge Technicolor bruise.

"This was his real birth mother," Joe assured them. "The police there got some prints out of his room and they match. His adoptive parents confirm it."

Helen brought the steaming cup to her lips, then set it back on the table to cool.

"How did you find out so quickly?" J.B. asked.

"Got in contact with the bank in Des Moines. They had two addresses—his birth mother's and his adoptive parents'." Joe rubbed his head and sighed. "His birth mother had no idea what he was doing to bring in all that money. All she knew was that her son was taking care of her, as well as his adoptive parents. Seems they were all in assisted-living facilities. He was the only one left to take care of them. With all the medical bills, I guess I can understand why he did what he did. He'd already had some experience with that sort of thing. Not that it's right."

"What's going to happen to them?" asked Helen. "Now that he's dead . . ."

Joe shrugged. "I have no idea."

Helen shook her head. "How sad. With as much effort as Alex—I mean, Derek expended, you'd think he could have come up with an honest way to make a living."

Images from the night before flooded her mind. "What's happening with the murder investigation? I assume you've arrested Eleanor."

"We have. Might have figured it all out sooner if I'd checked things out at the church myself. Hard to say. Deputy Jones verified that Eleanor had been there all right, but he neglected to determine when she'd left. Might not have picked up on it anyway. Eleanor left early. Claimed she had a headache and was going home."

"Only she didn't go home."

"She had it planned all along, then." J.B. glanced at Helen. "Are you in need of another pain pill? It's been four hours."

Helen nodded and J.B. headed for the kitchen again. "I finally figured that out," Helen said. "The problem I'm still having is how she got Rosie's letter opener. Unless she broke into the store."

"She didn't," said Joe. "She knew Ethan was seeing Rosie. Ethan had a key to Rosie's place. All she had to do was let herself in and look for a unique weapon. One that would tie Rosie to the murder."

"She certainly found that. Has Eleanor said anything?"

"Didn't need to. Jordan . . . er . . . Matthews wrote it all out for us."

J.B. returned with Helen's pills and a glass of water. When she'd downed them, she urged Joe to go on.

"Sunday night, Matthews came back to the restaurant to give Ethan his keys. Only, Ethan wasn't there. He was already dead. Matthews then saw Eleanor hurrying back from the beach with blood all over her hand and jacket. He wasn't sure what to do. So far she hadn't seen him. About that time, Chuck drove into the parking lot and started talking to her. He wanted to know what she'd done. He guessed right away that she'd killed Ethan. He told her nothing was worth killing a man for. Eleanor told Chuck she had to kill him to protect their interests. She'd done it for both of them, and he was in it as deeply as she was. Told Chuck if he didn't cooperate, she'd tell the police that he'd killed Ethan. Eleanor must have convinced him, as she talked him into driving Ethan's car up to the river to look for a place they could dump it. She followed him. According to Matthews' account, he was at her place, waiting for her to get back."

"So we really don't know what happened up there on the river," Helen mused.

"Nope. We have a number of blanks to fill in. Figure we'll get most of it when she gives us her formal statement this afternoon. Right now I'm not too worried about how she did it."

"So rather than going to the police with what he knew, Matthews resorted to blackmail." Helen leaned back against the pillows, looking at Joe through eyes she could barely keep open.

"Right. Near as we can tell, he went out to her place and waited for her to come back."

"At the house? You'd think Nancy would have noticed."

"Maybe she did. Who knows? Like I said before, Nancy's in her own world. She couldn't tell me when her mother got home that night. Couldn't say for sure she'd even gone to church. But Melissa told us Eleanor hadn't come back until around eleven. That would've given Alex plenty of time to talk to her. Probably waited outside the gate. He wouldn't have had the code to get in."

"Looks like he went a bit too far," J.B. commented. "Got a little too greedy."

"He picked the wrong woman, that's for sure. The day he got out of jail, he called Eleanor and wanted more money. By the way, it was Eleanor he was protecting, not Rosie. When he contacted her, she arranged to meet him up by Drift Creek—her idea. That was the last thing he wrote."

"Poor guy," J.B. said. "Didn't realize what great lengths Eleanor would go to, to protect her fortune."

"Joe, have you talked to Eleanor about Matthews' confession?" J.B. asked.

"She'd already seen it. Had it with her in the car. I imagine she took it out of the storage unit or maybe his van." Joe tossed Helen a half smile. "If you hadn't been there to stop her, she might have gotten away with it."

"I hope not." Helen picked up her ice bag and set it back on her face.

"All she told me was that it wasn't fair. She'd worked too hard to have you and Rosie mess things up for her. She was so close."

"Close to what?"

"Her dream of building a shopping center in Bay Village. Ethan wouldn't bend on the Riverside development project. She apparently made one last-ditch effort to change his mind. I don't know all the details, but I think she'd already decided to kill Ethan if he didn't back off."

"I don't understand why she was so desperate to have it go through. She was the primary investor, but—"

"Eleanor was broke," Joe said. "She sank everything she had into the development. She was desperate."

Despite her interest in the case, Helen yawned. "Sorry. Having a hard time staying awake."

"I have to go anyway. Need to get some sleep too. Got a big date with Annie tonight." His eyes twinkled when he said her name. "I think she's ready to talk marriage."

J.B. walked him to the door. Helen let her eyes drift closed. Things had worked out rather well, considering. Rosie had escaped unharmed and would be coming over after lunch. Eleanor wouldn't be getting her shopping center, but where she was going, she wouldn't need one.

Helen awoke the next morning to a ringing telephone. J.B. answered it. He listened intently, offering a couple of yeses and an agreement that he thought it would be a good idea. When he hung up, he went into the bathroom and closed the door.

"Not again." Helen groaned. She got up, shrugged into her

bathrobe, and went downstairs. Did he have another assignment? Too tired to cook, she set juice, cereal, and milk on the table, then brought in the morning paper. The headlines reported the U.S. had just received word that while the president had been traveling through Jordan, there had been an attempt on his life. That attempt had been averted by special forces headed up by Central Intelligence. No names were listed, but Helen couldn't help but wonder if J.B. hadn't somehow, at some level, been involved. She smiled, proud and at the same time a little saddened. Though they sometimes got in each other's way, she rather enjoyed having him around.

J.B. came into the room, kissed her on the cheek, then picked up his paper and sat down. He gave the headlines a cursory glance and then looked up at her. "I'll be driving into Portland this morning," he said.

"And you're not going to tell me why."

He picked up the granola and poured some into his bowl. "Nope."

As hard as she tried to accept his answer, she couldn't. "J.B., I have just been through a terrible ordeal. I know I'm not much to look at right now, but couldn't it wait a few days? You just got home. Let someone else save the world for a change."

He gave her an odd look, then scooped up a spoonful of grains. "Did I say the call was work related?"

"No, but . . ."

He pulled out another section of the paper and began to read.

Helen opened her mouth to protest but decided what she wanted to say to J.B. deserved action, not just words. She calmly set down her juice, rose from the table, and walked over to his chair. Without a word, she picked up his bowl and turned it upside down on his head.

"Wha . . . ?" He flicked the dish off his head and grabbed her arm as the bowl toppled to the floor. "What was that all about?"

"You . . . I know the work you do is confidential, but you could at least be civil! You come down to breakfast and read your paper like I don't even exist."

"I've always read the paper with my breakfast."

"Well, I don't like it."

For a moment he looked as though he'd like nothing more than to flatten her still-swollen nose. Instead he started to laugh.

"What's so funny?"

Milk dripped from his cereal-laden hair into his eyelashes and onto his clean shirt. Despite her anger, a chuckle rose inside her and leaked out.

He loosened his grip on her arm and pulled her against him. Taking some of the goop from his head, he smeared it into her hair.

Helen struggled to get away.

He brought her even closer and silenced her with a soppy kiss. Serious now, he raised his head. "I don't know about you, but I could use another shower. I should make you shampoo my hair."

Helen couldn't think of anything she'd rather do.

✢   ✢   ✢

Much later, while they were getting dressed, J.B. told her he had a confession to make. Helen sat on the edge of the bed and braced herself for what he might have to say.

"As I told you earlier, I'm going into Portland today. What I didn't tell you is that you're going with me."

"Really. Did you decide that before or after I dumped the cereal on your head?"

He came around to her side of the bed and knelt on the floor in front of her. Taking her hand in his, he said, "Before. I wanted to surprise you. Last night I called Kate and Jason. I made another call as well." He smiled. "Now, I won't accept any excuses. It's all arranged."

"What?"

"You and I are going to Portland, where we'll stay with Kate for a few days."

"Oh, J.B., I can't go anywhere looking like this."

"You can wear sunglasses."

"People will think you've been beating me up. Besides, no one wears sunglasses this time of year."

"Not here, but they do in Mexico."

"Mexico?" She grinned. "J.B., you sneak."

"We're taking a cruise. Then we'll go to Europe or wherever you'd like. For the next month you and I are going to do nothing but relax—together."

"It sounds wonderful, but . . ."

"No buts." He kissed her forehead as he rose, pulling her up with him. "I love you, Helen. You can't imagine how terrified I was the other night seeing you being carried out of that car." His Irish blue eyes filled with concern. "I don't want to lose you." He drew her into his arms and held her.

"You're not going to lose me, darling. I'm too tough."

"I know. We both are." He moved back and smiled. "What do you say? Are you with me, or do I have to make this trip by myself?"

She chuckled. "When do we leave?"

J.B. glanced at his watch. "Can you be ready in an hour?"

She was.